D0354312

# LAST Chance BOOKS

 **KELSEY RODKEY**

## HARPER TEEN
*An Imprint of HarperCollinsPublishers*

HarperTeen is an imprint of HarperCollins Publishers.

Last Chance Books
Copyright © 2021 by Kelsey Rodkey

Library of Congress Control Number: 2021932258
ISBN 978-0-06-299446-2

Typography by Jessie Gang
21 22 23 24 25   PC/LSCH   10 9 8 7 6 5 4 3 2 1
❖
First Edition

To Dylan,

Yes, I'm sure I'm a writer

# ONE

There's a bird in the store. A *bird*.

I've called Astrid three times since discovering it on top of the Self-Help shelf, but as usual, my aunt either doesn't hear her phone ringing, has misplaced it, or is too busy cross-stitching some new, aggressively positive quote onto a throw pillow, as one does.

My brother's shift starts in about five minutes, but he texted earlier to say he'd be stopping at Neato Burrito for lunch and I allowed him to be late if he brought me a Cowboy Crunch, but now I've decided that my growling stomach is not as important as getting this bird out of our bookstore.

But he doesn't pick up his phone either.

"Here, birdy-birdy." I start doing that sprinkle-finger thing people do to attract cats and it shoots me an unimpressed look. "Come on, I have books to put out. It's release day. Follow suit. Be free." I gesture to the front of the store, where the closed door starts to open.

The bird flies at the sound of the door chime and I lose sight of its gray feathers. I stumble over a warped floorboard—a gift given to us by two weeks of rain a few months back—when I try to track its movements farther into the store.

"Hello?" a voice calls from the front.

"Sorry! I'm back here. One second." I sweep the shelves one last time before I deem this bird a master of camouflage and abandon my search and rescue mission in exchange for making money. I grab a stack of new releases from the storage room and head to the front to rectify the embarrassingly empty New Arrivals table.

Every week, there's just one thing on the Tuesday-morning checklist, and that's to get the table up to par before a customer comes in and assumes that the New Arrivals table being empty means we don't have any new arrivals, which just about defeats the purpose of having a New Arrivals table, but who am I to judge someone for thinking that when we're a bookstore that can't even put out new books on time?

That entire hypothetical situation depends on a customer actually coming in, but that's been happening less and less since Prologue opened across the street.

But, naturally, someone would actually come in when there aren't books out *and* there's a chance of getting shit on by a scared bird. Why did I insist on switching shifts with Ravi today?

Oh yeah. Because Ravi never remembers to put out the new books on Tuesday mornings. The irony.

I guess the adrenaline was pumping too loudly in my body

for me to recognize the voice, but once I make it to the front of the store and see the customer waiting, I freeze. Jasper Hamada stands in the doorway, as artfully put together as every other day I've seen him, always here in Books & Moore, as if he doesn't exist outside these four walls—he was here three Mondays ago, two Thursdays ago, and last Saturday. Today, there's not a wrinkle within four miles of his powder-blue collared shirt with stitched white daisies, and his signature black jeans are as tight as ever. He finishes off the outfit with a pair of all-black Converses that look to have been freshly lint-rolled. He pushes away a few pieces of intentionally messy hair when they threaten to block his dark brown eyes.

"We have to stop meeting like this," he says, mock-serious. "It's like you're stalking me or something."

I'd usually play along—if there can be a "usually" in a semi-flirtatious acquaintanceship that's only half a second old—but: "There's a bird in here." I can't stop imagining the thing swooping toward his beautiful hair, mistaking it for a luxury bird nest.

He stills. "Is that—what does that mean?"

"Just a warning." I set the stack of books on the table. "And by the way, I hope we have what you're looking for. Our new releases flew off the shelf, so to speak—because it's a table." *Nailed it.* I guess my deadbeat mom isn't the only mediocre actress in this family.

He smiles, a faint scar next to his mouth disappearing when a dimple shows, and steps closer. "Any recommendations?"

I hold up what I've been calling *The Book That Shall Not Be*

*Named* by The Author Who Shall Not Be Named. I've been mentally preparing for this book's release for a few months now—it's a total white male savior narrative and that's just the beginning of the problems. I don't even want to put this flaming piece of garbage on a shelf, but Astrid says I have to and, because I want her to hand this store over to me after four unnecessary years of college, I will.

Behind the other new books. With its cover facing the wrong direction.

"Not this one," I say.

"Interesting sales tactic. Is this reverse psychology?"

I place the book facedown on the table. "No, unless that works on you?" I gesture around the store. "Don't buy any of these books. Definitely don't buy all the books."

"Actually, do you have the Discontent series?" he asks, and with that he wins my heart once and for all. Maybe today will be the day I finally work up the nerve to ask for his number. I like to tell myself that I was going to do it the last time he was in, but I was recovering from a summer cold and there's nothing cute about a sniffling, leaky girl begging for your attention. If I had asked, he probably would have never returned, and right now we desperately need the customers.

"I don't think I could in good conscience call this a bookstore without that staple of young adult literature somewhere inside."

I wind around the maze of shelves, stopping under my hand-painted sign marked *Young Adult—Current Events*, aka dystopian and postapocalyptic.

Jasper follows, nearly bumping into my back when I stop. It's a cooler day today, eighty-three degrees as opposed to the typical ninety or higher, but I can still feel the heat rolling off his body. Not a drop of sweat on his crisp shirt, though. Definitely no sweatstache, like the one I can feel pooling above my own lip.

The Discontent series by Isla Warbeck is my favorite. It's campy in the best way, like if *Guardians of the Galaxy* had taken place in a desert hell instead of space. The characters use funny phrases that fans have adopted to annoying levels—like, are you even an OG fan of the series if you're not eye-rolling at the people saying, "I feel half-past death"? The series is finally getting the recognition it deserves in the form of a film adaption of the first book, *The Magnificent Lies of Lasers*, out at the end of summer, and movie tie-in covers—though I think the old ones are better.

I pluck the first two books from the shelf and hand them to Jasper, our fingers grazing with an imaginary shock that buzzes through my limbs. He pulls his hand back fast, grip not tight enough on the books, and they fall.

And that's when the bird shows up again.

The flutter of wings causes me to duck, but by the way Jasper flails his arms around his head, the bird might have brushed him in its escape.

"There's a bird in here," he says with wide eyes. "I thought you were joking."

"Pidgey isn't a joke." I gather Jasper's fallen books and straighten, trying to see where the bird landed this time.

"You named the bird after a Pokémon?"

"I don't see you offering any names."

"Pidgey," he laughs. "I guess she's the 'more' in Books and Moore."

"No, that would be me." I cringe at my own comment. Back in middle school, a few boys liked to poke fun at my last name and the extra pounds I'm perpetually packing. "Madeline Moore."

I search around where the third book *should* be, but it's not there. Either misplaced or we sold it when I wasn't here. Disappointing, but I try to keep them in stock, so the next time—if he returns after the bird incident—he can pick it up.

"We're temporarily out of the third book, but it's on order."

"I'm a slow reader, so I'm sure you'll get it in before I even make a dent in the first."

We head toward the front of the store, my neck craning this way and that way to find the unwelcome visitor. To dodge any attacks it might be planning. A gentle little twitter echoes around the quiet store, but I can't tell from where. This bastard is taunting me.

I lay his books on the checkout counter.

"So," he starts, "this is a family-owned store, right? Like Prologue—or whatever it's called—across the street?"

"Not quite like the assholes across the street. We're an indie and they're just a franchise, like the shitty Subway a few blocks over that has watery soda and wilted lettuce."

He raises his eyebrows. "Wow, tell me how you really feel."

I smile brightly in my soon-to-be-manager way. "I feel

grateful that you choose to shop at Books and Moore instead. Your business is appreciated."

I've avoided looking at it as much as possible, but the cold and corporate-y vibes pull me in this time. It looks close enough to a Barnes & Noble to make people double take, kind of like the third Hemsworth brother—yes, there's a third Hemsworth brother—but enough like an indie to reel in the hipsters. Prologues are starter bookstores made for people who don't really like books, but want to seem like they do. This Prologue and the one about half an hour away are run by a local Japanese family. Their first location apparently did well enough to warrant this month-old one—as if we even needed the first, what with everything being available online, and, I don't know, the fact that B&M has been selling books here for, like, twenty years, thankyouverymuch. This Prologue is an unnecessary sequel following up a completely rude debut.

I shake the mouse on the ancient computer Astrid won't upgrade to check our Excel spreadsheet where she keeps inventory of the books. She's been like this for as long as I can remember—stuck in her ways with no real motivation to change. My aunt could be a visual inspiration for a Kate McKinnon sketch. She'd be stuffed to the point of exploding with paperbacks, have multiple reading glasses on her person that she could never seem to find, and she'd unintentionally whack everyone with her big bag . . . where she carries more paperbacks.

I guess I have to give her half credit for what she's done with the store because, when she took it over from my grandmother, she at least took it from a *paper* inventory to a computer.

"Where'd you buy your signs at?" He lifts his chin to the sign above me that says *Gateway to:* with a list of fictional getaways and an arrow pointing toward the register. He's always asking questions like this when he comes in, and they give me little heart palpitations. "I made them," I say.

He delivers a toothy smile, one of his canines sharper than the other. "They're cool. I like the 'You should be reading' one. I needed that above my desk when I should have been doing homework in high school."

"What were you doing instead? Disturbing internet searches? Would your history make the FBI agent assigned to you blush?"

He folds himself against the counter, which takes some effort because he's tall. I can rest my elbows comfortably on it without stooping too low.

"It wouldn't be appropriate to discuss in public," he says in a hushed voice, even though we're alone in the store.

"Curiosity is natural in young men."

He snorts, straightening. "What's my total?"

I glance at the register even though I know the price off the top of my head. "Seventeen dollars, please."

"For both?"

I point toward the sign in the display window. "Paperback sale. Fair pricing. Engaging conversations. Unlike Barnes and Un-Noble across the street."

"To be fair, I'm pretty sure you haven't actually gone over there to see how well they converse." He inserts his credit card in the reader and waits for it to beep. "You might be surprised."

"Bet they don't have a bird dive-bombing you, though." I

bag his books and set them on the counter. "Speaking of. I need to find some bread to lure out Pidgeotto."

"I thought it was just a Pidgey?"

"Well, if I don't do something to capture it soon, it's going to evolve into a Pidgeot and become too strong for me to handle." And that's the extent of my Pokémon knowledge.

He grabs for his bag, and time seems to slow. I have to do it. I can't let him leave without shooting my shot. Not this time. Clamminess be damned, I set my hand atop his to stall him.

"Um." I choke back fear vomit and wet my lips—and then start laughing nervously, withdrawing my hand. "Have a good day."

"Thanks." He pauses for a moment, half-turned toward the door. He spins back around and bites his lip. "Actually. Can I get your number?"

I stand there, staring, for a moment. Just trying to figure out when I lost track of reality and slipped into my daydreams. "My phone number?"

"Yes."

The word slips out of my mouth and I wish I could swallow it back in. "Why?"

"To . . . text you?"

"About what?" This can't be a casual thing, right? He wants *something* out of this. There's no way he just asked for the thing I was too scared to ask for.

"I don't know." He shifts from one foot to the other. "Updates on the bird?"

I shake myself more alert. "No, sorry, you can have it. This just feels like—" I can't say it feels like a fantasy because if I haven't scared him away yet, it's possible that will do it. "It feels like a mistake?"

I could smack myself with a paperback. "Just you getting my number. Not me getting yours. Me getting yours is like—" Finger guns. I do fucking finger guns. If the warped floorboards could please suck me in, that would be great.

He laughs, his scar melting into a smile line. "I'm sure me getting your number is—" He imitates my very terrible, hopefully soon-to-be-forgotten finger guns. "Unless all of this was a clever ploy to distract me so you didn't have to give me your number, in which case you could have told me honestly and I'll accept defeat—"

"No! You can have my number. I don't want it anyway." I gesture vaguely around the store. "I will provide you with photos of the bird's short life like a new mom on Facebook."

I relay my number to Jasper and then my phone vibrates in the back pocket of my overalls. Relief crashes over me like a wave. I wish Tristan Donahue, who misinterpreted my "come here often?" on our last day of AP English, could see how much my flirting has improved.

"Prove it was your number," Jasper says.

"But then you'd see my phone background and I don't want to scare you away." Don't underestimate me, Jasper; I could do it.

"Is it a picture of me?"

"Presumptuous," I say heavily, though I'm feeling lighter and lighter with each passing moment. Joking is easy. "Yet not incorrect. I snuck a photo of you when you were swatting at Books and Moore's new mascot."

He backs away from the counter, twinkles in the corners of his dark eyes. "I'll see you around, Madeline."

My name sounds like a beautiful language on his tongue, and I want to be fluent. Is there a Rosetta Stone course for Jasper just saying my name? I'd listen to it every night before bed.

He opens the door, holding it for—Benny! Benny with my burrito that I can't eat because my stomach is too full of butterflies. He wipes sweat from his brown skin and nods at Jasper in that way that dudes do, for whatever reason.

And then this damn bird dives toward Benny and Jasper, narrowly making it outside in the most spectacular and graceful move I've ever seen.

"Holy shit!" My brother swipes at his buzzed head, eyes wide.

"I want to make it known that that was all me. You're welcome." Jasper waves and lets the door close behind him.

"What the fuck? There was a bird in here?" Benny asks shakily. "You know I hate birds. The world is bad enough without giving little raccoons the ability to fly."

"They're more like rats."

"Not helping their case." Benny drops my burrito on the counter, and I notice Jasper left his bag. I dart around, swiping it up in a fluid motion, and hightail it out of the store before my brother can finish saying, "That guy was pretty cute."

"Jasper?" I squint in the midday sun, searching for him among the cars parked along the one-way street, the sidewalks full of people on their lunch breaks, but I don't see him.

Then a figure moves across the street. Tall, blue, handsome.

"Jasper!" I call as a car goes flying down the road, pushing hot air in my direction. I cut between parked cars, look left, right—despite the one-way limitation firmly in place—and left again. I dart across the street and see him duck into Prologue.

*Wait. What the actual* fuck?

Going in after him seems like a bad idea. Not only do I have a bag from another store, but it's a competitor. And going in could look bad for B&M. But my curiosity has gotten the better of me and Jasper paid for these books, so it's only right that I barge the hell in there and see what he's buying that B&M didn't offer.

About three times the size of B&M, this Prologue has an all-glass front with sliding doors, and a vestibule that bombards visitors with a steady blast of cool air. All my sweat chills on my body and the little bit of hips visible on the open sides of my overalls pebble with goose bumps. There are at least seven people shopping in here, but Jasper isn't one of them.

I take a spin to see if I missed him somewhere around the neatly arranged shelves at the front, but—*there*. He has his back toward me as he leans against the counter, talking to an older Asian man with chubby cheeks. I approach slowly, my shoes not making much noise against the compacted carpet, and tap Jasper on the shoulder.

He spins and I'm face-to-chest with him, the perfect height to read the name tag he's now pinned on his shirt, which reads:

Jasper Hamada

Supervisor

He has the audacity to smile stiffly and ask, "May I help you find something, miss?"

It takes a second to answer, the rage boiling inside me. My face heats, my head swims, and I want to shove him. I push the books into his hands instead. I want to do it ten times, once for every digit I stupidly provided him with, thinking he'd ever text me.

"You can help me find my shit because I just lost it." I stomp out without another word. What game did that asshole make me an unwilling pawn in? And why did he get my phone number when we are very clearly sworn enemies?

Jasper Hamada, welcome to my shit list.

# TWO

Jasper Hamada's stupidly symmetrical face haunts the rest of my day like the oniony smell of the pico de gallo Benny spilled behind the register while I was out tracking down that Prologue traitor.

I'm not even mad when he asks me to help him clean it up because it provides a good outlet for my frustration. I scrub and scrub and scrub the floor mat until my knuckles turn white and my fingers cramp in a curled position around the red-stained rag.

And before I know it, after hours of glaring out the window and restraining myself from texting Jasper horrible things—because I've officially deemed him Not Worth My Time—Ravi arrives to take over for Benny and me.

Fifteen minutes later, I swing into the driveway of our little three-bedroom rancher and park next to Sterling's Explorer. Benny's out of the car before I even shift to park—he goes to Sterling's every weekend during the school year, and whenever he feels like it during the summer, but his excitement to see his dad never goes away, even after sixteen years. Astrid's the shit, but it must be nice to have a real parent around. I've never even met my dad.

"How was work, baby?" Astrid asks when I go inside. She turns backward on the couch, *The Great British Baking Show* paused behind her, and gets one look at my face before she frowns. "That bad, huh?"

I hang my bag on a coat hook next to the door. "You remember that guy I told you about?"

I flop onto the couch next to her, grabbing one of her infamous throw pillows—this one reads: *Calm thine teats!* In the kitchen, Sterling instructs Benny on the next step to preparing whatever he's making, the faucet struggles to pump out water, and butter sizzles in a pan, the scent wafting into the living room.

"Jasper Hamada, the hottie?" Astrid pushes her glasses up her nose. She's only midthirties, but when she says things like "hottie," I can't help feeling like she's seventy and severely out of touch despite my best efforts. At least she's no longer using memes six months after they're over. "Jasper Hotmada?"

"I did not call him a hottie." My cheeks heat, definitely in anger and not embarrassment because I did *not* call him that. "In fact, that's the first time the word has ever come out of my mouth and now I think I need to go brush my teeth with sanitizer. *Especially* because it was in reference to him."

She frowns. "What happened?"

"Dinner's ready," Sterling calls in his deep, booming voice.

"Set the table, Madeline," Benny says, popping out of the kitchen.

I lean over the back of the couch to face him. "It's your turn."

"I made dinner." He ducks back into the kitchen.

I turn to Astrid, my mouth sagging open. "He just got home two minutes ago."

"Go set the table. I'll get drinks." She pats my cheek. "And then you tell me what Jasper did."

In our tiny kitchen, Sterling has prepared a veggie stir-fry soaked in so much butter that it counteracts any health benefits of the vegetables and chicken with it. He and Benny move the food to the table, Astrid fills up three glasses of water and one glass of orange juice—*why is she like this?*—and I put out silverware. Sterling takes pity on me and grabs the plates.

As soon as we're sitting and Astrid has taken a large and loud gulp of her orange juice, I jump into my Jasper story before Benny complains about how bored he was at work, or Sterling tells us a confusing story from his IT job that only he finds funny because he's the only one who understands, or Astrid wants to discuss what color we think things are when we, like, *really* look at them.

"So, Jasper Hamada."

"Oh yeah, go ahead," Astrid says with a nod.

"Is that the guy you ran after today?" Benny ask, asparagus hanging out of his mouth.

"I didn't *run* after him—"

"Yeah, you don't run unless you're getting paid. That's the Moore way," Astrid says.

"You shouldn't chase after boys regardless of the money," Sterling adds.

If they don't let me complain about Jasper this second, I'm going to explode. "Can I *please* finish my damn story?"

Sterling looks down his nose at me, his silverware clenched in his fists. "Madeline, was the D-word really necessary for that sentence to work?"

I can always count on Sterling to dad things up a bit. When my mother, Dahlia, was sixteen, she had me with Absentee Father Duncan Thomas, struggled for about two years, and then had Benny with Sterling. When she couldn't handle raising us "on her own"—as if Sterling wasn't doing everything he could to help take care of *both* her children (and her)—she flew us from California, where she had met Sterling on her failed journey to stardom, to Pennsylvania, where she dumped us with Astrid, her older sister by two years. Sterling was nineteen, had no car, worked minimum wage while taking online classes for a degree, but he followed us here and got his shit together—something Dahlia never did. The most responsible thing she did was stop sending us birthday cards in the mail, which always arrived late, and switched to scheduled, generic e-cards from some website that won't take me off their mailing list. At least it's eco-friendly.

"I felt like it added urgency and importance to the words that would follow, so yes." I push my plate away, my fingers catching on the chipped edge. "As I was saying, Jasper Hamada—the guy who came in not once, not twice, not three times, but *four*—works for the enemies."

Benny furrows his brow. "Fox News?"

"Prologue!" I search Astrid's face for some sign of betrayal—a gasp, narrowed eyes behind her too-big specs, the corners of her mouth turned down, anything—but she snorts into her OJ. "The obnoxious bookstore chain that moved in across the street and has single-handedly stolen all our customers."

She sets her drink down, her face tense. "They haven't stolen our customers—"

"They had tons of places to set up shop and they chose our street—"

"Let your aunt finish talking," Sterling says, cutting a piece of chicken.

I stare pointedly at her, my fingers tapping against the table-top.

"They haven't stolen our customers. We've always done better on weekends than weekdays, no matter the season, and if anything is making bookstores obsolete, it's the convenience of online shopping."

"Or maybe it's the wild bird Madeline let loose in the store."

"What?" Astrid looks to me, her glasses slipping.

"*Or*," I say, cutting a glare toward my brother, "it's the shiny, brand-new store across the street with the smarmy supervisor."

"He's not bad on the eyes, though," Benny says, taking a sip of his water. "A little lanky for my taste."

Why aren't they more worried about this? B&M is my whole life. I grew up playing hide-and-seek with Benny in that store. Learned how to read in it. It was my first job, the only reason I could afford my shitty 2008 Hyundai Elantra with the fancy paint that my best friend, Zelda, nicknamed "Edward Cullen" because it sparkles in the sun. Aside from Benny, Astrid, and Sterling, it's the one constant in my life—always there when I need it. It quite literally has our name written all over it.

"What was he doing in B and M if he works for Prologue?" Benny asks.

Astrid smiles. "Flirting with Madeline?"

"No. He was spying or something." I think back to how he asked the questions about my signs, how he complimented our setup near the front of the store. "What's the word? He was . . ."

"Doing reconnaissance!" Sterling chimes in like he figured out a particularly hard charade.

Benny's eyes bounce off the three of us. "What's there to gain from checking out our store?"

"Madeline," Sterling says.

"He was not flirting with me." Somehow, this conversation has taken a turn in the wrong direction. "He was sweet-talking for inside information, probably."

"They already have one successful store, so I doubt they need much intel from us," Astrid says, stabbing a green bean with her fork. "He was flirting, not spying. Embrace it, baby. You inherited the Moore good looks."

It's meant to be funny, but it just makes me think of Dahlia and how I'm nearly identical to her. Even when she's not around, I can't escape her—not if I want to ever look in a mirror. I once tried to convince myself that I intentionally gained weight just so we'd look a little different.

"We were having a sort of nice dinner," Benny says to Astrid.

"Why did you have to bring her up?"

"I didn't bring anyone up." Astrid gives him a hard stare, then looks my way, taking in my raised eyebrow and clenched jaw. "It's you who brought her up just now."

Sterling holds his hands up to ward us away from an argument. "Technically no one has brought her up, so if we'd like to switch topics, it's still doable."

We don't fight about Dahlia often. Usually just when she decides to pop back into the picture, be it through FaceTime calls she promises will be daily but are actually yearly; spur-of-the-moment five-day visits that disrupt our lives instead of enriching them; or even a random box of chocolate dicks she had anonymously delivered to our house because she thought it would be funny, but Benny's allergy to the peanut butter inside half the dicks made it entirely unfunny.

"We might as well tell them, Sterling." Astrid exchanges a heavy glance with him. He sighs, places his napkin on the table, and leans back in his chair.

Benny and I share our own cautious looks.

"Did she say she's coming to visit?" Benny asks, a resigned sigh stuck to his words. "I'm not missing soccer camp again because she says she's coming and doesn't ever show up."

It's been three years since we had a Dahlia visit—three blessed years—and now panic threatens to unfurl deep in my stomach.

"And I need to focus on B and M and, just, like, not Dahlia." I'm not giving up my summer—any part of it—so Dahlia can play mom for a bit. Whatever time's not spent at B&M should be focused on hanging with Zelda, reading, doing other things that make me happy during my last summer before college. Before everything changes.

"Was she dumped again?" Benny asks.

"Probably popped out another kid she can't handle," I mutter.

"She's not coming to visit or drop off any kids. I guess she learned her lesson with you two," Astrid says, standing and taking her empty plate with her. "She's coming . . . to stay."

"What?" I ask, my gut clenching. "Why?"

"Because she has children here she'd like to see."

"Since when?" I push my chair back from the table.

Astrid places her plate in the dishwasher and spins in my direction, her flowery blouse blowing like pages in a breeze. "Since always."

"Don't you get tired of defending her?" Benny asks. "She left us."

"All of us," I add with a sharp look at my aunt.

She releases a full-body sigh. "She's my little sister."

"That's not your fault," Sterling says stiffly. I've always wondered how he felt whenever Dahlia showed up for a visit, trying to be the cool, likable parent, while he was here not only for Benny but for me and Astrid, too. I've only seen him truly angry one time—and since Benny and I spilled paint across the cream carpet of his second apartment right after he moved in, we deserved it—but I imagine he's pretty pissed whenever my mom stops by. He probably resents her like I do. I can't imagine why anyone wouldn't, why *Astrid* of all people wouldn't.

"She's staying. At least until Benny goes to college."

"Ah, yes, the time when she gets to just magically stop being a parent." I skirt around Astrid and place my plate next to hers. "Does she know Benny's the younger child? Him going to college is two years away."

Benny drops his head into his hands. "Two years," he whispers, agonized.

I raise an eyebrow at him. "I bet she won't last a week."

"Enough," Astrid interjects.

Benny mouths: "A month."

Behind Astrid's back, I hold out my hand like I'm going to shake his. Under the table, he does the same. We bob our hands, unconnected, for a second. Bet made.

"She will be here next week," Astrid says in a clipped tone. "She will be staying in the basement and helping out with everything."

"What's there to help out with?" I ask.

Astrid and Sterling share another look I can't read. Instead of explaining further, they instruct Benny and me to clean up. Dahlia probably doesn't even know how to say "helping out," let alone do it. And if there was even anything for her to help with, she'd just ruin it. We have everything under control without her.

Later, when I should be sleeping but can't put down my book (i.e., have exhausted my means of internet stalking the apparently very private Jasper Hamada on Instagram, Twitter, and Facebook, so now I'm staring at words on a page, begging them to make sense), Benny knocks on my door. I almost don't hear it over the Kate Nash playing from the speaker on my bookshelf.

"Sterling left?" I ask him, bookmarking my place.

"Yeah, he got tired of me kicking his ass on every console we own." He brushes his shoulder off. I allow the brag to go unchecked.

His smirk disappears as he lies at the end of my bed, squeezing his arms around one of my extra pillows. "You don't think Dahlia's really coming, do you?"

"No. I mean, if she does show up, it won't last long. We've been through this before. She'll disappear as soon as something requiring an adult happens."

He snorts. "Like that time she insisted on showing me how to ride a bike—"

"When you were two!"

"And my foot got tangled in the pedal and I fell face-first to the ground." He pretend-crashes into the pillow.

"Blood everywhere."

"She bolted."

"She always does."

He offers me a small smile. "You were there, though."

"Four-year-old Madeline had her shit together better than Dahlia ever has."

He sighs, shaking his head. "And that time she convinced you to split your tooth fairy money with her—"

"And I agreed, because I was ten and she made it sound like I was getting double the money, not half—"

"And she helped you pull, like, three teeth in one go."

I sigh. "Another instance of blood everywhere."

"I wonder what she'll break this time."

"Probably just my spirit."

"A few laws," Benny adds.

I pause, thinking of Astrid's sagging face at dinner. "Astrid's heart when she bails again."

We stay up late, nearly until three in the morning, falling down various YouTube holes until we can't keep our eyes open anymore. My brother and I don't always get along, but if there's something we can agree about, it's how much better off we both are without our mother.

# THREE

B&M doesn't have a parking lot and on days like this, I really resent that. Because today, in its attempt to out-bad my previous shift, the only available spot along the street is right in front of Prologue.

It's half past eight in the morning on Thursday when Astrid and I arrive together, and only a few stores around B&M are open—Prologue not included. I go through the process of parallel parking without a look at the dark store windows. Even though I want to throw a rock through them.

Astrid doesn't normally work the same shift as I do, but last night she called for a mandatory staff meeting that surprised just about everyone, and asked if we could carpool since I was opening anyway. I woke to texts from my coworkers asking what was going on (Sofía and Zelda), if they were getting fired (Ravi), and whether the time of the staff meeting—nine in the morning the very next day—was a mistake (everyone, including Benny, who could have just asked Astrid himself).

A mistake it was not. An inconvenience it is.

There are hardly any cars driving down Oak Street at this hour, but we stop to check both ways before running across. I insert my key the entire way into the lock before pulling it out just slightly and turning. The smell of books has long since faded into a distant memory, but the sight of shelf after shelf, books crammed into any available space, and the quiet—except for the groan of the door shutting—feels magical.

I stuff my keys into my bag and throw it onto the counter, where it slides and hits the register, causing a jangling sound I hope Astrid didn't catch while she was setting down the doughnuts and coffee she bought for the staff. Ravi forgot to pull the coins from the register. I wonder if the bills are still in there, too. He's so forgetful I'm convinced that specific part of his brain just never existed. And if that were true, it would be okay. But it's not. I've never once seen a doctor's note about it.

While Astrid busies herself taking out the trash, something else Ravi should have done last night but probably has a great excuse for—like he forgot—I tally up the money left in the register and slip the excess into the safe. When she comes back, we go through the motions of cleaning and prepping the store, dancing around each other with practice and ease.

"Last Chance Books sales," she says while sweeping the floor. "Go."

It's a game we play when it's been a while since we last worked together. We try to see who can sell the most unfortunate-sounding books and/or books with terrible covers, and we have them secretly listed from I'd Pay A Quarter to Will Never Sell.

"I sold *How to Know if You're Bad at Kissing* to Jeffrey Peters's mom—you know, the lady that snipped at you for not coming to any football games last year?"

"Remind me," she says with a smile, "is that fiction or self-help?"

"I think she thought it was self-help and that's what really matters. And you owe me a dollar for it." I match her smile and flick the light switch, which kicks the ceiling fan on. "Your turn."

"You're going to be simultaneously happy and sad." She bends down to brush the dirt onto the dustpan. "I got *Wipe Front to Back*."

I stop organizing the window display and face her, my mouth sagged open. "Shut up."

"It was surprisingly easy. I just sat it by the register for an entire shift and waited until the right person happened upon it."

"Who could possibly be the right person?" *Wipe Front to Back: A Memoir by Neil Cusack, the Original Car Wash Guy* had the not-so-rare terrible title *and* cover combo. It's worth five dollars and rests in the subcategory under Will Never Sell called Maybe as a Joke Gift?

"A middle-aged man looking to start his own business. I said I read it before starting Books and Moore."

"Grandma started Books and Moore."

"We never said we couldn't lie to sell the book."

"Then I'm signing all of them and saying they're autographed by the author."

Astrid shrugs and dumps her dirt pile into the trash behind the counter. "If that's what you have to do. I always thought you were a stronger salesperson than that, though."

I shake my head as she lifts layer after layer of her sheer top until her jean pockets are visible. She pulls out her phone, holding it with two hands because she has a habit of dropping it, and checks the time. "Where is everyone?"

"It's not nine yet." I open the box of doughnuts and pick out the only brownie-batter-filled one, which I insisted she get. "Are you okay? You seem"—I search for the word, taking a bite—"tense? What's the meeting about?"

She waves away my question, which just makes *me* tense. "Where's Benny? He should be here by now."

"I'm not sure. The battery in my Brother Radar must have died." In the ultimate show of brattiness, he insisted on getting dropped off by Sterling just so he could get an extra thirty minutes of sleep.

But then the door slams in the back and he comes to the front with Sofía, who looks like she just stepped out of one of those really great makeup tutorials on YouTube. She smiles, revealing bright white teeth between her apple-red lips, and flips her hair over shoulder.

"Morning, Madeline. Astrid." She darts between us, shrugging her fringed bag to the floor, and searches for a doughnut, her hand moving over the box like a claw in one of those unbeatable games at the run-down bowling alley on Trindle.

"Thank you for your punctuality, Sofía," Astrid says, returning the smile. Sofía is always punctual. She's twenty-six and has twelve thousand dollars of student loan debt to pay off still—she keeps us updated on a weekly basis. Being late isn't an option for any of her three jobs, one of which is constantly trying to get her to work more. "You guys didn't happen to see anyone else when you were back there?"

Benny pushes Sofía out of the way so he can grab a doughnut before her. "Just Ravi, but he was debating not coming in because he thinks he's getting fired."

Ravi's worked at Books & Moore for three years, since he was my age, and even though he's in college, he comes home from YTI every other weekend plus his holiday breaks to work. Not even I plan to be that dedicated to B&M while I'm away at Shippensburg and I'm trying to get Astrid to make me manager.

"I'll go get him."

I move past the shelves to the staff room, which smells like burnt popcorn no matter how long we air it out, and through the door leading to the alley behind B&M. Ravi stands there, cigarette in hand, talking with Zelda, who plays with the strap of one of the five hundred totes she got at a recent book convention. They stop talking as soon as they see me.

"You guys coming in or do you need to talk more shit about me?"

"Oh please," Zelda says with an eye roll. "I'll talk shit about you to your face."

Ravi fidgets next to her. "It's not nine yet," he says in an agonized voice.

I struggle to pull my phone from my shorts—they weren't this tight last summer and I'm really regretting wearing them today. It's 8:58 a.m.

"You know if you were getting fired, Astrid wouldn't hold a staff meeting so everyone could witness it, right? This isn't some reality show elimination."

"Good point." He flicks his cigarette to the ground and stomps on it. There are way too many discarded butts back here, and I know they're not all from him because this alley plays host to all the businesses on this street, but he really has to stop doing that.

He wrings his hands. "Madeline, I, uh, I might have forgotten—"

"Already took care of it."

"Thanks." He smiles weakly and walks into the staff room.

"Did someone steal money or something?" Zelda twirls her long blonde hair around her fist. "Ravi probably just misplaced it."

I shrug, like it doesn't bother me. Like anxiety isn't pooling in my gut. "She didn't say."

"Oh, weird." She lets her hair unfurl. "I got *Hold for Applause* if you want to read it after me. I'm interviewing the author in two weeks."

Zelda's YouTube channel, Required Reading, started as a hobby after I introduced her to the Discontent series five years ago. Before that, she wasn't really a reader, but then that series changed her mind and she recorded a video spouting off her feelings about it in her general Zelda fashion, and her channel grew from one subscriber—me—to nearly ten thousand.

I nudge her playfully. "I knew I kept you around for a reason."

Publishers send Zelda a shit ton of advanced copies in hopes that she'll review the book on her channel as promotion. I could probably get my fair share as a bookseller, but it takes emails and crossed fingers, and rejection has never sat well with me. Zelda doesn't even have to ask anymore, so I pretty much use her as a library.

Our friendship's more than that, though. On the shifts that never seem to end, she and I play guilty-pleasure songs over the store speakers and see who can last the longest without laughing, especially when customers come in. My record is the entirety of "Gangnam Style" while Zelda did the dance behind someone I was helping. And, even though it makes my skin crawl to see books out of their rightful place, she sometimes leaves me messages on the shelves—she'll spell out words with the first letter of the book titles, usually swear words. Putting them back makes the time pass more quickly.

She walks inside, her hair whipping me in the face when it gets caught on a breeze. The only other worker missing is Henry, the fiftysomething pain in my ass with no spatial awareness. It's possible there's traffic, or he's walking from a poor parking spot, or some other totally reasonable excuse for running behind two minutes, but as I say: if you're not early, you're late.

"Henry came in the front door," Astrid says. I jump, heart thumping fast, and turn toward where she hangs out the doorway. "Come inside and we'll get started."

When we arrive back in the main room, there's an obvious tension that keeps my coworkers quiet and stiff. Random staff meetings could be very good or very bad. Obviously I'm hoping for good—an author visit, some kind of puff piece in the local paper about how great our generational bookstore is that leads to Astrid announcing me as manager, an implementation of a staff book club . . . I'm thinking of more reasons why Astrid would call this meeting when she spits out the worst sentence I've ever heard, and I've heard Dahlia say she likes the burnt edges of brownies.

"Thanks for being here today, everyone; I wish I had better news to deliver, but—I guess there's no reason to dance around the subject—our lease is up for renewal at the end of August and the price is increasing, by a lot."

There's an uncertain silence that fills the void her words leave. My coworkers exchange confused glances, but I stare straight at Astrid, unblinking. "Ooookay," I say, hoping she'll explain or tell us she's joking. "And?"

"We just don't make enough to renew at the new rate. Our monthly sales have decreased and we're not churning enough profit to stay afloat with more expensive bills and rent. The lease I signed ten years ago was at a much lower price."

"Okay, *and?*" Everyone looks at me like I just corrected a teacher. My heart hammers in my chest, creating a rude rhythm that speeds up my breathing. What is she getting at?

Astrid sighs. I can't believe she's saying this for the first time in front of everyone else. Benny and I deserved to know before the likes of Henry.

"Books and Moore will be closing at the end of summer," she says slowly, with a stern expression on her face that I haven't seen since I was fourteen and took her credit card to buy myself a new iPhone.

I was not expecting this when I woke up this morning—I

expected doughnuts and good news. Maybe I'm being dramatic and selfish, but it feels like my life is being destroyed in this very instant. This is the entire ruination of Astrid's past, and the entire ruination of my future.

No. I must have misunderstood. Misheard. Hallucinated. I'm still trying to process her first words when she's moved on to, like, her fourth sentence.

"It's Prologue's fault," I blurt out. I refuse to even glance in the store's direction.

"It's no one's fault," Astrid says, holding her hand up to stop me. "Times have changed. I wanted to let you all know, in case you wanted to start looking for employment elsewhere. I can't provide it for much longer, unless we have some miracle boom of sales—"

"There's a chance we could stay open, then?"

She looks like she's waffling between the truth and something sugarcoated that could rot my teeth. "Even if we could manage the rent, we still have to pay our bills and maintain a cushion. At this rate, that's probably not going to happen."

"Probably." Why am I the only one hanging on her every word? The only one looking for a positive spin to this. The rest of them are just standing and staring. "How much money do we need per month? What's the amount?"

She tilts her head. Maybe if she didn't want a pathetic meltdown, she should have told me in private. Before everyone else. I feel like a slap to the face would hurt less than finding out at the same time as the rest of the staff. As if I'm just a staff member. I'm one amazing display of responsibility away from being a manager. But with Astrid's defeatist attitude, I'm more likely to become a mythical creature than someone with skills to be commended for.

Henry steps forward into our little circle and bends in a weird little bow toward Astrid. "Thanks for everything, but I'm going to call it quits."

His eyes flick to the rest of us. "Bye, everyone." And that little shit just walks out the front door, a waft of armpit the only sign he was ever here. I should have known from the start that he'd be a flake when I saw him dog-ear a book page instead of using the perfectly good—and free—bookmarks available by the register.

"It's okay," Astrid says, almost sounding like she means it. "Anyone else?" She specifically turns toward Sofía, who avoids her gaze, her mouth falling into a frown.

If anyone else is going to leave, it'll be her. She has major bills to pay, while the rest of us, apart from Astrid, don't—at least not yet. Not seriously.

Zelda only ever used the store as her way of having street cred with the book community and some non-parent-funded things, like her septum piercing and the new hamsa tattoo— an intricate, black-and-white sort of hand with an eye in the palm that, in Judaism, is meant to ward off evil—she bought herself as a grad present. She's not going anywhere because she doesn't have to, because she's a book lover. If B&M did close, she probably wouldn't get another job since she's going to Penn State for film at the end of the summer anyway.

In less than a year, Ravi'll be looking for a new job, one that will utilize his culinary degree. Silently, he licks doughnut icing off his fingers, while probably ruminating on the taste and not the loss of his job.

Astrid is probably pulling a Dahlia and being dramatic, though. The store might not even be closing, not for certain.

"Let's get back to the money," I say. "How much?"

She leans against the counter, her arms crossed. "We need at least a thousand more each month when the new lease starts."

A part of me dies inside at hearing the actual number, but another more prominent part of me is angry at how resigned she already sounds. "So, the lease is up at the end of August. We have three months to save up—" I stop to do the math. *A shit ton of money.* How are we supposed to come up with a thousand dollars more a month, indefinitely?

"Well, we can—we just have to—if we tried . . ." My thoughts scramble and wither in agony. I don't know what to do. But this can't be the end. I'm supposed to be the third generation of Moore to run the store. I can't do that if there is no store.

"I don't want to keep you all any longer," Astrid says, perking up. "I'll see you when I see you. Thanks for coming in this morning. Take the doughnuts before I eat what's left all by myself."

She turns to me. "Madeline, open the store, please?"

Zelda and Ravi awkwardly exit out the front, my best friend miming that she'll text me as Astrid and Sofía move to the back. A customer comes in and starts asking me for book recommendations for her nephew who's turning twelve. I pull three different middle grade books for her and, without a care in the world, she buys all three. Like it's nothing. Like that sale didn't just deliver my crushed heart some blood to pump.

Sofía leaves the staff room a few minutes later, her mascara smeared around her eyes. She gives me a tight smile and an apology, then disappears. My anger mixes with sadness into a gross emotional stew in my stomach.

Benny works on restocking the shelves and organizing them, but I don't engage in conversation. He's quiet, but it doesn't feel the same as my quiet. I haven't seen Astrid since she met with Sofía. I don't forgive her for not telling me, but I won't say anything while I'm at work. All I can do today, during the longest shift of my life, is think about ways to save the store.

And that's what I do until five o'clock, when I leave without a word. About halfway through the day, when Astrid came out of the break room to give me my lunch, she told me that Sterling would be picking her and Benny up when the store closed so I could feel free to leave after my shift. I normally wouldn't care about spending my entire day here, but today it makes my skin crawl, so I accept this one little peace offering.

We didn't discuss sales, but I counted every single one of them. We made $178 while I was working. I'll solidify our plan at the end of the week when I have the totals and a list of expenses.

I exit B&M to the same humid temperature as I entered. My feet shuffle along the sun-cooked sidewalk, the heat radiating into the soles of my Vans, as I pass between two parked cars and check the road. In four giant strides, I'm at my car. Parked outside Prologue.

Only this time the store is open and Jasper's stupid face stares at me all wide-eyed and guilty through the window as he strings up a sign that reads *You should be reading* in hand-painted letters. My sign! He ripped off my sign and didn't even do a good job at it!

All the anger I've felt today comes rushing to the surface, making my skin hot and my face red. It's so bad that I can see it reflected back at me in the store window when I rush up and slam my fist against the glass.

"What the fuck?" I point to the sign, as if he didn't know he stole it from me. "That's my sign!"

Jasper leaves the window and appears outside in a heartbeat. He's wearing a lilac polo with trippy little triangles all over it. "Please don't bang on the glass, miss."

"I wouldn't if you didn't give me a reason to, *sir*." I step toward him, my finger pushing into his chest. "You stole my sign."

I look back to the window and see the same books displayed as what I put out on the New Arrivals table on Tuesday. "You stole everything!"

"Well, not everything. I didn't put out that book you told me not to buy." He scratches the back of his neck, awkwardly smiling at a woman who passes us. "Twenty percent off new releases until Friday," he tells her. She *oohs* and keeps walking.

"In my defense," he says to me, "they're new. If you go to Barnes and Noble, they'd have most of the same books out, too, and not because they stole the idea from you. I mean, that's a little conceited."

The rage—oh shit, I can't contain it. It's about to—"No, you stole everything, right down to our customers. Was that your store's goal from the start? Move to our street, steal our customers, do everything that we do so you keep them, and then, what? Run us out of business?"

He frowns. "No—"

"Prologue's got nothing on B and M, let me make that clear. If any store is going out of business, it's going to be yours. You guys are thieves and—and—not even real book people!" So, I fell a little flat on the ending there, but I think my point has been made. I will not stand idly by while this disgrace of a bookstore kills my store while trying to be us. They put out new releases early, for fuck's sake—I know because people on Yelp complimented them for it!

And sure, now as I'm looking at Jasper's bewildered face, maybe I recognize that I'm projecting some feelings onto him and Prologue, but ultimately . . . ultimately it is their fault, a little bit, in some way. They're not *not* to blame.

"I'm not sure what to say," Jasper says, deflating. He looks like he's a little scared of me—and he should be—all wide eyes and slack jaw. "You seem like the type of person who's calmed down by the smell of books; maybe you want to come inside and—"

I grab on to his polo right under the bottom button and yank him forward. He's got half a foot on me, but I feel taller. I look into his eyes, determination staring at him from mine, and ignore the way he smells like something less chemical than the body spray every other guy drowns himself in.

"Get ready to call your store Epilogue, because this is going to be its last chapter."

I shove him away, unlock my car, and drive away without another glance in his direction.

# FOUR

There's only one place I want to be from six to eight a.m. on a Sunday and that's my bed. But that's not where I am, not even close. No, Astrid woke me up at five thirty, stuffed me in her car with Pop-Tarts, and drove for two hours until she reached the airport in Philly to pick up Dahlia, who decided to come days earlier than expected to speed up the process of inconveniencing everyone. Five a.m. is not an hour I was meant to ever see.

It's moments like this I really wish Duncan had stuck around so I could be somewhere else on the weekends. Benny won't be awake until at least noon, and who knows if Sterling will make him come over to say hi to Dahlia. I wouldn't be surprised if I don't see my brother until I'm home on fall break from Shippensburg and Dahlia has skulked back to California.

After picking up Dahlia so many times, Astrid has this place memorized. She pulls into a spot and puts her Honda CR-V in park.

"I'm staying here," I say, hands tucked into my hoodie.

Things have been tense between Astrid and me since her announcement on Thursday, because she ridiculously thinks B&M closing is a done deal and I, very reasonably and smartly, think that's *preposterous*, but Dahlia has a way of making me redirect my negative feelings. As soon as I fully wake up and can focus on being mad about two things, I'm back to basically ignoring Astrid except at work. "I don't feel like putting my shoes back on." Even though they're slip-ons. "And I'm not dressed for public consumption." Even though my pajamas could pass as what half the airport population considers plane clothes.

She stares in that way she does, her blue eyes boring into mine, waiting for me to crack. But I can't put into words how queasy I feel. Any time I try to form a competent sentence in my head, my eyes start burning, probably from exhaustion.

"She wants to see your face, not mine," she says in a soft voice that feels like an apology.

"Then she shouldn't have left." I avoid her gaze. "And left and left and left and—"

Astrid grabs my hand. Her skin is always so soft, like velvet. "And now she's here to stay."

"Why should I believe her this time?" I ask the window.

She's at a loss for words and looks away. If Sterling resents Dahlia, I can't even come up with a word that could accurately describe how Astrid must feel toward her sister. Like getting a paper cut followed by a million paper cuts, just when the first one had stopped hurting. And yet, she keeps picking up the paper.

"I think we're better off without her." My throat starts

swelling up, my eyes prickle, and the queasiness turns into sharp, hot daggers. "I don't want her here. There's too much going on to deal with Dahlia, too."

How am I supposed to save our store with Dahlia breathing down my neck, clawing at me for attention she wants but doesn't need?

Astrid sighs, turning the car off and unbuckling her seat belt. "Come, or don't. It's your call."

She exits, slamming the door a little harder than she normally does. I watch her disappear behind parked cars before I slide into my shoes, unbuckle, and leave the car under the pretense that I'll suffocate in this summer heat in there. As soon as my door shuts, the car locks with a beep. She knows me too well.

I jog to catch up. I don't know why she believes Dahlia is trying this time, but I won't bring it up if she doesn't want me to. I will be civil until Dahlia realizes she hates being here, hates us. Then she'll leave again and I can go back to being perfectly fine without her.

Inside the airport, my aunt navigates us to the right place, her arm entwined with mine. At first, I think it's so she doesn't lose me, which is strange because it's not that crowded in this area and I'm not exactly prone to getting lost—that was always Benny's thing—but then I realize it's so I don't run away.

"When does her plane land?" I ask over an announcement that might as well be a foreign language with all of its numbers and directions.

"She's already here."

Awesome. I can barely contain my joy.

We round a corner and I guess I wasn't expecting her to be sitting right there, waiting for us with three suitcases large enough that I could comfortably fit inside, like her whole life is stuffed in them. Frustrated tears start running down my face and I can't stop them—every time I see her, my anger just comes barreling back full force with no notice, no warning that I'm about to explode. I unhook my arm from Astrid and walk away, rigid, through a crowd of people rushing in one direction. I don't want either of them to see me struggling. I sit down on the nearest empty bench and hold in my breath to prevent the full-body sobs that threaten to wrack me.

"Madeline?"

I'm expecting it to be Dahlia, but it's Astrid. Sometimes they sound so much alike that it sends a chill through my limbs. I forget the similarities in their voices, in their looks, up until the moment I see them together. And for weeks after Dahlia leaves or calls, I can't look at Astrid, can't listen to her speak without a weird feeling in my stomach, like my guts are being pulled out.

She sits down next to me, her arm circling around my shoulders, and pulls me close. She rubs my arm up and down up and down up and down until I can breathe again, though not through my nose because it's filled with snot that came out of nowhere and will haunt me the rest of the day.

"I was just . . ." I sniff. "I don't know. I don't want to see her."

"You already did. The shock should go away soon."

Shock. Yeah, maybe that's what I'm feeling. Shocked that

she's actually here. And with so much luggage. She usually only comes with a duffel bag and ends up stealing half my clothes when she leaves because she inadequately packed or because she just liked mine better than hers and mine were free, after all.

"I told her to wait over there," she says, indicating where we came from, "so you can take some time. Breathe in deep."

"I wish Benny was here." I wipe my face and sigh. "I feel like I'm stuck with her all by myself."

"I'm not going anywhere."

"No, but you're the one who welcomed the traitor into our home."

Astrid pinches my arm and I jerk away.

"Don't call her a traitor." She stands and offers her hand to me, winking. "Not to her face."

When we walk back to the waiting area, Dahlia's moved her suitcases into a row and stands in front of them, her fingers wrapped around the handles of two. Her blue eyes are wide, and her mouth hangs open like she froze mid-sentence. There's a brown stain on the front of her white camisole that she appears to be trying to hide with her dark hair, but it's too short.

"Hey, kid," she says, not moving toward me.

I wipe my face again, but I know the tears have dried because my skin feels too tight and itchy. "Hi."

"Good to see you." She almost drops one of her hands from the suitcase and I don't know, was she going to shake my hand? Reach in for a one-armed hug?

I ask about her flight instead of saying the same.

She gestures to her shirt. "Spilled coffee on myself, but I

managed to drink some before that. Couldn't really sleep."

"You're probably exhausted," Astrid says, stepping forward to hug her sister around the waist. Dahlia leans in, but keeps her hands on her suitcases.

"Time zone changes can do that," Dahlia laughs.

The last three years without her weren't long enough. I need more time to not deal with her.

Astrid grabs the other piece of luggage and wheels it closer to me. "How about we each take one?"

I do as Astrid says and follow the two of them around the airport. Astrid has maybe three inches on Dahlia and me, and her strides are longer, so it takes some effort for the two of us to keep up. I stay back, though, because I don't want to go too fast and end up next to Dahlia. She might want to talk then, and I like being behind her where I have the power to stay silent.

The backs of her top and yoga pants are wrinkled, there's a crease in her hair where she must have had a ponytail, and she switches hands on the suitcase more than Astrid and I combined, wiping her palms on her thighs. She looks back at me once and offers a smile that I habitually return, like when men say hi to me while I'm walking down the street. Just like those times, I want to smack myself for it. I am not happy, regardless of what my smile says.

There's an awkward shuffle for the front passenger seat when we reach the car. I let Dahlia have it to avoid conversation and sit in the back seat with one of her suitcases threatening to crush me the entire ride. I expect her to recline and pass out, but she insists on talking about her latest movie—she had two lines and got to meet Timothée Chalamet—and staying awake because she needs to get used to being on East Coast time.

It takes an hour and seventeen minutes for her to finally direct the conversation away from herself. Seventy-seven minutes for her to take a deep breath and realize she was speaking, uninterrupted, while two other humans, her family, sat there silent. And the only reason she stopped was to take a drink because her mouth was so dry and *isn't it so weird that my mouth is drier in humid PA than it is in hot-hot California? Isn't it, Madeline?*

"Yeah. Weird." The words stick to the roof of my mouth.

She turns in her seat, clearly encouraged by my speaking. "So, any boyfriends I should know about?"

Of course that's what she asks before anything else, before "How was graduation?"

Graduation was great, for her information. Zelda and I— along with her twin brother, Levi—got to sit next to each other thanks to alphabetization (Moore and Moscovitz) and kids threw beach balls and streamers while the teachers tried to get us to chill the fuck out, and it only started raining right as the ceremony ended.

"No significant other." I know she'll scoff at this because at my age she already had two kids, but I'm too busy with B&M to even think about romance or sex. My only attempt at a relationship—with Eric Washburn, the bassist of a popular, shitty local band called Solo and the Wookiee—lasted two months and for approximately seven instances of sex. All protected in multiple ways, thankyouverymuch. It was my decision that we were never technically together for anything other than the benefits part of a friendship, but the whole thing ended when he went away to college last year. The same goes for his band.

"Boring," she jokes, the sunlight making her eyes glow.

"There is a boy, though," Astrid says, glancing at me in the rearview mirror. "Jasper."

"Jasper?" Dahlia's grin doubles in size. "Tell me about Jasper."

I could tell her four things about Jasper Hamada from his locked down social media alone that would sum him up succinctly:

He graduated high school a year before me and went to a different school.

He actually listened when people said your online profiles should be private.

He works at Prologue.

He's The Worst.

I lean around the seat to get a better look at her. "There's no Jasper. I mean, there is a Jasper, but there's nothing there. He's an asshole and I hate him. He lied to me."

"My type," Dahlia sighs dreamily. "Stay away from him."

"I plan on it." Being around him is like finding your favorite book in a puddle of water. I cross my arms, flopping back into my seat and closing my eyes when a harsh patch of sun streams in through my window. "He's destroying B and M."

"Oh, he works for Prologue?"

My eyes snap open. "How do you know about Prologue?"

"Astrid told me. He works there?"

I hadn't realized Astrid and Dahlia spoke that much. Or about anything other than Dahlia.

"Yeah. He's a supervisor."

Astrid turns to Dahlia. "He's the owners' son."

"How do you—" I should have made the connection. That makes it even worse. It means he's extra invested in ruining my store just like I'm extra invested in seeing the demise of his.

My focus slams back into the car when I notice Dahlia leaning around her seat, staring at me with laser-focused eyes. "What?"

"You were thinking about him just then."

"No, I wasn't."

"You were. I saw it." She narrows her eyes. "I know that look."

Not on me, she doesn't. She hasn't been around to see it, to know any of my looks. "Well, we're talking about him! What do you expect me to be thinking about?"

"This is adorable. I can't wait to meet him." She faces forward.

"You won't be meeting him." I don't know why I feel so territorial. It's not like Jasper is anything to me but an enemy and a search history I need to clear. Maybe I just know that Dahlia would embarrass me or make things worse.

"You've got it bad, kid." She wiggles her eyebrows. "Come on, let's stop by the store. You can introduce me as your sister."

I've just about had it. I'm tired. I'm hungry. I am not in the mood for Dahlia. I don't need them joking around about Jasper, or her telling me how adorable my hatred for him is. Like I'm a little kid with a crush. He's a real problem. But, like always, a problem for us is not a problem for Dahlia. Bad things don't touch her because she doesn't get close enough for that to happen. She's a window shopper and we're the books inside. Well, I don't know about Astrid, but I'm tired of discounting myself in hopes that Dahlia will finally want to buy me.

I clench my teeth tight, release. "I'd introduce you as Dahlia because that's who you are. And nothing else."

The rest of the car ride is silent.

# FIVE

I wasn't supposed to work until Wednesday, but after the completely awkward welcome home dinner last night over undercooked spaghetti, I'm eager to leave the house and, because two of my coworkers quit, I have the perfect excuse to do so.

When I arrive at B&M at noon, half an hour early because I was that adamant about avoiding Dahlia, I'm stunned to find Jasper on my side of Oak Street, handing out coupons to people walking past B&M.

"What the hell do you think you're doing?"

His arm, extended to hand a coupon to a woman in workout clothes, drops and his head swivels in my direction, heart-shaped red sunglasses over his eyes. "Existing?"

"I obviously mean with the coupons." I glare at the stack in his hands, but I can't read what they say.

"Coupons? What coupons?" He moves his hands behind his back and grins at me.

"The paper in your hands," I grind out, stepping forward and ignoring the little flutter in my gut. It's just leftover feelings, an instinctual and uncontrollable reaction to seeing his smile.

"Oh, that's just paper."

"You're just handing out paper to people walking by my bookstore?"

He tilts his head to the side. "Is that a problem?"

"Yes, and you're a problem, too." I try to reach behind him, but he slides out of my reach. "Give me those!"

"One per person, Madeline."

I ram chin-first into his clavicle when I try to grab the paper again. He reaches out to steady me, his coupons flying across the asphalt, but at least it's not me.

"Sorry," he says, quickly pulling his hands off my arms as soon as I've balanced out. He bends to collect his *paper*.

I rub my chin. "You should be sorry about trying to steal our sales." I snatch a coupon wedged under the sole of his sneaker, tearing the corner. It's promoting a BOGO for their used books. "Are you guys ever not doing some sort of sale?"

He straightens, meeting my eyes—I assume—behind his glasses. "Jealous that you guys can't do the same?"

"You're setting Prologue up for failure by letting customers get used to it. Or you're charging way too much for your used books and it evens out to buying a brand-new one anyway." I stuff the coupon in my dress pocket. "What you guys should do is—"

He raises an eyebrow. "Yeah? What?"

"What you should do is—" Why am I offering advice to the enemy? "—*fuck off.*"

I snatch the coupons out of his hand and put them with the other one, moving toward B&M. "Stay on your own side of the street."

"My coupons?"

The doorknob is warm under my touch. I glance over my shoulder and smile. "I thought they were just bits of paper? I'll recycle them for you."

He runs his hands down his thighs, looking around as if he'll find an answer to his problem along the street. "Can I please have my coupons back? I'll go to my own side."

I'm struck by an idea. "You'll stay there permanently unless you want to come into B and M and buy a book."

He looks from Prologue to B&M. "What?"

It's a foolproof plan to keep him away. Sometimes my own genius astounds me.

"If you come over to this side of the road while you're working, you buy a book from my store," I say, facing him fully.

A woman passes between us, the little boy attached to her hand talking wildly about ice cream.

Jasper crosses his arms, waiting to move forward until they clear us. "Then the same goes for you."

"That won't be a problem."

He shrugs. "We'll see. I'm pretty irresistible."

"Yeah, well, *you're* the one over here. And you don't appear to be leaving anytime soon."

"You have my coupons." He points, as if I can't feel them

crumpled inside my flowy dress. I feel so ridiculous wearing this. I thought wearing something loose-fitting and cute today would be a good idea, especially after trying to shimmy into some pants that just wouldn't button comfortably, but now I feel ugly and bloated, like the hem is too short and he can see the fat dimples on my thighs.

"Come and get them if you want them so badly." I pat at the pockets, the paper crumpling inside, and hope he can't hear my heart hammering.

His foot slides forward reluctantly, a piece of gravel grinding beneath the rubber sole of his shoe. He stops. "You'd like that, wouldn't you? Because I'm irresistible." His scar recedes into his smirk.

My breath stutters, like I just ran any distance requiring more than thirty seconds of my time. "Oh, please. Do we have a deal?"

"The book-buying thing?"

"Yeah," I say, snapping. "Keep up."

"It starts once I agree and am on my own side of the street, sure." He holds out his hand. It's hot, sending goose bumps up my arm. "Should we seal it with a kiss?" he asks, tapping his smooth cheek with his free hand. "I hear that's the only way to make things official."

I rip my hand away. "I hear kicking someone in the dick is the *real* way to make things official. Go to your side of the street." I leave before he can say anything else, my heart clog dancing in my chest.

Inside the shop, Zelda poses for a photo with a girl who

looks about twelve. She has long red braids falling over her back and braces on her teeth.

"Hey, Mads," Zelda says, spotting me. She turns to the little girl and smiles. "Enjoy your books."

The girl, with a shopping bag and her braids swinging, skips out of the store with an older woman.

"Another fan?" I ask, raising my face toward the ceiling fan to cool down.

"It's so weird. Especially when they're young like that. I do not have a G-rated vocabulary." She sits on the counter. "Were you reading YA when you were, like, ten?"

"No, but that girl didn't look that young."

"My mom didn't want me on YouTube when I was her age." She bites a fingernail covered in chipped lime-green polish. "Sorry, Rhoda."

On occasion, shoppers recognize Zelda from her reviews. The wonder in their voices when they ask "Are you Zelda from Required Reading?" never ceases to amuse me. Usually they want pictures, but sometimes they ask her to sign books she's recommended—which she does not do, understandably.

"You missed it: Saturday night, Ravi made a list of things he wanted to do Sunday morning when he came in and, well, he forgot the list, but he remembered most of what was on it and actually did the things!"

"Holy shit. Old dog, meet new tricks." I stow my bag behind the counter. "How many customers have you had so far?"

"Five. That's not bad, right?"

"It's not good." Not good enough.

Turns out with Dahlia in the picture, breaking my vow of annoyance toward Astrid was a lot simpler than I expected it to be the day I enacted it. What does pretending I can't hear her or denying her solid eye contact do to save B&M? That's right, *nothing*. So, before I left this morning, I asked Astrid to get me reports on the last few months' worth of sales and expenses. I think she's hoping to put it off as long as possible—maybe thinking I'll forget I asked for them. But I'm not Ravi, and I'm not Astrid, either. I'm going to fight for this win, even if I have to drag her ass to the finish line with me.

The store is clean, brightly lit, cheerful. My signs are easy on the eyes, the books are new and old and sometimes loved a little more than others with funny annotations inside from previous owners. Zelda even has Eliza Doolittle playing quietly through the speakers in the corners of the store. There's nothing that's not appealing in here. Unlike Prologue, which has very unappealing ethics and a terrible supervisor. We don't need weekly BOGO coupons; we've got everything else.

I walk to the front window. It's large enough that I could stand on the wooden shelf and touch the top frame with outstretched arms, and it lets in a lot of natural light that shines down on the current book display. The cheapest book is nine dollars, which is a steal, but it's not our cheapest book in the store, and low prices will drive customers in. And if they don't, this might be a lost cause. Or maybe the people are a lost cause. Who doesn't jump at the chance for cheap books?

While Zelda does her thing—mostly answering YouTube

comments and tweets while behind the register—I set up a new display featuring some used books, all five dollars or less. These books have the most charm, but the least chance of being sold. Astrid and I both know that it's bad business to put any of the Will Never Sell books in the display, so I only use I'd Pay a Quarter books for it.

I add some under the following signs: *How to (for those who don't already know)*, *They should really pack up and leave*, and lastly, *Thanks, I love pain and suffering.*

Finally, to match the display, I take our dry-erase board and design a sign with the following words surrounding a giant, prettily written *$5*:

*Books about magic*
*Books about doin' it*
*Books about people who live in towns they should really consider moving out of because weird things are going down and people are dying JUST LEAVE ALREADY PEOPLE ARE DYING YOU COULD BE NEXT*

With some effort, I place the sign outside and come stare-to-stare with Jasper, who is doing the same outside Prologue. I notice the lack of care in designing his sign, which just reads *BUY ONE GET ONE FREE* with the last two *E*s squished against the side of the dry-erase board, and offer him an acidic smile. He could have left off that last word entirely and people would have gotten the message. I make sure not to tell him this because an ugly sign is not enticing—and totally resistible—and, therefore, it's good for B&M's business. My sign could hang in the bookstore version of the Guggenheim.

"Something wrong?" Zelda asks, making me jump. She holds up her hands. "Sorry. You're just standing out here. What are you doing?"

The doors to Prologue slide open and Jasper disappears inside.

"No. I'm good." I clear my throat, offering Zelda a distracted smile. "Nothing. I—what?"

Her eyes dart to Prologue before meeting mine, shutting the door behind her. "Our sign looks better."

"Our store is better." At least we don't have to move on someone else's turf and try to steal their customers with fancy sales.

An hour later, when I'm slumped over the counter and trying not to think about returning home to Dahlia, I get a text. From Jasper.

I read it aloud without meaning to. "Your move."

Zelda looks over her shoulder from where she was organizing book titles in the Nonfiction section to read HAMBURGER. She's only managed HAMBUR so far, but I know where she's going with it—she's hungry. "What?"

I lock my phone without answering, content in knowing I have my read receipts on and Jasper will see that I ignored his message.

"The asshole texted me."

"What did he say?"

"'Your move,' whatever that means."

Zelda glances out the display window. "Oh, hey. His sign."

I follow her gaze, moving toward the window to see it better. It now reads:

*Brand-new books with that brand-new-book smell you won't find anywhere, especially not across the street.*

"That's so unprofessional."

She joins me at the window, hands on her hips. "But how are we going to top it?"

I meet her eyes for a nanosecond, barely long enough for an expression to register across either of our faces. "Grab our sign."

She does, hauling in the sign with a bit of a struggle as I grab the markers and eraser. I wipe the sign clean and we stand in front of it, waiting.

"What are we going to write?" she asks.

"I don't know."

"Come on," she urges me, a hand clasped on my elbow. "You're smart. You're funny."

"So are you, so stop pressuring me." I motion toward the back of the store. "Go take your break or something."

She scoffs. "I'm taking an extra five for the attitude."

"Take an extra ten," I mutter, still staring at the vast emptiness of our sign.

By the time she returns eight minutes later, the only thing I've come up with is:

*BUY BOOKS FROM*
*BETTER-LOOKING EMPLOYEES.*

"Not bad," she says, eyeing it with a tight expression.

I sigh. "Just say it."

"It's stupid." She cringes when I glare at her. "You said to say it."

"Did you think of anything?"

"No, I got into an argument on Twitter with some troll about something stupid. And now it's this whole thing. Like, he saw in my bio that I say I'm half-past dead and he's all, 'What's the other half? Bitch?' and . . . he got me there. I've updated my bio to reflect this personal truth."

My phone buzzes on the counter.

### Ass-per Hamada

Today 1:06 PM

I'm waiting Madeline

1:06 PM

I decide to just go with it. At least my handwriting is nicer than his. Prologue's sign looks like it was put together in two seconds, most of the letters half-formed and stick thin. He probably can't hold a marker correctly with those long, slim fingers of his.

I place the sign outside.

Are we talking about all the
employees or just me and you?
1:08 PM

I type back all before he can point out that, between me and
him, he'd win.

Ok that might be true
1:08 PM

It doesn't hurt any less for him to say what I was thinking.

Zelda's a knockout and you wouldn't
stand a chance against her. Facts are facts.
1:08 PM

I'll only accept defeat this one time. All of your
employees are better-looking. I'm staring at a
worker with nose hair down to his bottom lip as I type.
1:09 PM

I refuse to laugh and instead ignore the weird feeling in my
stomach, probably too much adrenaline for how little physical
activity I'm getting; my body doesn't know how to process it.

Don't you have work to be doing?
I guess that BOGO isn't bringing in as
many customers as you'd like, huh?
1:09 PM

60

I get no response, but I see he's read my message. I peer out the window, hiding behind the revolving book display near the front. I watch as he darts out to his sign, takes it inside, and then returns it to its position a minute later with new words on it. It now reads:

New store.
New books.
No chance of bird attacks.

I whip the door open to collect our sign.

"I don't get it," Zelda says, brow furrowed, as she reads Prologue's sign. "Is bird attack a sex thing?"

"What? No."

She scrunches her nose. "Your face is really red; are you sure it's not a sex thing? You know I won't judge you."

"It's just hot out."

"Not really."

"Zelda."

She reads the look in my eyes and relents. "Fine, it's a little hot out; I'll give you that."

I grab the marker and my phone. I start writing, Zelda hovering over my shoulder.

"Whoa. Wait. Are you really—"

"Yes." I finish writing the words, double-checking my phone screen before placing the sign in our store window, blocking half of my cute display. Worth it.

It takes two minutes for Jasper to come storming into B&M. I hope he brought his wallet.

"Take that down," he says, out of breath and pointing toward the sign.

*For a terrible time, call (717) 555-9080*

aka Jasper Hamada's phone number.

I pause for a beat, my smile growing. "Can I help you, sir?"

He rolls his eyes. "Take that—" He charges toward the display, his hands outstretched to rip the dry-erase board down, but I cut him off.

Zelda watches with wide eyes from behind the register, her elbows propped on the counter. "Can I help you find something, sir?" She smiles cheekily when he ignores her.

He keeps his dark eyes on me.

I nod toward the bookshelves. "We had an agreement."

"I'll just post yours on our sign, then." He heads toward the door.

"Please do. I love making new friends. I'll let them know about the good deals we have here."

He stops, his hand on the doorknob. Without turning, he says, "Take it down now. I'll buy a book."

I wait until he moves past the first shelf to take down the dry-erase board. I store it behind the counter without erasing the message. I follow him into the stacks, keeping some distance between us but unable to stop the feeling of being led around with a leash of my own making.

After two minutes of silence, I ask, "Seriously, can I help you find something?"

He pulls a book I've never seen from the How To section in the back. He bypasses me without a word, without a glance, and heads to the register.

Zelda checks him out, but I stand so close to her that our upper arms touch from shoulder to elbow during most of the transaction. Jasper's buying a book called *Sew You Want to Design Clothes?* An interesting choice.

"That'll be twelve dollars even, please," Zelda says.

He feeds a credit card into the reader. As soon as she hands him his receipt, he grabs the book and flees toward the exit.

"Take down your sign," I say as he opens the door. He stares at me like he didn't hear me over the chime, but when I open my mouth to repeat my words, he smirks.

"Why don't you come over and do it yourself?"

I stand there glaring until he's across the busy street and tucked away inside his evil lair with his very intriguing twelve-dollar craft book.

# SIX

Dahlia insists on making me breakfast the next morning and I insist on poring over the sales and expense reports Astrid finally (and begrudgingly) hands me before she leaves for work.

Things aren't looking good. And I don't just mean that Dahlia is overcooking the pancakes and grease from the bacon is hitting the backsplash. The store is struggling to stay afloat. We're in over our heads. B&M is drowning. All the "oh shit" metaphors.

"Whatcha lookin' at?" Dahlia asks, her spatula in hand as she leans over my shoulder.

I sniff. "Something's burning."

"Shit." She rushes over to the stove and removes the pan holding burnt bacon from the coil. The smell fades as she powers the fan on the range hood and cracks open the window next to the sink.

She stares at the blackened bacon. "No problem. You said you like it crispy, right?"

"Crispy, not charred." What a waste of perfectly good food. And money.

"It's not that bad." She lifts a piece, nearly dropping it. "Hot."

She bites into it with a snap and flecks of black fall onto her chin and lips. Her teeth barely come together in small, disgusted bites, her face fighting a cringe.

"With a little syrup, it'll be fine," she says, turning toward the sink and trying to hide the fact that she spits it out. Typical. Trying to feed me something she wouldn't eat herself. And we don't even have a disposal in the sink.

"I'm"—I search for some excuse—"vegetarian."

"You said you liked bacon. And I saw you eat meatballs the other day."

I toss the reports onto the table. "They were vegetarian."

"No, they weren't. I ate them and they were pure . . . whatever meatballs are made of."

"I'm trying to spare your feelings."

She leans against the stove before recoiling and turning the burner off. "What do you mean?"

"I don't want to eat your terrible food. You don't have to cook while you're here. No one is expecting you to." I don't even know how she's taken care of herself all this time. Probably takeout, which would be a perfect excuse for why she didn't have funds to visit more often. Not that she wanted to.

My mind drifts to Buns, the bakery by B&M, and my stomach growls. Dahlia's pancakes are probably as hard and cold as ice by now.

"Well—" Dahlia starts, but I cut her off by pushing my chair away from the dining room table and collecting my papers.

"What?"

"How about lunch? We could go out to eat somewhere."

I grab my bag hanging on the chair and sling it over my shoulder. "Maybe, but not today. I'm busy."

"Do you think Benny will want to?" she calls after me when I head toward the front door. "Is he coming back from Sterling's soon?"

I pause, wondering the same thing. He was here for dinner on Sunday, but he didn't stick around. We're supposed to have our weekly dinner with Astrid and Sterling tonight, but I don't know if that's still the plan. All bets are off when Dahlia shows up. She throws everything into chaos.

I glance over my shoulder and shrug, grabbing my keys from the hook by the door. "Couldn't say."

"I thought he only stayed the weekends with Sterling."

"Well, it's summer and that's his dad. So . . ." I open the front door, expecting her to whine about how she's his mom and she never gets to see him (her own fault on both accounts), but she stays silent.

I bet the mess in the kitchen will still be there when I get back tonight, but for now, I choose not to think about it. I've got a different mess to deal with, one that involves money and potentially getting a new job.

"I don't think we can save it."

Benny looks up from his iced coffee, some light brown drink I didn't catch the name of, and raises his eyebrow. "But you were so sure the other day."

"Before I actually saw the numbers." I stab at the reports on the little table between us. "We are going under, fast."

I texted him on my way out of the house, thanks to Dahlia putting him on my mind, and met him at Buns for his first break from work. There's still a decent line for the register, despite the morning rush ending, but the bakery is pretty empty otherwise. I've been pacing myself with a warm chocolate chip muffin for the last ten minutes. Making it last.

It's unfortunate the same thing can't be done for B&M.

"So, what do you want to do?" he asks, his attention on whatever he's typing on his phone.

The answer eats away at my stomach, like acid instead of sweet, gooey chocolate. I can't say it. I wouldn't be able to take it back.

But life is expensive. I have car payments, a need for books, the desire to keep my clothes slightly stylish and gas in my car. I pay my own cell phone bill, have college to consider. The unnecessary and expensive textbooks won't pay for themselves. Neither will my as-yet-undecided major. Does Shippensburg have a major for if your plan was to run the family bookstore and now that might not be an option? Business with a minor in What a Fucking Waste?

"Obviously I want to keep the store open, but I just don't know how." It's times like these that I want an adult. It's times like this morning with Dahlia when I remember to be careful what I wish for. "Our sales just don't make up the expenses. And I can't find anything for us to drop. It's not like we pay for internet or anything. Just stuff we need. And Astrid hasn't given up so much as she's just . . . disappeared, managerially speaking."

He stares at me for a moment and then starts laughing to himself.

"What?"

"I was going to suggest we sell more books, but that's not really working for us right now."

I smack his arm. He leans out of my reach, taking his coffee with him.

"You should be more concerned about where the money for your soccer camp is going to come from." I pull off a chunk of muffin. "When are you coming home?"

"I don't know. I might just stay with Sterling. Let the ladies take home base."

"Those words came straight from Sterling's mouth." I gently tap my foot against his shin. "Seriously, though?"

He avoids my gaze by looking out the window. Visible at the very corner of the frame is Prologue. It makes the acid bubble in my stomach again.

"I don't know. I don't want to be around her."

"Well, so far you've managed just that. I'm the one stuck with her. By myself."

"Yeah, but if she stays, I'm the one stuck with her for years while you're away at school." He sips his drink. "The summer seems like a gracious trade."

I groan, laying my arms and head on the table. "Why can't we just suffer together?"

"Perks of being the baby, I guess," he says with a smirk.

"More like the perks of having a dad." I don't mean it as nastily as it comes out. I catch Benny's eye. His lips part, but he refrains from saying anything and then I feel even worse than I did a moment ago. He feels guilty and I feel guilty and there was no point in my comment because Sterling has always taken care of me and reminds me whenever Astrid and I get into little fights that his new apartment has three bedrooms. He even offered to paint the room rose gold—a color he vehemently insists does not actually exist outside outdated Apple products—and install bookshelves. Make it my little getaway.

"Sorry."

He drains his cup with a loud slurp. "You owe me a bagel now."

"I already bought you the coffee."

"You have to." He throws his empty coffee cup into the trash can behind me. "You have to take care of me. It's your one job in life that you can't quit."

"Oh, didn't you hear? Dahlia's back in town and very eager for someone to take care of. Go see her."

He mumbles something and checks his watch. He slides off his chair and joins the dwindling line. I watch his progress for a moment before my eyes fall on the *HELP WANTED* sign taped to the register.

That hot feeling rearranges my intestines again. If I don't tell anyone, if I don't say it aloud, maybe it's not as big a betrayal. Astrid holds no ill will toward Sofía or Henry for quitting and has mentally quit herself at this point. She's the one footing my tuition, anyway; she should want me to be making as much money as possible so I can afford to pay her back and not become a second burden living in her house.

I could totally be a barista. Or a baker. Or whatever. I bypass Benny before I realize my feet are moving. Ignoring the complaints behind me, all from Benny, I ask a worker selecting a cinnamon roll from the case if I can get an application when she has a moment. She's happy to oblige once the customer pays.

With the paperwork in hand, I pass Benny and he does the *my lips are sealed* motion. I ignore that, telling him I'll see him later for dinner, not really stopping to give him a chance to bail. I leave Buns, the application burning a hole in my palm as I walk down the street to my car. It's hard to tear my gaze away. One application isn't the end of the world. Maybe I'll apply and, when I don't get the job, I'll take it as a sign from the only god I believe in—Thor—that I'm not meant to leave B&M.

But if I'm taking random things as signs, I don't know what it means that I run into Jasper Hamada—literally.

"We need to get you a helmet or something," he says when I wobble.

"Or you could just watch where you're going."

He raises an eyebrow, no sunglasses today. "Or you could." He glances at the application in my hand. "What's so important you couldn't spare one glance before running full force into me?"

I put the application behind my back and narrow my eyes. "What's your excuse? You were just walking, completely attentive, and ran into me."

"She has a point." A random guy, probably close to my age, in a purple James Madison University shirt stops beside Jasper and smiles at me, his eyes squinting in the sunlight. His hair curls toward his chin and his nose is a bit big, but it suits him—kind of like how Adam Driver's does, but only when he played Kylo Ren. "Would it kill you to watch where you're going?"

Jasper shrugs. "She's not in my immediate line of sight."

"That's the problem with walking around with your nose turned up."

The guy cuts in front of Jasper. "Hi. I'm Grant. And you appear to know my butthead of a best friend."

"I've had the *pleasure*. I'm Madeline."

They share a look that I can't interpret, so quick that it's almost like it didn't happen by the time Grant is nodding. "Nice to meet you."

"Well, I have somewhere to be." I don't, not really, but I walk past them, not ready to dissect the fact that someone like Jasper can have friends. "You're lucky neither of us are working or else you'd be buying a book. This is my side of the street."

I spin and find him hunched over, staring at . . . my butt? Grant smacks Jasper's arm.

"What were you doing?" Heat blossoms painfully on my cheeks.

"Is that an application?" Jasper points down—I assume to where my hand still clutches the application behind my back. "And why do you assume I'm not working?"

I take in his tight Lorde T-shirt, dark blue jeans with holes in the knees that appear to be patched with some cartoon doughnut fabric, and his best friend practically glued to his hip. "Call it a hunch."

"Was it my lack of name tag that gave it away?" His lips

twitch while he tries to keep his face serious. "The fact that I'm not in the store?"

"You're hilarious," I say. "You should take your act on the road." I spin on the sidewalk and head toward my car again. "Seriously. Feel free to leave as soon as possible. Like, right now—what are you doing?"

It's a stupid question, really. He's walking next to me, his long strides cut in half so he doesn't pass me. A better question would have been why, why is he walking next to me, didn't he get my hint to leave? Grant catches up with a sigh.

I stop. Jasper stops. Grant stops.

Jasper frowns. "Are you that worried about your store closing?"

I glare at him, hating the paperwork in my hand, wishing Buns had online applications so no one would see proof of my treachery except for the person who would hopefully hire me to be a barista-baker-whatever.

"No."

"Then why are you filling out applications to work elsewhere?" He bites his lip. "Buns?"

"I like their food." I immediately regret saying it because it's not cute to talk about food with guys, right? But then again, why do I care? Everyone needs to eat, and I don't even like Jasper. "Bangin' chocolate chip muffins. Made fresh every day."

"Oh, that sounds good." Grant clutches his stomach and shoots Jasper a slack-jawed look. "I'm hungry, bud."

"You ate breakfast like an hour ago," Jasper says. He turns to me. "You sound like a walking advertisement for them. Did you get the job already? What else is *banging* there?"

It's not even that sunny or hot out yet, but the warmth on my face persists. A breeze flutters my threadbare tee and there I go feeling self-conscious about my body again, all because I admitted to liking a really delicious breakfast carb that anyone in their right mind would like.

"The coffee cake muffins," Grant says, answering him even though Jasper and I face each other, putting him on the outskirts of our tension.

"I probably won't even apply." I cross my arms over my chest, adjusting my shirt on the way.

"That's a shame," Jasper says. "I thought it was a smart move. Jumping ship."

"Excuse me?"

He shrugs, stupidly ignoring Grant's gesture to *abort abort do not speak* from beside him. "If you think the store is going to close, it's better to look for jobs while you still have one than to scramble for one after the place tanks."

Words fight for dominance in my mouth, but nothing is brave enough to come out. I struggle with my point, with an insult in the face of his self-assuredness.

"Prologue would be happy to have you on our team if you come to your senses," he says with a smile too conniving to be sincere. "I can put in a good word for you; I've got *connections*."

I can only imagine how gladly he would insist his parents should reject my application—no-fucking-thanks.

"I did say he was a butthead," Grant says, grimacing as he pulls Jasper away. "Sorry. Bye. Breakfast number two awaits."

I'm left on the sidewalk outside the yoga studio by myself, a crumpled application in my shaking hand and my face hot. I can't "jump ship" now. I can't let Jasper win. I can't let *Dahlia* win. If I learned one thing from her, it was how to quit. It's the one lesson I've struggled to unlearn my entire life. I mean, just to spite her, I wear my shoes until my toes literally poke out the front or I can no longer wear them in the rain. I've grown up to be a dedicated person, a passionate one who doesn't give up when things get tough. No one needs to know that I debated leaving B&M.

# SEVEN

I spend the rest of the day at Zelda's, reading her copy of *Hold for Applause* with goose bumps because her central air is set to sixty-six degrees year-round on account of her mother going through menopause. The things I suffer through just to avoid time with Dahlia, who is undeniably invited to the Sterling-Benny-Astrid-Madeline family dinner—Benny sent several confusing texts that hinted at Dahlia suggesting we meet at a winery.

Leave it to Dahlia to have family dinner night where she can get sloshed.

I bookmark my spot, not many pages since my last bookmark insertion thanks to air-conditioning and Jasper making me mad even when he's not here—I checked his Instagram again and it's still annoyingly private. I had been looking for a good photo of him to print out so I could take up dart-throwing.

If Astrid gets to invite Dahlia to our family dinner night, then I'm taking Zelda. I launch a pillow at her head, but instead it hits the framed bat mitzvah photo of us on her desk.

She stiffens in her computer chair and slowly spins to face me, a video mid-edit on the screen behind her. "How dare you disrespect the day I became a woman."

She says it as if she even enjoyed the day in question. She spent it crying because she got her first period and had shiny brace face in all the photos people posted online. On the other hand, Levi, who held his bar mitzvah at the same time, said it was great.

"Do you want to go to a winery with me and my dysfunctional family?"

"If I have to."

"You do. You can ask Dahlia about movie stuff for all I care. In fact, yes, do that. I don't have to talk to her then."

"What do I get out of this?" she asks, standing and adjusting her cheap plastic bracelets from her elbow to her wrist.

"A free meal? Information about the field you want to go into? More time with my lovely face?"

"Oh, well, if your face is included, count me in."


The drive over is just the right amount of time to play an entire album, but short enough that I don't have to repeat any songs and get them stuck in my head, no matter how badly Zelda wants to listen to track four more than once.

My family group chat lets me know Sterling has been here for at least ten minutes, ever the punctual guy, so we meet him around the back of the winery, where people chat in lawn chairs, play games, sip drinks, and eat from the food trucks.

String lights hang over wooden tables and wrap around tree branches, giving an otherworldly glow to the place, even with the last hours of sunlight in full force.

We claim a nice stretch of table and preoccupy ourselves with Guess Their Baggage, the game Sterling invented when Benny and I were younger to distract us during long wait times at restaurants. Zelda is exceptionally good at it.

"The lady in the green top. Glassy eyes and fanny pack." Sterling is careful to go unnoticed when he points at the woman behind us.

"She searches the lost-and-found pet Facebook pages every day in hopes of finding a cat she lost seven years ago," Zelda says suddenly in a low voice.

I blink. "I don't remember this game being so sad."

Sterling shrugs, a smile on his face. "You're old enough to handle the world's harsh realities now. What's yours?"

"She gets all of her drinks virgin and then pretends to be drunk to feel alive."

He nods with thoughtful eyes. "I have to go with Zelda's."

"Rude."

"He can't pick yours," she says. "That's practically nepotism. And it wasn't even that good, so get over yourself."

I search the crowd to find our target, because the loser always goes next. "Cowboy boots, in line for the bathroom."

"The one with the crop top?" Zelda asks, leaning across the table to get a closer look. "He for sure had someone in his life who vehemently hated the color puce, so now he wears a little bit of it each day to spite them."

Sterling points to Zelda. "I had a similar guess, actually. But with the boots."

They both look to me. "I mean, it's like you didn't even try, Sterling."

Scoffing, Sterling goes next and picks Dahlia, who has chosen that moment to make slow progress with Astrid and Benny toward us.

"How about I describe her?" I ask. "Desperate for attention, cares about no one but herself—"

"Okay, enough," Sterling says quickly. His mouth turns into a forced smile as he looks over my shoulder. "Hi, guys."

The false cheer in his voice reminds me of the awkwardness Sunday night when he and Benny showed up for dinner. Sterling had assumed he'd be cooking—I think he wanted the time to himself to acclimate to being around Dahlia without having to interact with her—but she'd already pulled the spaghetti off the burner by then. The dinner was tense and quiet, and I found myself gripping Sterling's hand under the table in a show of support.

Benny slides into the seat across from me, next to Sterling. When I stand to join him, to quietly tell him I didn't apply to Buns, Astrid puts her hand on my shoulder, forcing me down. Dahlia sits on my empty side, the two Moore sisters caging me in.

If Benny lied about keeping it a secret and told Astrid, she's going to tell me something wise and mature, sure to piss me off, like what Jasper said. Abandon ship before it sinks. But I threw that crumpled, traitorous piece of paper into the first recycling bin I could find and, therefore, I don't want to hear it. I am *not* leaving B&M, and no one can make me.

"How about the kids and Dahlia stay here to save our spot while Sterling and I go grab food?" Astrid gives Sterling a pointed look and he half rises from the bench.

"I'll go, too," Benny says, standing. "You can't carry food for six, let alone remember the orders."

"You're right. Text your order to the group chat and Zelda will help us carry the food," Astrid says, indicating that it's not really a question. Zelda nods, getting to her feet.

"Look, Madeline, there's a whole truck dedicated to cheese," Astrid says, nodding at a huge sign that reads: *Guarantees you'll like our cheese!*

I try not to roll my eyes and text Grilled macaroni and cheese sandwich to the group chat that now, unfortunately, includes Dahlia in it. It says Astrid added her a few minutes ago.

Sterling, Astrid, and Zelda leave, taking all conversation with them. I can only assume that since Astrid didn't immediately give me the *I'm proud you're making a good decision* face, Benny didn't mention the application, but it won't hurt to tell him I didn't actually apply. If this is the case, he—ignoring Jasper—is the only one who thinks I thought about leaving the store. I text this to him and try to get his attention, not so discreetly nodding to my phone.

"How were your days?" Dahlia asks, leaning on the table with both elbows. "What did you do all day, Maddy?"

"Madeline." Benny and I say it at the same time so the word comes out louder than intended.

Dahlia blinks. "Madeline. Sorry. You're right. It's a pretty name, after all."

It's probably the only thing she likes about me because it's the only thing she 100 percent had a say in since I was born. Her loss.

She smiles at Benny, a teasing tone escaping her mouth when she says, "And Benjamin is a nice name, too, but he doesn't seem to like it."

No, he prefers Benny and has since he was born—she'd know this if she'd stuck around. Just like she'd know I grew out of Maddy when I was twelve and she left me waiting for a ride home from my middle school book club two days in a row when she came for a visit. The second day was because she had just left. Gone back to California. There were only so many times I could hear "I'm sorry, Maddy" through the phone before the words and the name grated my ears. I was so pissed off that Zelda gave me the nickname Mads.

Benny finally picks up his phone, but I don't see the three dots on my screen indicating all the typing he's doing is to me. He stands.

"They need help."

Convenient.

Dahlia doesn't even get a word out before he disappears in the crowd, nearly upsetting a man with three drinks held precariously in his hands. What I wouldn't give to have one of them.

Awkward silence sits between Dahlia and me like an extra person.

"You still like reading?" she asks, tapping a fingernail on the table.

"It's not typically something people stop enjoying."

"True." She blows a piece of brown hair from her eyes. "Have you guys been here before? I thought it would be cool because we could all get whatever food we want. The reviews were really positive."

"It'd be cooler if I could get a wine slushie."

The other time I was here, I had to drive Astrid home because she had three of those things and couldn't walk straight. She claims it's because she never drinks, but I think the slushies are just strong.

Dahlia fights a smile. "Yeah, that would be cooler."

Without Astrid here to pull the Mom Card, I could probably get Dahlia to appease me, to get me a drink in hopes I'll think she's fun.

"You could get us some." A twentysomething girl walks behind me with a maroon slushie in a reusable tumbler. I nod in her direction. "I'd want that maroon one."

Dahlia spots the drink in question and glances at me. "You're not old enough."

"I'm barely three years shy."

"You drove here."

"You could drive me home. We're going to the same place." A drive with her would be more bearable if I were drunk anyway. "Come on." I lay the sweetness on thick. "Astrid would never do it, but she's so boring."

She grins. "I'll be right back."

And right back she comes, sliding her wristband off her thin wrist and onto my slightly bigger one. She places the frozen drink in front of me and winks. "It's nonalcoholic."

I think she's serious at first, but as soon as the drink hits my tongue, I know that was her way of saying she wants to keep this between her and me. I have no problem with that.

I raise my glass to the bottle of water she bought. "Cheers."

My cheeks are hot, my stomach feeling similar, by the time the others come back with our food cradled in their hands.

Zelda and Sterling take seats on opposite sides of Benny, and Astrid sits next to me, sliding my wrapped sandwich in my direction. Right now, it's the most perfect meal I could ask for. I want to marry this sandwich. This sandwich would never try to kill my bookstore.

Astrid eyes me, then the drink I can't seem to let go of. It's nearly to the dregs already. "Where did you get that?"

"Relax," Dahlia says, leaning around me. "It's nonalcoholic."

"It's definitely not. Look at her. She's swaying back and forth."

"You're being dramatic," I say in my most sober voice. I lift my drink. "It's a smoothie."

Astrid's face tightens. She latches onto my arm to show everyone my wristband.

Dahlia rolls her eyes. "She's fine. The drink is barely hitting her and I'm driving her home." She places a hand on my shoulder. "Let the kid have some fun."

I face Astrid. "Yeah, let me have some fun. Dahlia knows all about having fun."

"I'm her *mother*," Dahlia adds in a serious tone.

"You're doing a great job," Astrid says coldly. She and Sterling exchange a glance, like they're going to have a long, bitching phone call about Dahlia later, but stay quiet for now.

"So, Dahlia," Zelda says suddenly, cutting the tension, "I saw you in that music video, for that band."

Dahlia instantly relaxes, melting toward the table all casual. "Oh. Thanks," she says, as if Zelda complimented her just by having seen some of her work.

"I'm looking to go into film, actually," Zelda continues. "Behind the camera, not in front of it. Know anyone I could maybe intern with next summer?"

"I could ask around for you." Dahlia squeals a little. "It would be *so* fun to show you and Madeline around California. We could make it a girls' trip. There's this place in—"

"Yeah, *so fun*," I say sarcastically, knowing she'll be living there again by that time. "Except I'll be at the bookstore next summer."

"Boring," Dahlia says. "Why don't you want to do something fun? You're so young and have all these possibilities—and you want to work in the boring, dusty, *boring* bookstore?"

"It's not boring to me." Which reminds me. "Benny," I say, a few bites into my sandwich. Some cheese might be stuck to my cheek. "Will you go to the porta potty with me?"

Zelda raises her eyebrow at me, probably wondering why I'm asking my brother to go instead of her. She hates porta potties on principle, though, and there's also the matter of her not knowing I considered bailing on B&M. And that's why I need to talk to Benny.

"Interesting segue," she says, her eyes narrowed.

"I have a fear that the door won't lock and I need someone to stand guard. You're not very intimidating with your space buns and 'whatever' attitude."

Dahlia smiles when I use her shoulder to push myself up. Benny grabs on to my elbow and directs me toward the bathrooms, but I don't actually have to go, and I only *kind of* need his assistance. At some point recently, the world got all swirly around me.

"Let me have some of that," he says, nodding to what's left of my drink.

I hadn't even realized I had it with me.

"Sorry, you have to be at least twenty-one years of age to consume this smoothie in the United States."

He raises an impatient eyebrow, yanking me in time so that I don't run into an unattended child playing in the dirt. "You're seventeen."

I lift my wrist—no, wrong one. I lift the other. "Not according to this wristband."

"Let me have the rest and I won't tell Astrid about the application."

"You already said you wouldn't."

He smirks. "The situation has changed."

"Brat." I hand him the drink. "I got rid of the application. You know I'd never do that to the store."

When he finishes it, he grins. "And you know I wouldn't have told her."

I smirk. "You just drank my backwash."

"There's nothing wrong with applying somewhere else— Astrid wouldn't care." He levels me with a steady gaze. "But you really won't leave it, huh?"

"There's a lot wrong with applying somewhere else." I shouldn't be convincing him to rat on me—not that there's anything to rat on me about!—but the fact that he's trying to ease my guilt this way is unsettling. Like when Astrid basically gave the staff a big shrug after saying the store might be closing. Is he giving up, too?

"I don't agree. Just because your first words were 'books and Moore' doesn't mean they have to be your last words."

Then he excuses himself to use the bathroom, and I go up to the counter to order another drink. He should have played his cards right and asked for a brand-new one instead of my leftovers. But I wasn't about to tell him that, especially when he had been playing psychological warfare with my emotions. It's wild how they just hand the drink right over because of a little bit of lime-green paper wrapped around my arm.

It's after five minutes of standing outside the porta potties and no sign of Benny that I wonder if he got caught with my drink and was thrown out. Is that how it works? Can you get thrown out of a place that's outside?

Setting my drink down beside my foot, I free my phone to text him. Another child joins the unattended child from earlier and they run around me, upsetting my slushie. My phone slips from my grasp and lands on the dirt. I right the drink, pick up my phone, and text where are you.

I get an answer before I can even lock my phone.

**Ass-Per Hamada**

Today 6:58 PM

. . . at my house?

6:58 PM

I stare hard at the name on the text, confused for a second before it clicks, causing my face to grow hotter.

Wrong number

6:58 PM

That makes more sense

6:58 PM

I'm not ready to go back to my family and face the consequences of my actions. I've never been a huge drinker—not a lot of the stuff I can get my hands on tastes all that great—and I prefer to be the designated driver so that I know everyone will get where they need to be safely. But I have a ton of options for drivers tonight and I'm not drinking because I'm stressed; I just happen to be stressed and conveniently drunk. So, it's fine. This isn't coping, this isn't excessive. I will accept my lecture with a hazy head and then sleep it off.

Another sandwich sounds good. Or a taco. Or a cupcake. I pretty much want everything from every food truck I pass and I'm sure I should get a thank-you food for Zelda for accompanying me and distracting my mess of a mom. The options are endless and maybe Dahlia had a great idea by coming here. Not that I'd tell her.

Where are YOU?
7:00 PM

Spring gate winery
7:00 PM

The dots appear. Disappear. Appear again.

Are you drunk?
7:00 PM

Tipsy
7:00 PM

Do you need a ride?
7:00 PM

Got one
7:01 PM

Boyfriend?
7:01 PM

Huh. Now that's an interesting question. And it strikes me as more interesting that I debate lying to him.

My mom—

Delete.

Yup—

Delete.

I have a ride

7:03 PM

You said. Am I supposed to keep guessing?

7:03 PM

The food trucks hum with the sound of generators or motors or whatever it is that they use to power their grills and stoves and magic food-cooking tools. I'm a truck away from double-fisting grilled macaroni and cheese sandwiches when a book catches my eye.

It's perched on the counter-window thing that pops out when food trucks are open for business and it's called *Finding My Identity with Food*. It has some delicious-looking wrap on the cover. I approach the truck and find a lady, hairnet and all, cooking up some kind of fusion food for the two people in line. The graffiti words on the truck read *On the Menu*.

I watch the woman work, sipping my drink and letting the phone vibrate in my hand. There's a music to her movements, an art to the expressions her face holds as she preps, flips, and spices the food. The menu says she serves Korean-Mexican-inspired dishes.

"How much for the book?" I ask her through the window as she hands two meals to the people waiting.

She raises a dark eyebrow at me. "'Scuse me?"

"The book." I nod at it. "How much are you selling it for?"

She glances at the book, like she forgot it was there. "How much would you buy it for?"

"Fifteen dolla—"

"It's yours."

I pull my leftover cash from my pocket and hand it to her. She drops the book into my hand and hesitates.

"And I'll give you my favorite dish in the book." She gets to work and I go back to my phone, thinking about how all books should come with food. I check Yelp to see if any of the reviews mention this truck's food. I should have done that before buying the book, probably, but I have a feeling I won't be disappointed.

When I open my app, Prologue pops up as my last search. It sours my mood instantly and reminds me that Jasper texted again.

I started reading the magnificent lies of lasers

7:06 PM

I call bullshit because if you had started you would not be able to look away

7:11 PM

On page 78

7:11 PM

Tell me a line from that page

7:11 PM

Wait no you could just flip open to that page

7:11 PM

Tell me the name of the inventor

7:11 PM

There's a pause, just a brief one, and then the three dots indicating his typing appear.

Crafter

7:12 PM

You could have googled that

7:12 PM

Then ask me another question, fandom gatekeeper

7:12 PM

"Here you go," the woman says, pulling me away from my phone and handing over a paper dish with a smile.

Her signature Newchos, according to the menu, hit the spot just as well as my sandwich did earlier. The homemade tortilla chips are warm and the pork strips are chopped into small enough pieces that I can scoop them up with the kimchi and cheese. I devour the dish in a few bites while sitting on the ground and flipping through the book. I finish my drink as my phone vibrates.

You've got nothing huh?
7:14 PM

I'm busy
7:14 PM

And you're the enemy
7:14 PM

I'm not tipsy enough to forget that. What's his plan here? To get me to drop my guard more, weasel his way into my head and heart by loving a series I love? He's not special. Everyone who reads those books loves them. Just don't go on Goodreads to fact-check me.

I go to force-quit my message app and all my running apps pop up. Yelp practically screams for my attention. I open it again, taking in the five-star reviews of Prologue, and decide to leave my own.

Prologue not only has really rude workers, but they put books out early. They sell their used books at the same price as new books. Prologue's air condition blows too roughly when you walk in. The ceilings are too high and the carpet is slippery. 1 star because I can't give 0.

The entire family group chat wants to know where I am, plus Zelda asks if my "drunk ass got lost." I ignore them and tuck the cookbook under my arm, an idea inspired by my second maroon-colored—I don't even know what flavor—slushie and bangin' nachos brewing in my head. A book event. But with food. Because people like food, right? And because nothing goes better with a book than free food, or vice versa.

I knock my knuckle gently on the food truck counter to get the woman's attention. "What inspired you to mix Mexican with Korean food? It's really good."

"Thanks." She leans out the window. "My mom is Mexican and my dad is Korean. They both made such great food when I was a kid, but it was always a Mexican dish or a Korean dish, and it seemed a shame not to mix 'em. My food's a way for me to share my identity with people."

I hold up the book. "Yeah. Do you want to bring your truck to my bookstore and sell food and books?" Didn't quite nail the proposal there, but my head's a little foggy. "I'm Madeline Moore. I work at Books and Moore."

She gives me a strange look, her tanned cheeks pinking. "Sure? I'm Melisa."

"Cool." I'm two steps away before I swing back. "I should probably get your number."

She nods, a grin fighting its way onto her face. "And maybe some water?"

# EIGHT

The best part of having a food truck parked outside B&M is surprisingly not the food, but instead the fact that it blocks my entire view of Prologue and, therefore, Jasper Hamada's stupid smirk.

Not that I've seen much of it in the last two weeks while planning for tonight anyway—just a few instances of glaring from across the street, slightly less intense sign wars than before, and an order of unpaid veggie pizzas, but the joke was on Jasper: I love veggie pizza and had forgotten my lunch that day. It's been nice focusing on this event, instead of a war with Prologue or Dahlia's incessant attempts at being friends. I've barely seen her, too, and we live together.

I did lose the bet, though. Benny rubs it in my face every time he happens to be around Dahlia and me at the same time, which hasn't been much. He gives me a cheeky grin and says, "Hi, Dahlia. Fancy seeing you here," and then he whispers "still" to me. I'm not sold on the fact that she'll be staying, though. It's one of those I'll-believe-it-when-I-see-it things. I try not to think of what the twenty dollars I forked over to Benny could have bought—two burritos and a brownie, one or two or even *three* books depending where I got them, a new pair of jeans, gas for the next two weeks. The list could go on forever.

Today's event, while meticulously planned by Melisa and me under the reluctant help of Astrid, could still be a flop for so many reasons. Right now, the main cause for concern is the weather. Melisa's doing food prep in her truck, her window and door open so she won't cook herself alive in the heat, and I worry people won't be interested in hot food today. We're having the event from noon until three thirty, and it's a Saturday, so we're hoping whoever is out shopping will want to take a moment to get some lunch and maybe come inside where it's air-conditioned and check out Melisa's—or literally any other—book. If someone buys her book, though, B&M will get 10 percent of the profit, which turns out to be, like, one dollar, but still!

I'm tweaking our dry-erase board to read *Purchase Finding My Identity with Food & receive: water bottle and excuse to bask in AC* when Dahlia enters through the front door, all smiles. It's probably her third time in the store in as many weeks despite her last name being on the building. She's wearing bright orange wedge sandals, cuffed, light blue jeans with holes in the knees, and a white V-neck that was probably tailored for her torso because she read about that in a magazine once; she told me so—twice—while criticizing my own wardrobe for all the untrendy holes and faded colors most of my clothes sport. Yet she still steals my clothes.

"Hey, Maddy—*Madeline*." She raises her eyebrows at me, like I'm going to give her praise for catching herself after the fact. I like it better when she just calls me "kid" because at least then it feels like we have the right amount of distance between us. Familiar strangers. "Are you excited?"

I lift the sign with some effort and bypass her with a tight smile, until I'm pushing through the door and I can let the expression drop as heavily as the sign does. I make sure to place it in an inconvenient spot, right in the middle of the sidewalk, so people have to acknowledge it when they walk by. Maybe they'll feel guilty. It's what I'm going for.

Ravi arrives while I'm looking over the sign for any spelling mistakes or letters that could be written more strongly.

"Reporting for duty, ma'am," he says, saluting me with one hand. His other holds a plate of what looks like homemade white chocolate macadamia nut cookies. A daring, and somewhat problematic, choice.

"Where's the water?" I ask, wiping my sweating palms on my thighs.

"What?"

"We agreed last night that you'd buy water on the way here, the bulk kind."

His eyes widen. "Oh. Shit."

"Ravi." I try not to glare at the cookies. I'll for sure end up eating one or four, but I can't forgive him for showing up with something other than what we agreed on.

Melisa leans out her window. "I'm just about all set up with cold and hot options. Ready?"

"No . . ."

We probably won't get a customer as soon as Melisa starts taking orders, but there are two people waiting for food already. Apparently, she has a large social media presence, thanks mostly to her teenage son, Matt, who makes surprisingly funny memes. He's helping her in the truck today, when he's not staring at my boobs. Normally, I'd be grossed out or even flattered—for me, there's a fine line between the two—but today I just don't care. I'm too stressed and it's too hot, so a loose camisole is what I'm working with, even though it puts my entire torso on full display.

"I'm going to get some water, but start taking orders," I tell her. I turn to Ravi and, against my better judgment, say, "You're in charge until Astrid or I get here." I run into the store, ignoring Dahlia's "Can I help with anything?" as she sits uselessly on the counter, and grab my small cross-body bag from the staff room. I pass Ravi on my way outside. "Don't listen to Dahlia. You're in charge."

The closest place that sells water is conveniently located just around the corner, but so, so unfortunately located on the corner off Jasper's side. Carrying two large cases of water to the store is certainly going to put a strain on my back and arms, but what makes the situation worse is that I'm working and I know Jasper's working because his car pulled into—and quickly out of—the reserved parking spot for Melisa's truck as soon as he arrived this morning. I was half a minute away from going out and yelling at him, maybe kicking at his sleek black Mazda 3 because dealing with the parking authority for that permit was no joke, but he saw the sign and actually decided to be a decent human being.

I don't have the time, patience, or energy to get the water and deal with him seeing me and making me spend money I don't have at his terrible store. I should have sent Ravi, but the thought of dealing with Dahlia and the potential lack of customers at the same time was not an appealing one. Plus, if you want something done right, you do it yourself. I look left and right and left again, before running across the street and sliding between parked cars. I swing around the block and into the convenience store. I lug two cases of water to the register and I'm out within three minutes. Before I take the corner, I set the cases down on the hot sidewalk and pull out my phone to text for help. A shadow falls over me.

"Hi, do you need help?" The guy is Asian, kind of bulky—like he's intimately aware of what a gym is—and maybe half a foot taller than me. He's wearing Nikes, a tight shirt, and a smile with a bit of mischief in the corner as he lazily spins his car keys around his finger.

The smile twitches, like it's about to disappear forever. My stare is probably freaking him out.

"What?" I ask.

He nods to the cases of water. "Do you need help putting those into your car?"

I glance at the waters and then peek around the corner to B&M, barely visible behind Melisa's big silver food truck. I hate that I'm so worried to step foot on Jasper's side of Oak Street. This was my street before it was half his. "Do you work—" I point at the convenience store behind me.

He laughs. "No, sorry, I saw you put them down and they looked heavy."

I consider his offer. They are heavy, especially two. I can't imagine even picking up one right now when holding my phone is draining what little energy I have left. If ever an arm muscle were unlucky enough to find its way onto my body, I'd handcuff it and threaten its family to keep it there.

"That's really nice of you, but I can get someone to help me. I'm taking them to my job across the street." I point vaguely in the direction of B&M through the brick wall of Carson Convenience.

"Oh," he says, perking up. "Do you work on the food truck? I've always thought that would be a cool job."

"No—"

"Luke?"

I peek around the guy's frame even though I know—and dread—who the voice belongs to.

"What are you doing?" Jasper asks, and I'm not sure if he's talking to "Luke" or to me.

*Oh fuck. Then it hits me. Is this beefy dude another Hamada?*

"I'm just gonna help her with her waters and then I'll be there."

Jasper hesitates a moment as Luke turns back to me and bends to grab both cases at the same time. I'd be lying if I said it wasn't extremely impressive.

"Where to?" he asks, barely winded.

"The shop around the corner," Jasper says, coming to a stop next to Luke and straightening the hipster suspenders he's wearing. "Books and Moore."

Luke raises an eyebrow at Jasper and then turns to me, mouth open a little. A smirk starts forming—apparently a family trait, but Luke's is without a scar to conceal. "So, this is Madeline, huh?" He readjusts his hands on the waters so he's cradling them in one arm, like it's no big deal, and offers me a hand to shake. I take it out of pure shock that he can hold both cases like that, and from fear that him waiting on me will cause them to fall. "Hi. I'm Luke, Jasper's brother."

Luke is technically the enemy, but he's been so polite that I really can't help smiling back. Jasper avoids my eyes. Luke knowing my name means Jasper's talked about me before. I mean, I talked about Jasper before I knew he was the enemy—okay, and after I knew he was the enemy, but that was to bitch about him. Does he bitch about me to his family? I can only imagine . . .

*Madeline, the book troll from Books & Moore, put my phone number on their display sign today. Madeline, the chubby pest from Books & Moore, ran into me today and gave my shirt one whole wrinkle.*

"Nice to meet you," I say, stomping down my desire to flee. "I can handle the waters, but thanks." Luke can definitely handle the waters, though. He's already been standing with them in one hand longer than I had with two hands.

Jasper steps toward his brother, holding out his arms for the waters. "Dad's waiting for you to start the staff meeting. I'll take them."

My feet certainly don't make any effort to step forward so I can take the cases, but I say, "I've got them."

Luke hesitates for a moment, like he's not sure who to give the waters to, but he could stand around waiting all day without breaking a sweat over it. Maybe the Hamadas don't sweat. Jasper pulls the cases from his brother's arms and takes off around the corner without a word.

As soon as Jasper's foot touches the asphalt of Oak Street, he speeds up, but I latch onto one suspender strap, pulling him back as a car rushes by. It had been completely blocked by the parked SUV Jasper was walking in front of, but I saw it coming from the sidewalk. This idiot is going to get himself hit one of these days.

He looks at me over his shoulder, something unreadable flickering in his eyes. "Thanks," he says in a breathless voice.

I look around him, right and left and right again, before letting go and crossing the street.

When we arrive at B&M, there's a line of at least four people waiting for food and I spot Dahlia inside, talking to someone I don't recognize—oh shit, probably a customer. And it's not just them and Ravi either. There are at least three other people I can see.

I lay a hand on Jasper's shoulder to stop him from entering the store. "Out here is fine. Thanks."

He places the cases on the ground with more care than I did before.

"You didn't have to help," I say.

"I know," he says, looking toward Melisa's truck, "but I wanted to see what was going on over here. I needed an excuse."

"Hasn't stopped you before."

"Your *rules* have stopped me before."

"Rules?" I bat my lashes in innocence.

He narrows his eyes. "Don't be cute. You have to buy a book from Prologue. You were on my side of the street."

I want to argue that I meant for the rules to be like if I were over there trying to sabotage his store, like with *coupons* or something, but I know even if he were helping an old lady cross the street to this side, I'd hold him to buying a book.

*Maybe if I can distract him . . .* "I can't help it."

"Help what?"

I shrug, knowing my next words are a gamble. "Being cute."

A pause takes place in which I fear I've taken my last non-blushing breath in front of Jasper Hamada.

Then he smirks. "What about humble?"

I scowl and pull cash from my bag. All I have is five bucks. My last five bucks until I get my meager paycheck. "Here. Get one of your coworkers with taste to pick me out a used book and send it over." I bend for one of the cases of water, but spin back to Jasper, who stares at the money. "If you've got nothing for that price, which I'm sure you don't, you'll have to deal."

I take the waters inside the store and don't go back outside until I'm sure he's left.

I'm not sure what or who I have to thank, but something was working today. Maybe it was all Matt's doing because he's a little social media savant—we should consider hiring him. Dahlia even managed to stay sequestered on the sidelines for most of it, content with not having to help, but also being able to give off the vibes that she had something to do with the event whenever she managed to rope someone into talking with her.

Zelda showed up for her regular four-to-nine shift after one of those family-friendly, middle-of-the-day graduation parties she was invited to, and Ravi stuck around an extra hour just to see the sales total—and to pick Melisa's brain on her recipes. Astrid revealed, with one of her squinty smiles, that B&M should scrape by our new monthly sales goal, even with the waters and Melisa's cut taken out, and nine days left in the month. I double-checked her numbers and estimates before getting too relieved, but it was a success. We turned our store into an event and it paid off; we know how to build a cushion to work with from now on.

So now, as Zelda and I sit in the staff room stabbing what's left of Melisa's thank-you cake with a fork and Astrid and Dahlia—or more realistically, just Astrid—close up the store, I dare to think of the possibilities.

One event a month could keep us afloat. Possibly. They'd have to be incredible events that never get redundant—or maybe we could lean into redundancy and host book clubs and writing groups. It certainly wouldn't hurt to make connections with other small business owners in town, especially the ones selling food. Positive collaborations will bring positive word of mouth and mutually beneficial outcomes.

I want to chase that feeling of success, even if it was small, for as long as I can.

I slide a forkful of cake into my mouth as Zelda groans again, holding her stomach. Her nausea won't scare me off. The cake's still moist and sweet despite having been sitting out for hours. It looks like a pack of wolves got to it before me, but I don't even care. I couldn't eat lunch because my nerves were so high and then there wasn't time because we actually had customers to take care of. I sold all our copies of the Discontent series and ordered in three more of the first book in the new cover for customers, even though they wouldn't be out for nearly two months. I even chatted with a girl my age who was so excited for the movie that she nearly started happy-crying—

New covers.

Movie.

I push the sales reports away to unearth my phone.

"What the hell?" Zelda says as the papers fall into her lap.

I shush her and visit Isla Warbeck's website, clicking her "Tour" link. She's out promoting the books before the movie comes out this summer and it looks like she'll be closest to my area . . . at the end of August. Two months from now. She's wrapping up her tour in Philly, her hometown.

But, theoretically, if I could get in touch with her agent or her PR person, maybe I could get Books & Moore in little old Mechanicsburg added to her tour; it's only two hours away.

"Mads, what's up?" Zelda asks, watching me as a smile splits across my face.

"I have an idea."

I'm halfway out of my seat to tell Astrid about my plan when she and Dahlia come into the room. Astrid looks cautious. Dahlia looks like she just learned she can breathe money into existence.

"We have good news," Dahlia says. From their expressions, I can tell that it's good news for Dahlia only. Maybe her agent called her with another "big break" and she'll leave.

"Same." I'm unable to hold it back any longer.

Dahlia cuts me off, though, throwing her arms wide open as if I'm going to rush into her for a hug. "I'm the newest member of the Books and Moore staff! I can't wait to work with you all summer!"

She pulls me into a hug that I don't reciprocate as I glare at Astrid over Dahlia's shoulder. Behind me, Zelda chokes back a laugh.

"Do we really have the money for another staff member, Astrid?" I ask tightly.

"I'm working for free, duh," Dahlia says. "I just feel like I never see you because you're always here."

I grit my teeth. "Problem solved."

# NINE

I open my blank Word document and wait for inspiration to strike, but after a minute of willing the keys on my laptop to depress themselves and start typing eloquent sentences, nothing happens. This email is too important for me to mess up, but my words all jumble together in my head, none of my phrasing coming out coherently. I need Zelda, but her day off from work is being spent doing "family stuff," which could mean she's cleaning the house, running errands, or visiting her dad at his Maryland rehab. When she doesn't elaborate, I don't ask questions.

I've been at Neato Burrito for almost an hour now and the only progress I've made is through a Cowboy Crunch, a bottle of Dr Pepper, and a peanut butter brownie thanks to the gift card I unearthed from the dark abyss that is the space under my driver's seat. I tried to work at home, but if Dahlia wasn't standing in my door frame, sitting on my bed, or attempting to vacuum my floor despite the clothes and books strewn all over, she was talking my ear off. I had to leave.

And then when nothing magical happened while I was here trying to be productive, I tried to look Jasper up on social media again—for the second, or third, or twenty-ninth time. There's no Wi-Fi at Neato so it proved fruitless at first. But then I remembered I don't need Wi-Fi to cyber stalk him on my phone. That's how I found out the loser with the slick clothes requested me on Facebook, Twitter, *and* Instagram, which I had made private to match his because if I can't stalk him, he can't stalk me. Now the temptation is killing me. We're obviously *not* friends, but seeing his profiles might help me find a way to take him down. It would be purely research if I accepted. Though holding these requests over his head would fill me with sick pleasure and power.

I let this eat away at me like diet soda before switching to my messages to avoid having to respond to his requests at all.

**Zelda from YouTube**

Today 2:33 PM

Can you help me with an
email to Isla Warbeck's agent?

2:33 PM

DID YOU WRITE A BOOK
AND NOT TELL ME??

2:33 PM

No, of course not. When would I have
had time to write a book? I'm
going to contact her and see if she
can add B&M to Warbeck's tour stop

2:34 PM

OMG why didn't I have that idea

2:34 PM

Because you're too busy
having a million famous author friends

2:34 PM

How do you even do that?

2:34 PM

I pretty much interact with all their social media
until they acknowledge me. Then BAM!

2:34 PM

Btw have you and

2:34 PM

What does Astrid call him

2:34 PM

Hotmada?

2:34 PM

Dyingggg

2:34 PM

Have you and Hotmada cut the tension
yet? You said you had a story for me
involving him and I assume if you had
made out or something I would have
heard about it by now

2:34 PM

Excuse me. My email. Help.

2:35 PM

And no, of course not. He's evil.

2:35 PM

Cute brother, though.

2:35 PM

How am I supposed to help you with
an email when you say something like that

2:35 PM

Not much of a story. I bought waters on
his side of the street, his big muscle-y
brother was going to help me carry them,
but then Jasper did.

2:35 PM

Anticlimactic

2:36 PM

Okay fine. The email

2:36 PM

You'll want to kind of phrase it like you
would an email asking for advanced copies probably

2:36 PM

So . . . I'm very excited to see Isla Warbeck.
I would appreciate if you sent her to me to review?

2:36 PM

If I were her agent I'd say yes

2:36 PM

Approved

2:36 PM

I'll overnight her to you ASAP

2:36 PM

I play with the tinfoil my burrito came in, squeezing it
together, then carefully pulling it apart. I switch back to my
Word document and type:

Hello, Ms. Li.

I'm emailing today to

To what? I delete everything but the greeting. Zelda says to write like it's a request for an advanced copy, but I've only ever done that once—and got rejected. I cannot be rejected this time. What would my big idea to save B&M be then?

I wanted to start off by saying I'm an extremely big fan of Isla Warbeck's and can't wait for the new paperback movie tie-ins and the film! I am the assistant manager at my family's indie bookstore in Pennsylvania called Books & Moore.

Not bad. Zelda can help me clean it up before I send, but first I need to figure out how to phrase my request.

I noticed that Ms. Warbeck will be near our location at the end of her tour and was wondering if we could set up an author event with her before she leaves the area.

I email it to Zelda. She calls me after a few minutes.

"Is it that bad?" I ask quietly, my phone tucked between my ear and shoulder as I pointlessly change the font and size of my words.

"Sorry," she grunts, "my mom wants me to do the laundry." A pause. "I put you on speaker; can you hear me?"

"Yes."

"So, maybe you should mention you're in a bookstore battle

with the competition across the street and having Warbeck come could help save the store."

I scoff. "We'd sound so desperate."

"Aren't we?"

I squeeze the tinfoil again. "And then we'd just put Prologue on her radar and she'd be all 'Well, why wouldn't we just send the author to the better bookstore?'"

"You could mention I'm available to moderate the event or something."

"Conceited."

She huffs on the other end. "You don't really feel that way, right?"

"That you're conceited?"

"We both know you think I'm conceited. I mean that our store isn't better. Prologue is just a less-funded Barnes and Noble wannabe. We're better."

Funds. I don't even want to think about it. Everything boils down to money, or the lack thereof. One event a month will only get us ambling by. We need more so that it's not even a question that we have enough emergency money to fall back on to renew the lease and keep the store open.

"We should do a fundraiser," I say. "Or is that equally as pathetic as begging Warbeck to come because we're struggling to stay open?" I type "GoFundMe" into my Notes app.

"A fundraiser! The online book community would go wild for it. Save the indie! Long live books! Down with the Hotmadas!"

I pull the phone away from my ear, smiling. Her enthusiasm

is appreciated, but the fundraiser will have to wait for now. One thing at a time. The one thing currently being cleaning up and sending my email.

She starts yelling something on her end and I reluctantly return the phone to my ear.

"Levi, these are clean clothes you just threw your dirty uniform on!"

"Zelda," I say patiently.

"I don't roll around in dirt and then jump on your bed!"

"Z."

"I'm being nice and you do that? I'm going to buy a used jockstrap from Craigslist and put it in your pillowcase."

"Zelda, focus."

"Sorry, Mads. I'm here." She grumbles a bit. "What an ass."

After internal and external debate with a mostly focused Zelda, this is what I end up sending to Samantha Li:

Hello, Ms. Li.

I am the assistant manager at an indie bookstore called Books & Moore in Mechanicsburg, Pennsylvania. Ms. Warbeck will be nearby in August, and Books & Moore would love to set up an event with her before she leaves the area. Please let me know if we can discuss the details by email or phone, at your convenience.

Thanks for your time and I look forward to hearing from you,

Madeline Moore

Assistant Manager, Books & Moore

As I'm throwing out my trash, a familiar face walks into Neato, a box in her arms. I can't place exactly where I know her from. She's Indian, I think, middle-aged, pear-shaped, and has dark hair braided around her head. It's not until she walks nearby that I smell it.

Chocolate.

She's the owner of Buns. Guilt thuds heavy in my stomach, even though I didn't fill out the application. Even though I'm the only one who would care if I applied elsewhere.

Her box is full of the brownies that Neato stocks at the register. She sets it down on the counter and the worker, Davis, this kid I went to school with who tried to go commando under his graduation gown, greets her. They begin counting the brownies or something, marking things on a clipboard, and I shut my laptop and shove it into my bag.

I watch them for a minute longer, straining to overhear their conversation.

"So, we sold all two hundred last week," Davis says slowly, reading something on his clipboard. "So, that means Neato gets one eighty and you get four twenty." It must kill him not to make a joke about that number.

He glances at the owner, like he wants her to tell him if he did the math wrong, but she nods. One hundred and eighty dollars just to let her sell her three-dollar brownies here. And she makes *four hundred and twenty dollars*. This is a cash grab. Everyone from soccer moms to stoners comes here and none of them are impervious to fresh brownies. I mean, I buy a brownie 90 percent of the time I'm here and I'm here 90 percent of the time.

I wait outside in the midday humidity, staying underneath the overhang of the strip mall to keep out of the sun. When the owner comes out five minutes later, I pounce.

"Hi!" I nearly scream, scaring even myself.

She twitches, turning around. "Uh, hi."

"Sorry." I laugh, stepping forward. "You're the owner of Buns, right?"

She faces me fully, no longer looking like she's about to run for it. She can probably smell the money potential. "I am."

She outstretches her hand and I take it.

"I'm Madeline. I work at Books and Moore down the street from you."

"Oh, hello. I'm Preeti."

"Nice to meet you." I clasp my hands together. "I was wondering—sorry if this isn't the proper way to go about it—but I'm the assistant manager"—I'm getting too comfortable using the self-given title—"and I would love to strike up some kind of deal like you have with Neato. Selling your food at our register."

She raises her thick eyebrows. "Really? I'd love to discuss that with your boss sometime."

It doesn't go unnoticed that she doesn't want to discuss it with me. Probably because I look fifteen and already admitted to not being in charge. And I jumped at her.

"Do you have a business card or . . . ?" I should probably be giving her my information, but Preeti seems charmed by my moxie or something and hands hers over.

"And your boss's name?"

"Astrid. Astrid Moore. My aunt." I don't know why I said that. I'm only further discrediting myself. *Nepotism, yay!* "We're trying to highlight other businesses in the area. Maybe you saw that we had an event this past weekend with On the Menu, the food truck? Great fusion food and a cookbook." I'm rambling. "I'll have Astrid give you a call! What hours work best for you?"

"I'm at Buns basically every day from six in the morning to seven at night, with the occasional lunch break or work trip exception." She hikes her bag higher on her shoulder with a smile. "She can call anytime during those hours and I'd be very happy to speak with her."

"Great." I smile and it makes Preeti smile. "I look forward to . . . this."

Classic. Horrible ending. Doesn't matter.

Preeti leaves and I stand there basking in the glow of my own genius. Maybe if we start this partnership, we can also get a discount to have Buns cater the Warbeck author event. If that even happens.

But things are looking up. So maybe it will. And maybe we'll do the fundraiser, too. Every little bit helps and so far my ideas are helping. We can save B&M. I can save B&M.

# TEN

I'm probably going to kill my little brother, but whatever. It's my fault anyway.

I should have actually thought about taking his shift before I agreed to it. But when he shook me awake from my nightmare this morning, I was so confused as to why he wasn't Jasper Hamada, why I wasn't in my dream version of the Buns basement, and why I no longer had all the pages from my latest Last Chance Books sale stuffed in my mouth. Then when I came to my senses, I was additionally confused by why he was home. So, when he asked me to cover his shift today, I didn't think twice.

Had I been able to comprehend what I was signing up for, or even what day it was, I would have flat-out told him no. Because working a double today is the worst thing I could possibly do. Not only has today been a nightmare—a screaming and puking child, a man who wouldn't get off his phone while I was ringing him up, and an attempted theft, to name a few events—but it's the first day of the *Magnificent Lies of Lasers* pre-sale and I desperately need those midnight tickets! The film won't be out for at least a month and a half still, but I need that very first showing.

But have I been able to even look at my phone, let alone pick it up to order tickets? No. Does Astrid have a semi-working computer connected to the internet? No. Is Zelda allowed to input credit card information into the computer? No, because Rhoda lives in perpetual fear of identity fraud, and the internet in general. I'm not sure I blame her lately.

The ticket ordering was up to me.

And what makes everything feel less worth it is the fact that I don't know why Benny needed off—not that he needs to tell me, but I feel like I haven't really spoken to him since Dahlia arrived. He's always at Sterling's or we're working opposite shifts. And when I do see him, he never wants to talk. His soccer camp is next month, for like a week, and then I'm off to college for months. This is our last summer together—morbidly assuming we'll grow apart during the next school year—and it's going to end with me hating him for not being around and, more important, making me miss my chance to see a midnight premiere of my favorite book-turned-film. There are only two theaters within thirty minutes of my house offering the midnight showing and I can't go farther than that because Astrid will have a conniption with me driving so late. Plus, I actually hate staying up late. I'm not a Morning Person, per se, but I am definitely not a Night Person. I'm barely a Person these days. I'm just a vessel for stress and mania.

There are five minutes until B&M closes and this woman with dyed red hair poorly covering her black roots has been here for an hour. I don't want to rush her, but I also need to get the hell out of here and to a computer with internet access. The presale started six hours ago and there hasn't been buzz for a movie like this since—well, okay, since the last Marvel movie, but still!

"Hi, ma'am." *Me again*, I want to say. "Is there a particular book or author or genre you're looking for? I want to make sure you leave the store"—*now*—"with exactly what you're looking for."

She shakes her head, her short hair hitting her chin. "No, but thank you. I'm just looking."

Astrid strictly forbids us from "scaring customers away" by mentioning that we're closing or hovering around them, so I'm stuck here.

"Actually," the woman says, getting my hopes up, "do you have anything similar in tone to W. B. Hertzler?"

"I'm not familiar with that author. Can you name a book by them?"

"*Sunrise, Sunset.* A woman travels across the country after her husband dies to meet the half sister he never knew he had."

Oh god. Grief road trips.

"Are you looking for road trip books or kind of . . . sad ones?"

She thinks for a moment. "Road trip, maybe?"

I search "road trip" in our Excel file because I've been making slow progress putting in keywords for easy searching and find one book. I walk the woman to the bookshelf and pluck it free.

"Here's *Fuel Low*." I skim the back of the jacket quickly. "It's about two ladies who used to be friends, but grew apart after some mysterious fight, taking to the open road when their third friend, who lives far away, tells them she has cancer."

She takes it from my hands with a smile. "I'll take it."

And I'll be taking my leave.

Dahlia pounces as soon as I get home, but I completely ignore her, racing up the stairs and into my bedroom. I slam the door shut, unintentionally, but at least it sends a clear Do Not Disturb message, and open my laptop.

The site is slow to load, which gives me hope there are still tickets and people are still able to buy them. I fill in all my criteria: two tickets, theater, date, and time.

Cold fizzles in my stomach, quickly overtaken by angry heat.

Sold out.

I try the next closest theater.

Sold out.

I try for one ticket at each theater, hoping maybe they just didn't have two tickets or there was some buying limit I didn't know of.

Sold out sold out sold out.

Fucking Benny.

If he has the nerve to show up here tonight, I'm going to give him a piece of my mind. This premiere, this book, means so much to me. I could get a ticket for a later date and time, but it's just not the same.

Someone—let's be real, it's Dahlia—knocks on my door. I don't tell her to come in, but she cracks the door open anyway, peeking in.

"Everything okay?"

"I'm finally ready to be an only child," I mumble, closing my laptop.

"What did he do?" She takes a seat at the end of my bed.

I swivel in my chair to face her. "I took his shift today and I missed my chance at getting presale tickets for a movie I really want to see."

Maybe Dahlia will shit talk Zelda-style with me, even if it's against her own son. She's never shown loyalty to him—to either of us—so why start now? Any chance to be a cool, relatable, likable mother, right?

"That was really nice of you," she says, "but that sucks. I'm sorry."

I nod.

"Can you go another time?"

I nod again.

"You really wanted to go to the midnight show, huh?"

"Yeah. It's a big deal." Something in my gut squeezes. I've been waiting for this for so long. I've never gone to a midnight showing of anything ever. Nothing has been important enough. It was the *one thing* I wanted this summer before I knew I'd have to want the store to stay open, for Prologue to close, and for Dahlia to leave.

"Maybe the radio stations will be doing giveaways or something."

I lean back in my chair, crossing my arms over my chest. "How does that work?"

She laughs, scooting forward in her flannel pants and oversized Anza-Borrego Desert State Park shirt. She sent the same shirts to Benny and me for our birthdays one year. I donated mine.

"Well, radio stations sometimes get the tickets and do giveaways on air. Like, they'll ask a question and the first person to call in with the right answer will win the tickets."

"It's not like on a website or something?"

She gives me a pointed stare. "As a millennial, I feel I can say this. You are giving your generation a bad name."

"My generation likes convenience. And a well-thought-out meme that can change the world."

"Sure, Jan."

"God, you're old. At least my generation didn't kill napkins and Applebee's."

She throws her head back, laughing loudly and fully. It makes me smile.

"Don't blame me for that. I love napkins and Applebee's. I think I single-handedly kept both in business back in California."

We sit in content silence for a moment before I turn back to my desk. "I have to cross-post some reviews, so . . ."

What I really mean is that I need some mind-numbing work to do requiring no original thought and to possibly have a mental breakdown. Plus, there's nothing more embarrassing than the thought of *me* wanting to continue the conversation past when *she's* ready to be done.

She stands. "Okay. What's the name of the movie? I'll keep my ears out for any tickets."

I tell her and she leaves, but I don't think she'll even remember this conversation by tomorrow. It doesn't benefit her, so why would she?

Still, this didn't feel as tense as it usually does. As awkward.

It was almost nice.

# ELEVEN

I wake up to my cream-colored walls drenched in sunlight, a bird chirping outside, and Astrid hovering over me with a brownie-batter doughnut in her hand. It smells like winning the lottery.

"I thought that might wake you up," she says with a squinty smile behind her glasses. "Are you excited for your first parents-free Hershey trip?" She hands me the doughnut before I can accidentally take her hand off with it.

I throw my legs over the side of my bed, my back cracking, and take a bite. "We're rescheduling."

At one point, I would have been excited to spend a day, sans parents, at Hersheypark with Zelda and a ton of roller coasters. Levi works the bag check station and was going to let us in with vodka in some water bottles—Zelda's adventurous idea. But right now, my life is a bit of a roller coaster itself and making a video to go with our fundraiser we're launching is a better use of our time than throwing up in public.

But it's for the best, if my Weather app is to be believed. It's going to be sunny, humid, and ninety-two degrees today, which is the actual worst weather—rain included—to stand in lines all day at Hersheypark. Because that's what a summer trip to the park is. Standing in lines for roller coasters. All day. Staying in line when they break down. Leaning against the scorching metal rails when your back starts to hurt. Sitting on them when your feet start to hurt. Counting your blessings when the queue has protection from the sun and those fans that spray water enough to disguise the disgusting amounts of sweat on your face, arms, and general everywhere area.

Thoughts of B&M's impending closure wouldn't be so easily lost in a loop or corkscrew turn, anyway.

"Why? This has been on the schedule since before graduation." Astrid sits on my bed.

I gather clean clothes with one hand and devour my doughnut in the other.

"Zelda's making a video for her channel to promote the fundraiser," I manage to say around a mouthful of chocolate.

"But neither of you work today. Don't you want to enjoy a day off together?"

I stop. "We'll have plenty of days off together when B&M's secure."

She sighs. "I really hate how stressed this whole thing is making you. You should be enjoying your last summer before college, not working nonstop."

That's laughable. This is her business—her family legacy—I'm trying to save. Why isn't *she* stressed? "Someone has to be."

I grab a tissue from my desk and clean icing off my hands.

"I'd feel worse if I just sat there and watched the store die." I try not to glare at her. "Just want to get this video done."

She stays quiet, watching me, a frown pushing lines onto her young face. "You don't have to do a fundraiser or any of this, you know? You don't need to add extra work to your plate."

It certainly doesn't feel like that. It feels like I'm eating for two since she's apparently fasting.

Zelda takes another long gulp of "water" until the bottle is empty. She shrugs at my pointed and disgusted stare.

"I already had the vodka ready for Hershey. What was I supposed to do? Funnel it back into my mom's bottle and hope she didn't notice that the amount increased after she supposedly drank it?"

"Or maybe you could have saved it for another day, not the one we're filming an important video on?"

She tosses the empty bottle into the little green recycling bin behind the counter, where Ravi doesn't even budge from his hunched position. He flips the page on his graphic novel, or maybe it's a comic. I don't really know the difference and now it makes me feel like I'm not as good a bookseller as I think I am, but I can't ask him and admit defeat. I'll ask Google later.

"Sorry, Mom," Zelda says, rolling her eyes. "Would you feel better if you had some?"

"What, are you going to regurgitate it and spit into my mouth?"

She gives me a pointed stare so heavy her golden messy bun shifts forward on her head. "I have the other bottle."

The store is empty except for the three of us, and I'm not technically working, but being drunk here feels like sacrilege, and one of us needs to be able to drive after the video's over. I imagine it's not actually going to take the two hours Zelda predicted, but then again, she's the one used to making videos. Maybe they usually take this long. Or maybe she's low-key drunk in all of them and that's why they take so long to make—

"Madeline," Zelda says again, shaking the extra bottle in my face. "Yes or no?"

"No. Can we set up for the video now?"

"You're so antsy." She zips the bottle into her small white backpack and tosses it over Ravi's head. He finally looks up. "Isn't she so antsy?"

"He's not even paying attention. The actual Avengers could have stopped in the store by now and he wouldn't have noticed."

He raises an eyebrow at me and then mutters to Zelda, "She *is* antsy."

A drop of sweat drips down my back despite the AC. I pat my shirt against the area, soaking it up.

"What's your deal?" She sets up her tripod and camera, moving them both in front of the window facing the bookshelves where the first thing she did was organize the books to spell out her name as an "Easter egg" for her fans.

"No deal. It's just hot."

"It's always hot." She turns her camera on and a little square of B&M is visible in the viewfinder. "What's going on? You're killing my buzz."

"I'm frustrated."

"Sexually?"

"No, with Astrid."

"Definitely not sexually, then," Ravi interjects, flipping a page.

The door chimes and a middle-aged man wearing glasses and a Hawaiian-style shirt steps inside. We all freeze, nodding at him, but he just smiles and heads into the stacks.

"Please let me know if you need any assistance," Ravi calls after him, already reengaged in his comic.

By the time the man checks out with Ravi, I've told her everything, just let the dam loose or whatever the phrase is. And instead of offering insight or sharing my frustration, she says, "Astrid's dealt with the store for a long time. Maybe she's just done." She adjusts her Peter Pan collar. "Oh, hey, when you drop me off at home, do you want to stay to Drunk Dive?"

I tilt my head. "Not giving me much of a choice if I want you to live."

"So, you'll be Sober Swimming?"

"Zelda." I hate feeling like a nag, but lately, it seems like I'm the only person taking this seriously. Yes, I should be spending my summer having (safe) fun with my best friend, but that's not in the cards I was dealt. It's just not an option and I wish she'd get on board.

She grins, nodding toward the shelf. "Let me fix the focus. Stand a foot in front of the shelf."

I do, squinting in the bright light from outside. "What do you think? Should I say something to Astrid? Tell her to get her head in the game?"

"I think she's your aunt, and your boss, and you should let her process what's happening to *her* store in her own way." She twists the lens a little, squinting at the viewfinder.

"Maybe she just needs someone to snap their finger in front of her face, get her to come to her senses. Maybe she's *in shock*."

She offers a sympathetic look. "Oh, Mads. Get real."

I step forward to, I don't know, smack her, but she waves her hands at me. "A foot away from the bookshelf! I have to redo my focus now."

"Are you sure you can even see clearly with how much vodka you just chugged?"

She waves away my statement. "It hasn't hit me quite yet. Stay right there." She grabs tape from her backpack and marks the floor where the toes of my sneakers—what used to be her sneakers—rest. "It's Astrid. You can't tell her what to do, and it's a waste of time to try."

"What you're saying is, I should let her sabotage the store— what should one day be *my* store—by not doing anything?"

She laughs, laying another piece of tape next to my feet. "Not exactly. But she has to *want* to save the store. She's been open to what you've suggested so far." She straightens. "Are you sure you don't want some vodka? It'll loosen you up."

"I'm sure." It's only now that I realize how stiffly I'm stand- ing. I roll out my shoulders and neck with a sigh. "This is just so important to me."

"I *know*," she says, shaking me gently by the shoulders. "Now, let's shoot this video before the vodka fully kicks in or you'll be holding me up scarecrow-style."

She presses the record button on her camera and I wish I were anywhere but here. Not now. I can't seem to force my face muscles into anything other than a blank expression, but I try.

"Hey, students," Zelda says, waving the camera. I've seen her film before, but she hadn't shot the introduction while I was around. I want to laugh but suck it in, using the feeling to create a smile. "This is Zelda from Required Reading, here with my best friend and book wizard, Madeline."

I wave at the camera and, fuck, it's so awkward. I know Ravi's watching us, but if I look in his direction, I'll burst into laughter.

"I know I normally post videos on Tuesdays and Thursdays, but this video is a little special. It actually has nothing to do with one specific book, but everything to do with a whole bunch of books." She gestures to the books on the shelf behind us, then turns to me. "I'll cut this out and put confetti or something on the title card." Back to the camera: "I've mentioned it before, but I work at a local indie bookstore with Madeline and we have created a GoFundMe page to basically ask the amazing book community to help us save it."

She points at the camera. "You guys can't see it, but—maybe I'll show you later—there's another bookstore across the street that's trying to run us out of business and we can't let that happen. Books and Moore is an institution, if I'm even using that word correctly. Basically, it's kick-ass and the store across the street is just ass."

I shift next to her. Is it going too far to slander them to ten thousand or more people online? Did I even need to be in this video if I don't have to say anything? Will people be able to tell I'm sweating in 1080p? I can imagine the comments now, the ones that focus on my appearance instead of the message.

"Do you want to say anything specific?" Zelda waits for me to answer.

"Um." I glance at the camera and then to her. "To the camera or you?"

"As hilarious as it would be if you only addressed me in the video, I meant to the camera."

"Like what?"

"Anything you want to say. About B and M or Prologue, or if you wanted to turn this into one of those videos where you come to the realization that you have feelings for—"

"Z."

"I'm just saying. My viewers would definitely ship hashtag . . . Jadeline."

My face grows hot as I look to the camera, Zelda doing the same, and think of how badly I want to squash Jasper beneath my Vans.

"Books and Moore is my family's store, but it's kind of more than that. It's another family member. A place I go when I want to feel useful or safe or just to escape. I want to run this store after college, but now that might not be a possibility. We need some extra funding to stay open, so any donations would be really appreciated. We've even—" I glance at Zelda now, who smiles encouragingly, but not entirely like my best friend, more like the YouTube personality version of her. "We've even set up a system so that you can order certain books from us if you'd prefer your money be spent that way."

"A link to a list of the available books will be posted in the description below and on my Twitter, and each purchase will come with a signed Required Reading bookmark," she adds.

I nod, feeling sick to my stomach for being so honest and needy and out of my depth. These strangers don't owe us anything. I could just be putting myself out there to be trolled.

She turns to me again. "Anything else?"

"Date and time of the fundraiser?"

"Oh, yeah. Duh." To the camera. "Our GoFundMe page is officially live now. Please click the link here." She gestures vaguely above her, then looks to me and points to my nose. "Or here." Now she does a sweeping gesture below our torsos, a giggle escaping her lips. "Or here. Or in the description of the video below." She points down. I think the vodka is hitting her.

"And, as always"—she starts to slur—"tune in on Tuesdays and Thursdays for more book interviews, author reviews, and general bookishness from me, Zelda from Required Reading." She winks and delivers a heavy glance in my direction. I wave to the camera, unsure. She bursts into laughter and rushes forward to stop recording. I can't tell if the mess-up was on purpose or because of the alcohol.

"I want to transfer it to my computer and see if it's as terrible as I think it might be. Then get some interior and exterior shots of the store. Maybe some of Prologue. Do some fancy focus shift shit for the intro and outro."

She spins toward me with the camera clenched in her hands. "We should record a prank on Prologue!"

Part of me screams *Yes!* but the other part reminds me that I'm not drunk, or that senseless.

"No. That seems like it wouldn't really win people over in terms of helping us?" Not that it isn't completely tempting.

She deflates. "Fiiiine. I'll have the video edited tonight and post it tomorrow. Are you ready?"

"I'm not expecting much." You can hope for it, but not expect it. The only thing I can control is how I help B&M personally. I'm hoping to be so busy planning the next event that I won't even notice when the fundraiser tanks.

"Just wait. A few donations and you'll feel differently." She turns to Ravi, who stares at us with a smile and his chin perched in his palm. "Books and Moore," she chants. "Books and Moore! Books and Moore!"

# TWELVE

Isla Warbeck Book Tour

Yesterday at 10:32 AM

From Amy Jones

To Madeline Moore

Dear Madeline,

Thanks so much for reaching out about hosting Isla Warbeck at your store! Things are looking positive on our end, but I'd like to gather some information about your store. Could you please send me the owner's contact information, your contact information, and the store's location for starters? Also, if you have a preferred date and time from the list attached. Thanks!

    Best,

    Amy Jones

    Publicity Consultant

    Carvington Books

Re: Isla Warbeck Book Tour

Yesterday at 10:47 AM

From Madeline Moore

To Amy Jones


Hello Ms. Jones,

I'm so glad to hear we can try to schedule something. I've attached all the information you requested. Any of the suggested days and times would work, but ideally Saturday, August 22, would be best!

Sincerely,

Madeline


Re: Isla Warbeck Book Tour

Today at 9:57 AM

From Amy Jones

To Madeline Moore


Dear Madeline,

Great! We'll add that date to the books, then. I'll be in touch with Astrid and you with more details, but you can go ahead and consider this confirmed.

Best,

Amy Jones

Publicity Consultant

Carvington Books


"What are you doing?" I ask for the four thousandth time. I can't keep the annoyance from weighing down my tone despite the good news I got an hour ago.

Dahlia stops her second lap around the store. "Just trying to memorize where everything is." She raises her wrist so I can see the slim purple band around it. "And get my steps in."

It's been a rough morning so far. First, she barged into my room at seven o'clock asking if she could borrow my never-worn white dress that had been meant for graduation—to which I had to tell her I wanted to wear it today, forcing me to actually commit and remove the tag—and second, she insisted we listen to the radio, which I forgot I even had in my car until she turned it to some pop-country crossover station. Third, she's been aimlessly walking around the store, nitpicking placements and saying the section titles aloud instead of putting books on the shelves, cleaning, or staying really really really quiet.

I cap the marker I've been using to design flyers for the War-beck event. "Why don't you take a break? Get us something from Buns?"

Her eyes light up. "Coffee? I'm really needing a pick-me-up today."

*Debatable.*

"Sure, get coffee." *You can have all the coffee in the world if it'll get you out of here.*

"What do you want?" She bends behind the counter and pulls out her wallet. I don't know where she's getting her money, but I won't complain if she's paying. It's not like she ever offered any child support over my near-eighteen years of life.

"Something small and carb-y." I'll take a break while she's gone. Really enjoy it, too. "Chocolate is a must."

She heads to the door. "Anything to drink?"

"Strawberry banana smoothie. Take your time."

"Sure thing, kid." She opens the door, the chime ringing throughout the store, but from the corner of my eye, I see her standing still.

"What's—what the hell?" I round the counter and stand next to her, confusion bleeding into anger.

Someone—let's be real, *Jasper Fucking Hamada*—has placed caution tape all over our entrance. For how long, I don't know. No wonder it's been a slower morning than even our slowest of mornings. People couldn't get in the door. God, the store probably looks like it's condemned or something.

I rip through the tape and stomp outside to check the rest of the storefront. Thankfully, it's just the caution tape over the door, but someone—*Jasper Fucking Hamada*—owes me a book sale. And deserves some retaliation.

Back in the store, I run my flyer through our outdated scanner, printing a stack as thick as the paperback Astrid's been slowly reading on her breaks the last two months. By the time the last page spits out, warm to the touch, the device is shaking and clunking and humming, on its last legs.

"Stay here," I tell Dahlia, ripping the rest of the caution tape free and throwing it into our trash can. I grab my stack of flyers and a dry-erase marker.

"Do you want some help?"

I try my best to hold back my glare when I look at her, but it's clear I failed by the way she shrinks back. "Just watch the store, please. And if Jasper comes over, tell him I said he has to buy a book and that I'm—I don't know. Say I'm on my break. At Buns."

I cross the street out of sight of any smug and watchful Prologue eyes, stopping at Jasper's car. I write "Shop at Books & Moore" on each of his windows. And when that doesn't set off his alarm, I hip-check his driver door, pull on the handle, and attempt to shake the car. The alarm shrieks to life and I fling myself a few cars away, closer to the entrance of Prologue, but out of sight.

Nothing happens immediately, so I pull my phone out of my pocket and dial Jasper's number.

He picks up instantly. "You've reached the best person in the world, Jasper Hamada."

"Keep lying to yourself." I eye the door to Prologue. "You've got a black Mazda, right?"

". . . yeaaah?" The suspicion is heavy in his tone.

"Parked on Oak Street?"

"What did you do to my car?" He's no longer calm. No longer cocky. No longer suspicious, but angry.

"Oh, I have to go. I think there's a customer coming in." The customer is him. He just doesn't know it yet.

I hang up and wait two seconds before Jasper zooms out of the store and heads for his car. I make a beeline for Prologue, slipping in unnoticed. I should have a minute or two before he heads over to B&M—how could he resist?—and I have to use my time wisely.

I start in the Young Adult section because the Discontent series is YA. I start folding and tucking the flyer into every single book I can get my hands on. My knuckles and fingers hurt from working so quickly, under so much pressure, but eventually I get down to two flyers. I sneak toward the nearest wall, where several flyers advertising Prologue events are posted, remove two, and stick up my own flyers. Chances are it'll take a few days for anyone to notice. I crumple up the old flyers and throw them in the nearest trash can. I doubt they recycle here anyway.

It's as I'm deciding I should use B&M's old display sign to advertise "Free dildos at Prologue" outside the store's neighbor, an antique shop constantly filled with granny-aged women and twentysomethings—there is no in-between—my phone vibrates.

"You've reached the *actual* best person in the world, Madeline Moore."

"You're not at the store and you're not at Buns. Where are you hiding? You crossed a line. That was—that was vandalism." He sounds out of breath, like he's hustling wherever he's going.

"It's erasable marker on glass, calm down. It doesn't even affect your customers from entering the store," I say in a pointed tone. I head to the front in a hurry, my feet padding softly across the carpet. "I'm at B&M. What book did you buy?"

"I bought a book called *If You Want a War, I'll Give You a War*."

"Sounds stupid. I would have recommended not buying anything before buying that."

"You're still doing that thing where you talk people out of purchases? No wonder you guys are going under." A car honks on his end. Shit, he's crossing the street. "I just want to make sure you're clear that my purchases alone won't keep your store in business."

"They sure don't hurt, though." I pass a young Black woman organizing the POS display at the counter. She tells me to have a nice day and the smile I give her is more of a cringe.

"And a fundraiser? Donations taper off. Your cause will lose momentum."

He saw the video. Heat fills my cheeks at the thought of him seeing me that vulnerable.

"You sound scared." I keep my own fear out of my voice, knowing that once I step through this vestibule, I'll either walk right into Jasper or he'll see me, or I could make it out without him ever knowing. The air pushes down on me as the door slides open.

"Not scared. Annoyed—"

I wasn't fast enough.

He tilts his head to the side, tucking his phone into his pocket. He has a Books & Moore bag dangling in his hand. "Up until now, I've mostly been doing my job, but if you want to give my phone number out to people, sabotage my car, or make a video calling Prologue 'ass,' make sure you can handle it when I do the same."

With my heart flailing in my chest, I try to sidestep him, but he blocks my way. I've never wanted to escape into the heat more than now. "You're more than welcome to give my phone number to people, as I said before," I say, "and if you want to make a video calling Prologue 'ass,' I'm not going to stop you.

Zelda might even be able to get it trending on Twitter."

Again, I attempt to get past him. "And I wasn't the one who called Prologue 'ass' in that video."

He nearly frowns. The action isn't enough to hide his pale scar. "I didn't realize your friend was, like, internet famous."

"Famous enough to ruin your store. If you had known, would you have waved your white flag sooner?"

"You say that like I'm waving it now. I told you I'm ready to go all in." He crosses his arms and fights a smile. "Your rules indicate you have to buy a book."

I huff, spinning back into the store, just to get away from him. He follows behind closely—too closely. I throw on the brakes and he rams into my back.

"Give me some space," I hiss. "Do you hover over all the customers in here?"

He looks me up and down. "Only the ones who might set the place on fire if given the chance. Don't happen to have a lighter on you, do you?"

"Arson isn't my sabotage of choice. If I need help finding something, I'll be sure not to ask you."

"Yeah, you could ask him," Jasper says, pointing over my head. I follow his direction and my stomach drops.

Benny, dressed in a Prologue polo with a name tag pinned to his chest, looks as shocked as I feel when his eyes land on me.

# THIRTEEN

*What. The. Fuck.*

*WHAT THE FUCK.*

I've never wanted to pulverize my little brother more than in this moment, right now. I could literally strangle him, not to death, but right to the point before death so I could stop and scream in his face, "WHAT THE FUCK?" This is so much worse than the day he ruined my chances of a midnight showing.

I can't even justify this moment like: maybe he's buying a book—because I've never seen him with a book that wasn't a textbook or one at B&M, and he's wearing the fucking uniform—or I'm totally fucking hallucinating, sleeping, being pranked again. This can't be real.

"Shit," he mutters, eyes sweeping the floor. "Hey."

"What the fucking fuck, Benny?" I step forward and latch onto his polo at both shoulders. I look at the red, cottony material and shake it a little, pulling it loose from his stupid fucking khakis. "What are you doing?"

He pulls his shirt free and I'm happy to say there are clench marks in it now. "I realize I should have said something sooner—"

"Or at all. You should have said something at all." I take a step back, sizing him up. This can't be my brother. "Or just not done this at all. Does Astrid know?"

"Of course Astrid knows."

So, it's just me, then. My own brother, my automatic best friend, didn't tell me that he was leaving us. The little backstabbing coward. "When did this happen?"

"Does it matter?"

"Yeah," I say too loudly, "it does. I want to know exactly when you betrayed your family."

He wants to roll his eyes. I can see it, can practically feel the itching in my own eye sockets.

"That day I asked you to cover for me, I had an interview."

Oh, it just keeps getting better. That day I was missing out on midnight tickets to a movie I've waited forever to see? That day? I could fucking scream.

First, he leaves me at home with Dahlia. Then he leaves me at the store with Dahlia. Now he's leaving me and the store and Astrid and Dahlia and what the fuck. I feel like I'm trying to choke down one of Dahlia's attempts at breakfast.

"I hate you," I croak out. "How could you do this to us? To me?"

A customer walks in and I want to scream at her to turn around, go to the store across the street where the workers are actually trying to save the store instead of sabotage it. She eyes the two of us even though we're locked in silence for the time being.

"Please let me know if you need any help," Jasper says to her, reminding me that he's here to witness what could possibly be the most heartbreaking moment of my life. To us, he says, "Maybe you should talk in the break room or something."

As if I'd give him that. He doesn't care about me or my reaction. He wanted me to be pissed, so I want to cause a scene. I want Benny to be embarrassed and Jasper to panic. I want to deter anyone from walking into this store, this place where Benny decided to throw away years of our family's hard work.

I glare at Jasper. "No."

"Madeline," Benny says with a sigh. "Books and Moore is just a store, and it's closing. You *have* to accept that."

"No, I don't. And it won't. You'll see. And then you'll feel like shit for leaving. And when I become the manager, I'm making sure we never hire you back, even when you come crawling across the street with your stupid polo set on fire."

He shakes his head, eyes going to the ceiling in a half roll. It only makes me angrier.

"B and M was never my identity like it was yours. It was just a job. Astrid's not mad at me for leaving, so you definitely shouldn't be. It's not your store—"

"Not yet."

"It's just a fucking store!" he hisses. "I needed something stable, so I'm here. I want a car, clothes, to help pay for college. I won't apologize for doing the right thing. Get over it."

I stare at him for a moment longer, searching for what's left of my brother. All I see before I stomp out is another Prologue robot here to destroy my world.

"Don't hound your brother about this, okay?" Astrid says, sipping water from a mug Benny and I hand-painted as kids. Our little handprints wrap around it and I want to take it and smash it against everything left of his at the house. "He made a good decision."

"How can you say that?"

I left Dahlia at the store alone to finish out the remainder of both our shifts, too angry to wait to see Astrid. I only went in to grab my bag and keys, then drove too quickly home, my Hyundai nearly out of gas.

Astrid sighs, setting the mug down. Benny's lime-green handprint with the blurry pinkie finger is faced toward me. I spin the mug so I don't see it. "He's allowed to work elsewhere."

"Elsewhere would be fine. But he's not working elsewhere, he's working at Prologue."

I've been texting Benny, but no response. I can't tell if he's ignoring me or if Prologue actually has a working no-texting policy. I'm not sure what I'd say to seventeen variations of "What the hell," but I'd at least try to form a response.

"I'm home," Dahlia calls, opening the front door and souring my mood, if possible, even more. "And I know just what will cheer you up!" She comes into the kitchen, a smile on her face. "Dorm shopping. Let's go today."

Zelda's texts about us raising nearly a thousand dollars in a few days didn't cheer me up—even her "I have no pants and no chill" text didn't—so I really doubt dorm shopping, or Dahlia, could. I've never been this mad. I feel like my organs are all screaming and melting inside my body, and my head is pounding. How could he just leave? Like it's not part of him like it is me. He said it's not his identity like it's mine, but how can that be true? We have so many shared memories there. I pulled out his first tooth in that store. Taught him how to tie his shoelaces while Astrid hosted a local author.

"I don't think so," I say, pushing my chair away from the table. "I just want to trash Benny's room."

"Madeline," Astrid says. "You need dorm stuff."

I reluctantly meet her eyes, then look at Dahlia. There's a pinch to her face.

"Not right this second." I shrug. "We don't have the money to buy a bunch of things anyway. I could probably just take Benny's stuff from his room since he's totally fucking abandoned us."

"Stop."

I'm shocked into silence. Because it wasn't Astrid reprimanding me, but Dahlia. Her face is stern, her eyes unblinking. Hot anger fills my veins. Who does she think she is?

"Your brother did not abandon anyone," she says stiffly. "I think him taking the initiative to get another job when he's worried about his current one is respectable."

Of course she does. She's an abandoner, too. Must be where he got it from. "So, you knew about this, too?" *He fucking told Dahlia before me? Dahlia?*

She ignores me to say, "You will go with me to Target and

wherever else we need to go in order to cross a few things off your dorm list." She puts her hands on her hips. "Got it?"

I'm so annoyed I could scream. Is there no one in my family I can vent to? Sterling definitely wouldn't agree because he's Team Benny all the way. Where the fuck is Duncan when he's actually needed?

Astrid nods. "Dear Old Duncan's final child support payment came through, just in time."

Oh, there he is. Not helping at all, making matters worse, that sounds about right for my life.

I grit my teeth and force an acidic smile, meeting Dahlia's eyes. I can't even begin to process how I feel knowing Duncan is officially out of my life, sans DNA, right now. "Fine. I'll go. Only because Astrid says I have to."

The Target on the Carlisle Pike is busy. Dahlia wants me to push the cart while she stays in control of the list, but I'm too busy willing Benny to answer my texts to watch where I'm going, and there are a lot of shoppers here collecting last-minute dorm items. You'd think halfway through summer they'd still be putting out those supplies, but apparently they're eager to replace bedspreads and mini vacuums with notebooks and superhero backpacks for the non-college back-to-school season. Everything is on sale, so there's that at least.

Dahlia turns a corner and stops beside a wall of matching sheets and bedspread sets. "What about this one?"

I glance away from my phone for one second to tell her "No," even though I kind of like the pattern she picked out.

"You know, I worked at a Target for a while in California. It was probably my favorite of the odd jobs I had between acting gigs."

I'm sure she means for, like, a month. "Cool."

"I didn't care for the uniform—I don't look good in all colors like you do—so I left." She points to a different pattern, her marigold-painted nails reflecting the harsh overhead lighting. "This one?"

"No." I text Benny again. My own rage has exhausted me to the point where I'm asking him to please text me back, can we please talk about this?

"Madeline," Dahlia sighs. I lower my phone and give her my almost undivided attention. "Could you please engage with me? With this experience? You should be excited about college. You'll be moving out." I'll be away from her. And Benny. "Making friends."

I don't need more friends. If my family can hurt me this badly, why would I welcome anyone else into my life? Zelda's enough.

I point at the pattern she picked out originally. "I like that one."

She smiles gratefully, tugging the rolled-up bedspread off the shelf. "Thank you."

"Can you get me a little trash can, one with the step pedal thingy, that matches? I'll watch the cart." I gesture to all the people around and Dahlia seems to think this is a valid excuse to separate. She nods and backs out of the aisle.

I swipe to my messages and fire flickers in my gut when I

see my last message to Jasper. That asshole stole Benny from me. He crossed the line.

### Ass-per Hamada

Today 1:27 PM

So we're stealing employees now? I can't believe you were insinuating that a harmless prank on your car was crossing the line when you did THAT.

1:27 PM

I move the cart when an insistent woman refuses to back out the aisle in the other direction. Her perfume stings my nose.

Is it stealing when they come willingly to us and ask for a job?

1:27 PM

Maybe if your brother started working at my store, you'd know how I feel.

1:28 PM

My brother?

1:28 PM

I think that's a little different

1:28 PM

How?

1:28 PM

I know you might think your store
is like a family but come on . . . mine actually is

1:28 PM

He . . . he doesn't know that Benny's my brother? So, they hired him just because? Or because he's a B&M employee. Regardless, that has to feel good for them. Stealing from the competition. Again. I bet he loved seeing me so disoriented, so upset—a loser.

Benny is my brother. Same mom,
different dads. You think I'd care that much
if some random employee left us?

1:29 PM

When you called him family I just
assumed it was a kitschy bookstore thing

1:29 PM

Still, he doesn't owe your store anything if he
doesn't have the last name in my opinion

1:29 PM

I feel like I've been slapped. Did Benny say this to Jasper? Does he not feel like he's part of this family, this store? He *and*

Sterling are as much a part of it as my grandmother was. Is he standing there next to Jasper, feeding him these words, knowing they'd hurt me? Knowing I'd hurt because he hurts?

"Madeline? Are you okay?" Dahlia's returned and her hand immediately goes to my forehead. I want to sob. It's the most maternal thing she's ever done, even though I'm sure she doesn't know how to tell if I'm sick just from a forehead touch. "You're pale."

> I doubt him leaving has anything to do with not feeling part of our family, asshole.
>
> 1:30 PM

> Regardless, you guys are closing and he did the right thing
>
> 1:30 PM

"I don't feel well." I pocket my phone, nausea pooling in my gut. "I want to go home."

It's after we've checked out—new bed stuff, a trash can, and notebooks that cost way too much—that my phone vibrates again. If I have to see Jasper's venom all over my screen, I might lose it.

**Benny**

Today 1:48 PM

> It's nothing personal
>
> 1:48 PM

B&M is dying. Astrid knows it. I know it.
Even Dahlia knows it. Why else would
she start working there FOR FREE if she
didn't think it would be temporary?

1:48 PM


You're leaving at the end of summer, so
it's okay if the store closes. I NEED a job
though. Better sooner rather than later or
whatever. Don't take it so personally. I didn't
tell you because I didn't know how. I knew
you'd act like this.

1:48 PM


But how do I not take it personally when my brother has left
me and our family's store all in one move?

# FOURTEEN

It's been about a week since I caught Benny working at Pro-logue. My shock has worn off, only to be replaced with a cold serial-killer-like focus—no murder, just the premeditated plan-ning stuff.

Three days ago, I asked him for his schedule so we could coordinate shifts and ride to work together, even though it meant I would need to pick him up from Sterling's. He didn't find anything suspicious about this. In fact, I think he was grate-ful and relieved. First mistake. He knows me better than this.

His second mistake was providing me a copy of his schedule that not only included his shifts, but Jasper's as well. *He knows me better than this.*

I've been biding my time. Pretending things are fine, that I've mellowed out, that I'm totally over the rage simmering in my stomach and forming malicious plans in the back of my mind. I even accepted all of Jasper's social media requests to catch him off guard and make him think that I'm coming around on him. But as soon as Benny walked into Prologue, he became my enemy, and I knew I had to plot against him. Jasper wanted to up the stakes anyway—he acted like I spray-painted his car instead of doing something totally harmless.

Today's the day for *me* to up the stakes.

Jasper works at one o'clock, so I need to get into Prologue before then without it being suspicious. He hasn't said a word about how I didn't buy a book that day, but I don't think he'd be so kind this time. Noon is when Prologue sees an uptick in customers, people shopping on their lunch breaks, so I'll strike now, at 12:45, while there are still others to distract the workers, namely my brother.

I pull the bagged lunch I asked Dahlia to make for Benny from behind the counter. I "forgot" to give it to him when we parted ways this morning. At 12:46, Ravi comes back from his first fifteen-minute break, precisely one minute late. I'm so tightly wound that I could yell at him, but then I'd just waste more time.

"I'll be back!" Benny's lunch swings in my hand, hitting my bare thigh with each step as I exit B&M into a wall of thick air. Today, I'm wearing brown ankle boots and a burgundy romper Dahlia tried to get her hands on. At this rate, all the clothes I've been too self-conscious to wear will get their fifteen minutes of fame just to avoid ending up in Dahlia's checked luggage back to California.

The doors to Prologue slide open and the cool air pours down, brushing my hair over my shoulders. I take a deep breath and enter.

There are a few customers milling about, some at the tables with coffees, books, and computers, while others wander the shelves slowly. At the register, Benny checks out an older woman in a sun visor. She's buying five books in one go. The only person who's left B&M with five books in one go was me. My record is seven.

The woman leaves, giving me a smile as she goes, and then it's just my brother and me.

Benny frowns. "What's up?"

I hold up his lunch. "I forgot to give this to you. Dahlia made it. You're probably safer not eating it, but I promised I would deliver it."

He laughs, taking the bag, and peeks inside.

"An Uncrustable. Chips. Brownies." He raises an eyebrow at me. "I can't tell if I should be offended she packed me an eight-year-old's lunch or happy that she stuck with prepackaged foods so I don't die eating her cooking."

"Yeah, well, don't get ahead of yourself. I'll take the Uncrustable." *Because he can't fucking eat peanut butter, Dahlia.* "And check the brownies for peanuts and the chips for peanut oil."

"Yes, I know, Madeline. I've kept myself alive this long."

I shrug. "I had a hand in that. You used to try to eat rocks because you thought they were big Nerds."

"Because *someone* told me they were."

"Well," I say, scooting down the counter, "that was all I came for. Actually . . ." I hesitate, like I rehearsed in my head all morning. I glance around the store, lean over the counter, and whisper, "Could I . . . Could I order a book here?"

He shakes the mouse connected to the computer, unfazed by my request. "What's it called?"

"That's the thing. I can't remember. I can just vaguely remember the cover. And Astrid isn't ordering any more books until we sell, like, all of the ones we have now, so I can't do it at B and M. Don't tell her I asked, though, okay?"

I play up the embarrassment, the shame, the guilt—all the feelings he should be having for leaving us. He stares at me.

"What?" I ask, my heart rate kicking up.

His eyes narrow. "You don't know the name of the book."

"Look, it's been a very stressful week, month, summer. Give me a break. Can I just peek through your ordering system—you have one of those, right?"

"Of course we have one," he says with an indignant scoff. He glances around and then jerks his head to the side. I flit behind the counter, standing arm to arm with him. The computer is stuck at the log-in page, which is exactly where I hoped it would be. He pushes the keyboard forward on the counter, revealing a taped note there—the password. Sterling would shit himself if he knew how unsecure they were.

He types it in slowly and pulls up an ordering system way more advanced than ours. He begins scrolling down the page of "Upcoming Books."

I lay a hand on his forearm. "Wait, you're going too fast."

He sighs, slowing his scroll. "What category is it? Genre?"

I tilt my head to the side in thought. "YA. I can't really remember. There was a lot going on in the blurb."

He filters it to only upcoming YA releases.

"Maybe it's already out."

He sighs again.

"Sorry," I mumble. I have to make him as annoyed as possible, so he'll leave me alone with the computer.

As if sent by the gods themselves, a middle-aged lady with a sequined top and too-long capris approaches the counter. Her flip-flops *clack clack clack* against the soles of her feet when she walks.

"Can I help you, ma'am?" Benny asks professionally, smoothing the front of his tucked-in polo.

"I'm having trouble finding a book. Another worker checked your inventory and said you had it, but I can't find him anymore."

"Oh, yeah. It's just me now. I can help you." He hesitates, giving me a sharp look. "I'll be right back. You can't be here when Jasper shows up."

I don't plan on it. I nod, placing myself in front of the computer and pretending to search for the nonexistent book I want.

He leaves and I quit the ordering program to open the computer's settings. I click into the password and security options, my heart thumping violently in my chest. No one is watching me. Benny said he's the only employee here until Jasper shows up. Exhale.

I type in the old password, Pr07ogu3, and then enter a new one, 3ugo70rP, into the Change Password section. I save the changes and log out. The password written under the keyboard doesn't work when I try it. In case I typed it in wrong, I try again, but nope. It's officially changed. I'll celebrate when I'm safely across the street. Maybe I'll even get a burrito today.

I hustle out from behind the counter and make a beeline toward the doors. They slide open with a whoosh and put me face-to-chest with a bad case of déjà vu.

"Hi, Jasper," I say, addressing his shiny name tag, "I'd love to stay and chat, but, actually, I wouldn't."

"Madeline—where's your purchase?" He gestures to my empty hands. "I'm not really feeling generous again." As predicted.

His short-sleeved floral button-up is wrinkled near the bottom, where it's tucked into his black jeans and secured with a simple black belt. Wrinkled. Huh.

"You're not on the clock. Those are the rules. Bye."

He wraps a hand around my upper arm and pulls me back, gently, when I try to exit. The doors slide open to the hot air outside and, despite the sweat building between our skin, I'd rather be out there away from him.

"The rules are you can't prank if *you're* on the clock. What did you do this time?" he asks with a sigh. "I had to stay late to pull out all those flyers you put in the books before. The least you could do is tell me what part of the store to look for your sabotage in."

"I dropped off Benny's lunch." I flick my eyes to his hand, but I say nothing, even when his thumb flicks against my skin and causes goose bumps. If he continues to hold me hostage right here, customers will get weirded out and decide not to walk into the store. "Sorry I didn't make you anything. I figured all the fun-sucking you do probably fills you up."

He removes his hand, exposing my skin to a cool burst of air, and the bumps on my arm multiply. His brown eyes lock on mine and his lips part like he's going to say something, so I turn on my heel.

"Okay, bye," I say, practically throwing myself out the door. I glance back as my feet hit the sidewalk. He stands in the vestibule, eyes narrowed. Probably thinking of inappropriate responses centering around my "fun-sucking" comment, but joke's on him because it'll be too late and too pathetic to retort now.

I cut across the street quickly and join Ravi inside B&M. He swipes past picture after picture on Instagram, going too fast to actually be looking, and cuts his eyes to me.

"Was that your lunch? You were gone, like, ten minutes. You know, it's not healthy to eat that fast."

Out of breath and heart pounding, I force out, "I'll take my last twenty later." Even though my stomach growls in protest, like me as kid begging Astrid to read one more chapter before I had to go to sleep.

I'm sure Jasper will be able to link me to his malfunctioning computer now that he saw me—anybody would—and I can't miss the chance to stand here smugly, ready to greet him when he stomps into the store to yell at me. And buy another book. Because those are the rules and I don't have to reciprocate his generosity because it was his choice to do so.

It's a harmless prank, one he could never replicate because he has no insider help at B&M. He'll come over, I'll ring up his book and tell him the password is just the backward version of what they had before. No real harm unless he doesn't associate the change with me, which would be a rookie mistake.

And if that were to happen, it's not the end of the world. They'd get it fixed eventually, only a little disrupted by it. It would serve Benny right. He's the son of an IT professional. He knows better and should say something to the Hamadas.

A man approaches and asks if I can help him reach a book. I stare at him for a moment, blinking, and then nudge Ravi, who is a foot taller than me, to help. I lean over the counter, watching the doors to Prologue for the next two minutes.

Eventually, Jasper stomps out, his face pink, and heads directly for B&M. I scurry around the counter with glee dancing in my stomach and watch as he steps out from behind a parked F-150.

Right into the path of a car speeding down Oak Street.

They collide.

Oh my god—*they collide.*

Jasper flies a few feet in front of the hastily stopped car, and lands with a thud I can hear from inside the shop.

"Holy shit." I tear the door open with a garbled chime and push past two men stopped on the sidewalk to gawk. My heart is in my throat and I can't seem to breathe past it.

I fling myself onto the street and kneel next to a motionless Jasper, gravel digging into my exposed skin. Blood is blooming from a crack cutting down his forehead.

A harmless prank. Right.

# FIFTEEN

I grab his shoulder and shake, immediately recoiling because what if his neck is broken and I shake it into a more broken state, like death? What if he's dead? Holy shit, if I killed him—

He groans.

"Oh," I say, my body sagging over his. I grip his shoulders, my eyes closed for a moment of relief, though my heart falters in my chest. His breath tickles my neck. "You're not dead."

The driver gets out of the car.

"What the hell?" are the first words out of this asshole's mouth. "You weren't in the crosswalk, dude."

I whip my head in his direction. "You hit him, you fucking idiot. He's bleeding."

Jasper groans again, his hand traveling toward the cut on his head. I stop him, pulling his hand back to his side. His eyes stay closed.

"Is he okay?" the guy asks, barely sounding like he cares. He glances at the crowd forming on the sidewalks. A car comes to a stop behind his and honks the horn. "Can we get him out of the road?"

I glare at him. "I want your information. We're not getting out of the road until I have it."

"Who are you?"

"I'm his friend and I'm going to make sure you pay for his medical expenses. Get your stuff now!"

He dashes into his car, his too-big sneakers flapping on the hot road. My bare legs are burning up, rocks sticking to my sweaty skin, but I don't move.

"Jasper," I say quietly, my heart beating in my throat. "Hey, can you hear me?"

"What happened?"

I look up. Benny. His eyes are wide and his mouth falls open when he spots the blood on Jasper's forehead.

"Go watch the store. I've got this."

He takes a half step forward before shifting backward. "Are you sure?"

"It's fine. I'm going to take him to the hospital." I watch him go back to Prologue before I lean over Jasper, my head casting his face into shadow. His eyelids twitch, one eye opening a sliver.

"Ow." He tries to reach for the cut again, but I place my hand over both of his, resting all three on his stomach gently. And that's when I see how badly his arm is torn up, blood running any way it can escape.

"Shit. Don't touch." I check on the driver. He's still in his car. "Can you tell me your name?"

"Jasper."

"Last name."

"Hamada."

"Favorite color?"

He raises an eyebrow, only to drop it with a wince. "What?"

"What's your favorite color?"

"Blue?"

"You don't sound sure."

"That's not one of the questions you ask." He exhales forcefully. "That's too subjective. You can't tell if my brain is scrambled by asking a subjective question."

He's fine. The attitude says it all. I push some hair away from his forehead with my free hand. "Well, if you know the official questions, why don't you ask them to me?"

"How many fingers am I holding up?" He wiggles his within my grip.

"Funny." I let go, twisting my fingers together in my lap.

"Here's my information," the driver says, kneeling. He's probably early thirties. He has some wrinkles around his eyes and mouth, a layer of stubble on his jaw. He hands me his driver's license, a copy of his insurance information, and a phone number written on the back of a McDonald's receipt—McNuggets and a McFlurry. It looks like the pen ran out of ink toward the end, but the basic shapes of the numbers are there.

I take a photo of it all, along with Jasper, and one of the man, who freezes as I aim my phone at him.

"Should we call the police?" he asks uncertainly. As if I'm the adult.

"Jasper, do you want me to call the police?" Regardless, he needs to go to the hospital. He hasn't made a move to sit up. I place my palm to his warm cheek, angling his face toward me. "Jasper."

"Hospital first," he mumbles. It sounds like it takes some effort. He licks his lips. "Please."

"Should I take you?" the driver asks. His white skin is pale and shiny with sweat. He wipes some away from his upper lip.

"Yeah, you're a great driver. I really trust you to do that." I stand, dusting off my knees. "We'll be in touch."

I hope I sound menacing and not just scared.

"I can take you to the hospital or we can call an ambulance. I don't know if you should be moving or not," I say to Jasper.

"I'm going to try to stand."

I help him, holding on to his uninjured arm and tugging. I turn to the driver, who stands there gaping instead of helping, and repeat, "We'll be in touch," with a pointed look toward his dent-free car that won't even need any repairs. I'm not sure the doctors will say the same about Jasper.

Slowly, Jasper pulls his car keys from his pocket. "My car's right there."

He attempts to point, but doesn't get his arm very far into the air. It's literally right there, though, so I shuffle him carefully to the passenger seat and get behind the wheel. I have to move the seat up, a lot, to reach the pedals, so much so that the steering wheel is practically kissing my gut. I adjust the mirrors and see the bystanders disperse. A few cars drive past us before I can turn on the car and pull out.

"Please don't hit anyone," Jasper says quietly, his eyes closed.

The drive to the hospital is silent, but every time it gets too quiet—like, my ears are ringing, hairs standing on end—I reach out to touch Jasper's shoulder, giving it a little shake.

"Still with me? How do you feel?"

"Head hurts." He raises a shaky arm and flips the visor down. I think he's trying to block out the sun at first, but then he slides the piece of plastic covering the mirror and leans forward, getting a good look at the deep gash on his head. "That's why."

I make a left at the next light and pull into the hospital parking lot. When we clamber inside, Jasper's arm over my shoulders even though he's walking fine, just slowly, we're given a clipboard with paperwork and a few tissues for Jasper's cuts.

Then we wait in silence.

I have to wait longer than Jasper to find out how he's doing because I'm not allowed to go back with him. Even though I brought him here and filled out his paperwork to the best of my ability. An hour after he's taken back to see a doctor, he's wheeled out, forehead and arm bandaged. His eyes widen when he sees me.

"What are you doing here still?" His mouth is slow to move.

"Is this your ride?" the nurse asks, raising his bushy eyebrow at me. "I'll help you into the car."

Is he assuming I wouldn't be able to help Jasper? Or is it protocol? Is the whole point of having a nurse this intimidating just to transport people into cars? He's built thicker than Jasper's brother.

"No, I have to call my parents—"

"I'm his ride," I tell the nurse. I glance at Jasper. "I have your car anyway. We can call your parents on the way." Since I forgot to do that the entire time I sat here worrying. I don't exactly have a plan on getting back to B&M after I drop him off at home, but figuring it out later is better than taking his car and making his family pick it back up and think about how this is all my fucking fault any more than they already will.

Jasper eyes me for a moment and then sighs, a weird slackness to his face. He's buzzed. "Sure."

I pull his car up to the sidewalk and the nurse helps him move from the wheelchair to the front passenger seat. I'm told that Jasper is on painkillers, but that he's good to take the maximum dose of over-the-counter pain medicine if he needs it after today—Tylenol preferred. As if I'm going to be taking care of him. The nurse hands me his paperwork and then we head out of the parking lot in uncomfortable silence. Jasper clears his throat, but says nothing.

I should have just called 9-1-1 and ditched him, but . . . could I have really done that, morally? He might be a brother-stealing asshole, but he's a human being and this is my fault.

"Can you call your parents?" I ask.

"I'll just shoot my mom a text."

"'Hey, Mom, got hit by a car but I'm fine' isn't exactly something you should text." I watch as he ignores me and types slowly on his phone anyway. I sigh. "What's your address?"

He rolls his head in my direction, giving me a pointed stare. "The thing listed on my license."

I come to a stop sign and return the look. "Are you concussed or just a troll?"

He only lazily smirks in reply. He gives me his address and stays quiet the rest of the drive. The only sign of life he gives me is his fingers tapping against his thighs to the quiet sounds of whatever station he listened to last.

After a short drive into New Cumberland, we pull up to the corner of Fourth and Forge, where his two-story Victorian-esque house sits, looking eerily like the funeral home a few streets away, sans hearse and signs. It's huge and white, with a porch wrapped around the sides and large windows every few feet. I had been hoping to see at least one car in the driveway, but there are none. Unfortunately, I can't just leave him here, make him someone else's responsibility while I try to squelch my guilt.

Even though staying with him would be the least I could do.

A bead of sweat trickles down the side of my neck despite the AC on full blast. I pull into the driveway and slam the car into park. Jasper's halfway out of his seat by the time I reach his door and offer help. He politely declines and takes a step. He sways, clenching his paperwork so hard it crinkles. I latch my arm around his waist. It's weird, but I fit nicely here, tucked under his good arm.

"You smell nice," he says quietly, begrudgingly.

Goose bumps pop up all over my skin, a traitor to the heat. "What?"

I glance at him, miscalculating a step and twisting my ankle. He has his head angled down toward me.

"You smell like vanilla."

"Thanks?" I have no clue how he can smell my ChapStick, but it's good to know the scent can power through the day.

He shoots me a shining half smile. "What do I smell like?"

With my head so close to his armpit, I'm ready to give him a truthful answer, but he smells good. Not vanilla good, thankyouverymuch, but good. Clean. Crisp. A gentler scent than the one that filled his car.

"Like fresh laundry." I gesture toward his front door with my free hand. "Let's go. Which key is the house key?"

His eyes narrow mischievously. How strong were the meds his doctor gave him? "If I said none of them, would you take me home?"

"You are home." I try not to twitch as his thumb flicks against the skin at my shoulder. It's rough, probably a little calloused. It sends shivers down my spine.

"I meant your home."

I laugh, because what else am I supposed to do? He's not flirting—or, I mean, he's not meaning to flirt. He's just a little high, maybe confused. I offer him the lanyard with his keys on it and thankfully he puts me out of my misery by selecting the one to open the front door.

"Okay, where's your bedroom?" I ask, my eyes taking in a shit ton of potted plants. It's stuffy inside and smells like syrup.

"You like to get right down to it, huh?"

I roll my eyes.

"Shoes off first." He uses me to keep balance as he bends to unlace his Chucks. "Yours, too."

I do as he tells me, placing my Vans on a shoe rack by the door, and then let him direct me to the small part of the house that is entirely his and his alone. The room is painted cobalt, with two large windows shrouded in sheer curtains, an unlit neon-light on one wall reading *Imagine me and you* and beside it on the other wall, *I do.* There is a powder-blue sewing machine across from the bed, next to his desk where he used to do "homework," and an overturned hamper pukes out black jeans and T-shirts directly in the center of his gray carpet. On the nightstand by his bed, some pamphlet lays open on top of . . . *The Magnificent Lies of Lasers.* Huh. Maybe he really was reading the book when he said he was.

He flops onto his unmade bed, fluffing the white comforter with a few punches, and buries his face in it, stitches not included.

"Is this what you imagined?" he asks, keeping his one visible eye on me. His voice is muffled in the fabric, and I can't stop myself from imagining hearing it late at night over the phone, or when I wake up in the mornings. I need to get out of here. My skin is buzzing. I must be allergic to something in this house.

"What makes you think I imagined your bedroom?" I step lightly toward his sewing machine, gliding my fingertips over his sharp steel scissors, and then over the spools of thread sitting nearby. The opposite of what I should be doing. A picture frame with two photo slots hangs on the wall—the photo on the left shows Jasper and a person I recognize as his friend Grant, in matching outfits striking muscle-man poses with big cheesy smiles, maybe a few years ago; the photo on the right is of two little boys, definitely Jasper and Grant again, in similar matching outfits, striking the same poses.

"I imagined yours." His voice is clearer now. When I snap my head in his direction, he's staring at me. Then he blinks fast and laughs. "I imagine everyone's."

I will my heart to stop square-dancing in my chest. "Weird."

He raises an eyebrow, adjusting his position on the bed so he's belly-up. His shirt has come loose from his jeans and a sliver of his stomach is— "You don't do something like that?"

"No." I try to wipe some sweat on my thighs, but remember as soon as my skin touches skin that I'm wearing a short-as-fuck romper. I'm so glad I shaved my legs this morning. "Or I guess I do. With Benny's dad. We have this game where we guess different people's baggage."

He scrunches his face up as much as he can.

"Emotional baggage."

He cracks a smile, nodding to himself. "I like that. Do me."

My breathing stutters, turning into a laugh. "Oh, uh. I can't. I—" I shrug. This is weird weird weird.

"I guess I put you on the spot."

I step toward his bed, my fingers now walking the back of his chair by his desk. "So, what do you think my room looks like?"

No, Madeline. Leave. *Leave. What are you* doing?

His tongue darts out to wet his bottom lip and I can't help but track the motion. "Lots of light because it's good for reading. It's probably covered in bookshelves—every wall. Then there's probably books on your nightstand, too. Whatever you're reading at the time—I imagine you read multiple books at once because you can't ever take a minute to just breathe. Pictures of you and Zelda and your family on the walls, but not in frames. Probably clipped on a clothesline or something like that. Aaaand clothes all over the floor, like mine, because you have no time for laundry."

I perch on the edge of his bed—his *bed*—with his legs behind me. "That was scarily close."

"What was I wrong about?" He sits up slowly, until his chin nearly hovers over my shoulder. I can feel his breath on my face.

"I'll never tell. Hopefully the uncertainty eats away at you."

He smirks, his scar disappearing. "Maybe I'll see it in real life to figure out the differences myself."

My face heats in a nanosecond and I'm sure he can hear how loudly my heart thumps. "And why do you think that'll happen?"

He looks down at my lips and then meets my eyes. "Because we're friends now."

"Says who?"

"You."

"I clearly remember saying we were *not* friends. But I'll let it slide since your brain got scrambled today." And it was *my* fault. My fault my fault my fault.

"No, I heard you tell the guy that hit me that you're my friend."

I angle toward him, putting our faces closer than they've ever been. I'm happy to see some pink creep onto his cheeks;

it's the least he can do to equalize this strange moment. "What else was I supposed to say? I'm your mortal enemy?"

He tilts his head playfully. "There has to be a middle ground."

"Does there?"

"Yeah. Why don't you meet me in the middle?"

My breath hitches, just a little. I don't think he's talking about putting a name on our relationship anymore. In fact, he's leaning toward me—as if there's even space to do that—and he stops. An inch from my mouth. Blinking too hard could propel me forward enough to close the gap, place my lips on his. But he's leaving me the option, letting the choice be mine.

He glances at my lips. "Oh. That's where the vanilla smell is coming from."

And then, as I'm thinking maybe I'll close the space between us, someone clears their throat from the hallway and brings me to my senses.

# SIXTEEN

"Mom." Jasper jerks away from me, fixing his hair to cover the bandage. He stuffs his arm under the blanket before facing her. "Hey. Did you get my text?"

"No, I forgot my phone at home. Was it important?" she asks hesitantly, a smile creeping into the corners of her mouth. She's Japanese, I assume, with long black hair braided over her shoulder. She holds a huge package of bulk tissues.

"Not really. Don't worry about it."

I whip my head in his direction. Is he really going to try to hide his injuries?

"So, who's your friend?" she asks, her smile completely transformed into a shit-eating grin.

Jasper raises an eyebrow at me. "See? Friends. This is Madeline."

She damn near gasps in excitement. "Madeline. Oh, hi." She rushes forward, the tissues still in her arms, and offers me a hand. Jasper pats down his hair again, but resistance is futile.

Even without the bandage, a few stitches on his forehead are likely to draw attention and his arm is cut to shit.

"Hi." I allow her to roughly shake my hand, up and down and up and down and up and down.

"I'm Kira, Jasper's mother." She rolls her eyes. "You knew that. He called me Mom."

She grins at me, then looks at Jasper, wiggling her eyebrows suggestively. "She's cute."

My stomach lurches.

"Mom."

"Okay, fine," she laughs, stepping away but keeping an eye on me. "I won't even mention how adorable you look together."

"Mom, seriously?"

My face heats as I stare down at my lap. It might have looked like we were about to kiss when she walked in, but we didn't. We didn't kiss. I don't know why disappointment pangs deep in my gut at the reminder. Has it really been so long since I kissed someone that kissing Jasper seems like a good option? Sure, before I found out he worked for Prologue and was a total tool, I might have fancied the idea of putting my mouth on his, but now, in this version of reality, it would never work between us. We're enemies and I'm leaving for college and he's hopped up on painkillers; he probably doesn't even mean what he was implying. If he tried to kiss me while sober, that would be another story . . . Maybe one with a happy ending—but no. There's no happy ending for us. There isn't even an *us*.

"I'm going, I'm going." When she thinks I'm not looking, I see her mouth "So cute!" to Jasper.

She spins toward us when she gets to the door. "Oh," she says, lifting the tissues higher like she just noticed them. "These are for you, bud. I got that kind you like, you know, with the lotion, for your special times."

"I might murder you if you don't leave," Jasper says, a twitch starting in his eye.

"I'm just kidding." She deadpans, "But really, where do you want me to put them?"

He drops his head into his hands and then hisses in pain.

"What's wrong?" his mom asks, her face dropping.

He sighs. "Don't overreact, okay?"

"Too late." She pins his face between her palms, pushing back his hair. "What happened? Who am I suing?"

"Some dude in a car," he says, flicking his eyes to me. "Madeline has his information."

She turns to me, dark eyes frantic.

"Some guy hit him when he was crossing the street." To enact some type of revenge and/or yell at me. "I took him to the hospital," I rush to say. "I'll text the driver's information so you guys have it."

I should leave. I should have left forever ago. Just plopped Jasper onto his bed with a water and a protein bar and disappeared—the Hungover Dahlia Special. Jasper's mom places a soft, small hand on my forearm when I stand, my message reading Delivered. A wrinkle forms between her brows.

"You saw it happen?"

"I was at my store, across the street."

"She ripped the guy a new asshole," Jasper says.

"You know I don't like that expression," she says to him. She releases me. "Thank you for helping him. I'm so glad you were there."

"What are friends for?" I ask, shooting a bewildered look toward Jasper. "I should get back to the store, since you have someone here to look after you."

"What did the doctors say? Is anything else hurt?"

He rolls his eyes, settling back on his bed, and shows her his arm. I avoid the stretch of exposed skin on his stomach again. "The paperwork's on my desk."

His mom starts flipping through the papers and I step toward the door. "Bye, Jasper. Nice meeting you, Mrs. Hamada."

She looks over her shoulder at me, a giant smile gracing her features. "Kira. It was lovely to meet you. Please stop by whenever. And thank you for taking care of my baby."

"Mom."

"You are my baby. Do you need anything? Water? Food? Painkillers? What's hiding behind those bandages? Will it make me cry?"

Jasper bites back a laugh as she creeps closer, her fingers extended for poking and prodding. He grabs the pillow behind his head and uses it to ward her off. I step out of the room and feel the warmth drain from me, just a little bit, as their laughter echoes around Jasper's room.

I make my way to the door in a hurry, eager to get away from the weird feelings being in this house has given me, and slide into my shoes. As soon as my hand falls on the doorknob of the front door, it flies open. I recognize Mr. Hamada from my first time in Prologue. He was the man talking to Jasper when I interrupted. Luke stands behind him, eyes wide.

I take a step back, trying to figure out what to say to someone who opens the door and finds a stranger in their house, but Mr. Hamada sighs in relief. He rushes forward, wrapping thick arms around my shoulders. My body goes stiff and I pat him awkwardly on the arm. Luke laughs.

"I'm sorry," Mr. Hamada says, pulling away. His eyes have those red threads in the whites. "Benny called to let me know what happened and I was so worried. Jasper's here, right?"

I point up. "He's with your wife."

Luke steps inside. "And he's okay?"

I nod vigorously. "Oh, yeah. Same old Jasper. He'll probably be super sore, but the ability to be snarky is still there."

He grins. "What a shame."

Mr. Hamada swats at Luke and then delivers one steady, long look into my eyes. "I'm so glad you were there to help. I don't know what I'd do if he didn't have someone there."

If I hear one more time how grateful people are that I was there, when I was the reason Jasper got hit, I am going to throw myself in front of a car.

I force a smile. "I'm glad I was there, too. I should get back to the store." *The one yours is running out of business, ring a bell?*

I jut my thumb in the direction of the door, having made my way slowly toward it to indicate I'm done talking and accepting praise and thinking about Jasper's injuries, how sore he's going to be because he was literally hit by a car while trying to confront me over a prank they probably still haven't fixed at Prologue.

I'm the worst. I took it too far. I upped the stakes so high that a fall from them would result in certain death.

"Of course. Thank you again." He latches onto my hand long enough to squeeze and then I make a break for the door, stopping just outside when I remember my car isn't here. I whip out my phone, ready to start begging Zelda for a ride. She'll ask questions, but if I just clam up for a bit she'll fill the car with her voice—singing or talking or screaming the words written on the traffic signs, just to cheer me up and enact revenge for my tight-lipped demeanor. But it'll be free and beats potentially riding in a Lyft with a stranger.

Would the Hamadas be so nice to me if they knew why Jasper was crossing the street? Would they be willing to joke around and thank me if they knew I've been trying, poorly, to sabotage them enough that B&M gets the upper hand?

*Yes*, I realize as my finger hovers over Zelda's number. Yes, they probably would. They seem like nice people. Real people. They didn't set up shop to ruin my life, they did it as a business decision, just like Astrid thinks closing B&M could be a good business decision.

The door behind me cracks open and Luke's head pops out. "Need a ride?"

"Oh." I hold my phone up. "Just about to call one."

"I'm heading back out since the idiot's okay. I'll drop you off on the way."

"That's really nice, but—"

"You don't know how to say yes fast enough?" He closes the door behind him, thrusting his hands into his pockets. "No need. It would be my pleasure."

He leads me toward a white Nissan parked in front of the house and opens the passenger door for me. I slide in, the interior cool, the leather seats warm, and the scent of pine strong. He starts the car, and the AC powers on and blasts my hair, even the strands sticky with sweat. He pulls a U-turn and heads toward B&M.

The car is quiet except for the dull hum of a Green Day song through the speakers.

"Thanks for the ride." I feel so awkward. So guilty. "Do you work at the other Prologue?"

He smiles, keeping his eyes on the road. "Yeah, I'm a manager there."

"Do you like it?"

"Yeah, it's nice."

Must be. His car is nice. All the Hamadas' things are nice.

"I get to make the schedules." His fingers tap against the steering wheel and he darts his eyes to me quickly. "Don't tell my dad, but I give myself off every other Saturday."

"Your secret is safe with me. I'd do the same." Yeah, right. My hands would be too tight on the reins to even scratch my nose, let alone step away from the store for a weekend day.

"Really? Seems like you're always at the store from what Jasper says. I assumed it was by choice."

It's one thing to know you're controlling, but for a near stranger to point it out . . . "Sometimes."

"What would you do with your Saturdays off?" He spins the wheel with one hand, turning us into Camp Hill. A few kids bike down the sidewalk.

"I don't know." I laugh to myself, but it's not funny. I have no life outside of the store. "Have a life, maybe?"

He laughs loud, like the sound is coming from his gut without having to travel up his throat. "I can't say the same. I use mine to duel at a card shop."

"Duel? What's that mean?"

He bites his lip with straight, bright white teeth. "Like, Yu-Gi-Oh! card games. Bunch of nerds gather and we have tournaments."

I can't control it. Hysterical laughter erupts from my mouth. I wipe at the tears forming in my eyes. "I'm sorry. I don't mean to laugh—oh my god, yes I do."

He turns onto Oak Street, me having entirely missed the part where Camp Hill turned into Mechanicsburg. He pulls into a spot near B&M and puts the car in park. "Yeah, yeah. Whatever. It stimulates the mind."

I grin, imagining this big guy hunched over a table with trading cards or whatever spread out in front of him. "Dueling" a ten-year-old. "Reading does, too, but I don't look like such a loser when I do it."

He raises an eyebrow. "You saw my little brother get hit by a car while coming over to flirt with you and I'm the loser? At least I can keep myself in one piece."

My mouth snaps closed. "He wasn't—that's not—no." I can't admit what I did, but I can't let them think it's Jasper's fault, either. Or that there's something going on between us. There is definitely not. We're enemies. *We're enemies, right?* Just because I didn't let him bleed out in the street doesn't mean we're actually friends. Just because we maybe, kind of, sort of, almost kissed doesn't mean we're anything more than we were yesterday. . . .

The look he shoots me is dripping with sympathy. *Oh, Madeline, you're so naive.*

"Sure. Okay." He winks.

I nod—not sure why—and unbuckle the seat belt. "Thanks for the ride."

I grip the door handle and he stops me, staring off into the distance for a minute. "It's a sign, him getting hit. I mean, I'm glad he's okay. I obviously don't want anything to happen to my little brother, but this'll probably set him straight. Get his head in the game, you know?"

"Okay . . ."

"It's just not in his—or Prologue's—best interest if he's wasting time pulling pranks instead of doing his job." He sighs, releasing tension, while my stomach clenches. "I want him to come to my store and work as my assistant manager and that's not going to happen if he's out of commission with a concussion or worse. My dad needs to see him as worthy of the nepotism, you know? And he's not doing anything else with his life— no college, not pursuing any passions besides video games and all-nighters—so he really needs this."

I nod, unsure what to say. Is he blaming me? He's not wrong, but I can't control what Jasper chooses to do—crossing the street in a blind rage aside. My hand sweats around the handle.

"If you were anyone else, this probably wouldn't be a

problem, but you're you. You work for the competition. You work across the street. You're a distraction whether you try to be or not." He bends his head, meeting my eyes condescendingly. "You get what I'm saying?"

"I think . . ." *that I don't.*

"It's just better for everyone involved if you guys steer clear of each other, okay? I don't want anyone else getting hurt or either of the stores having to escalate things, you know, like, legally speaking."

My joy at Luke's confession has been completely smothered. I think I hate him. I don't necessarily disagree with anything he's saying, but I'm so mad that he feels like his say in the matter, well, matters. I just nod and stomp my way toward B&M. He doesn't drive by until I'm inside, the door shut. Like the metaphorical one he just attempted to slam and bolt behind me.

# SEVENTEEN

Unfortunately for Luke, I don't take kindly to being told what to do, especially when the thing I'm being told to do is something I don't want to do. Example being: staying away from Jasper. I have an apology to issue before we can go our separate ways, but I've been waiting to reach out to him because he hurt his arm and probably can't text.

And, okay, I might also be waiting because I'm a little nervous. I mean, I got him hit by a car. I wouldn't be so eager to forgive in his case, so maybe I'm just delaying the inevitable yell-fest I have coming for me. The last time I saw him, sure, he was friendly, but he was also not thinking clearly. I can't allow myself any butterflies over what might have happened if his mother hadn't interrupted. I didn't earn what was going to happen. I was part of some drug-induced haze that he's definitely come down from thanks to over-the-counter painkiller and time to wallow in his hatred.

And besides, I didn't really want to kiss him—did I? It was just the moment.

Either way, I've been begging Benny for status updates on Jasper and one finally came in this morning, four days post-accident: Jasper back at work.

Not as detailed as I would have liked, and Benny didn't answer me when I asked what time Jasper would be leaving, but I need to get this over with. Armed with a pan of homemade brownies with TRUCE? written in blue frosting left over from Astrid's birthday, I make my way to Prologue.

I step into a nearly empty store. It's quiet, except for the tinny sounds of music and gentle clicking coming from the front desk, where Benny hunches over the keyboard, typing. This visit feels so different from my last. I'm more nervous and I can't even relish the lack of business properly because I'm too busy searching for Jasper, my heart hammering.

Benny looks up from the computer and spots me. "Here to get me nearly fired again?"

My body can only hold so much guilt. Maybe once I talk to Jasper, I can move on to Benny. Until then, though, I have little to no sympathy for the boy who grew up with me and should have seen my blatant attempt at sabotage coming before I even crossed the street.

"Is Jasper still here?"

Benny leans over the desk to peek into the pan. He smirks. "I'll tell you for a brownie."

I return his smirk. "They have nuts in them." *They definitely don't.*

His face falls. "You get him hit by a car and then you serve him disgusting brownies? Isn't this supposed to be an apology?"

"Where is he, Benny?" My palms start sweating and I can't

blame the warm pan for it. I'm about to see Jasper, face my consequences, *and* lose fresh brownies. This is the worst day and I need to get it over with quickly.

"Fine. The break room." He goes back to typing.

"And where's that?"

"In the back." He gestures loosely with one hand, his eyes on the screen. "'Employees Only' door."

When I arrive, the door is closed and I don't know if I should knock, so I stand outside for a good ten seconds before settling on slowly peeking inside.

*Please forgive me please forgive me please forgive me.*

The room is dimly lit, but I see a few collapsible tables, a television on the wall, a black refrigerator, an armchair, and a shelf full of books marked *RETURN TO SHELVES* pressed against a squishy-looking couch . . . where Jasper is lying, eyes closed and injured arm cradled to his chest.

"Need something?" His limbs splay across the couch similarly to how he lay on his bed a few days ago and my heart flies to my throat.

"Um."

He cracks open an eye. The blue-green tinge to his skin around his stitches is horrifying, but it makes him look rugged in a way I didn't know I liked.

"Sorry. I wanted to give you this," I say, offering my modest attempt at baked goods. "And to say sorry. In addition to being sorry that I'm now interrupting your break."

I wait, my breath stalled and my heart doing a dance number.

He shifts into a seated position. "What's the catch? Poisoned? Ex-Lax?"

In his defense, they're not the most appetizing-looking brownies. But it's the only thing I made that turned out edible. The marshmallow treats were too mushy, the cookies burnt. Apparently being terrible at cooking is genetic, and I wasn't about to stumble through making a fourth dessert when Jasper could very easily, and with much pleasure, reject my apology despite my efforts and intentions.

"The only catch is that they might suck."

For a moment, he just watches me, his face slowly but surely softening from annoyance to something more open, less tension in his jawline. "You can set them on the table," he says, nodding to the one behind me.

"I hope we can agree that things went a little . . . too far," I say quietly, setting the brownies down.

"A little?" He glances at his freshly bandaged arm. "Yeah, I'll agree to that."

"And maybe we can agree to stop?"

His eyes narrow. "A truce, just when I was about to step up my game to finally take down Books and Moron. Convenient."

I sigh, resisting the urge to roll my eyes. Of course he wouldn't make this easy. Not that I *deserve* this to be easy.

"The least you could do is buy a book," he says, "per our old agreement."

"I'm here to call a truce!"

"In the grand scheme of things, it seems fair, though. You pulled shenanigans, what, twice? Without buying a book? And those were *your* rules." He swivels into a seated position and reaches behind him, wincing with the movement, to the utility shelf. "Are you sure I couldn't interest you in"—he reads the title of the paperback he grabbed randomly—"*The Duke's Dirty Secret?*"

On the cover, a woman clenches a well-dressed man who appears not to give one single fuck about how sad she looks.

I hover closer to the couch. "Depends on what the dirty secret is."

"I haven't read it, but I think it might be this woman attempting to mind-control him into having sex with her."

"Pass. Consent or bust."

He tosses the book behind him with a breathy snort, keeping his eyes on mine even when the book misses the shelf and slides to the floor, taking another book with it. That was almost a laugh, right?

"We can call a truce," he says. "But only because my Tylenol is wearing off and arguing gives me a headache." His eyes flick to the table behind me. "And because brownies are my favorite, even when they suck."

Thank god I ruined the other stuff I tried to make. I slowly take the seat across from him, watching how his feet slide between mine when he stretches out. "How are you doing?"

He raises an eyebrow and it's impressive how quickly his disdain cuts through me. Okay, noted. This is clearly not how things are going to go. I should just take the win and skedaddle.

"I'll leave." I make to stand, because what am I even doing here, but he cuts me off.

"Wait," he says. "You don't have to leave. I wouldn't have handled the whole thing like you did, if it had happened to you. The accident part. I would have been begging you for forgiveness instead of verbally kicking the ass of the idiot who hit you. You could have just called an ambulance and left me, but you didn't."

What does it say about me that I thought of doing just that, though? Will the guilt never end? Do I even deserve for the guilt to end? I take in his smile, the twinkle in his eyes somehow fighting the darkness of the room. My heart stammers harder, with more nerves. It feels like a fog has lifted and I'm seeing him with the same eyes as the first time he walked into Books & Moore. *Oh, fuck. He's cute. Really, really cute.*

"Is this your way of saying you not only accept my truce, but also forgive me?"

His smile rips into a smirk. "You didn't even text me to see if I was okay and I know for a fact that you have my number. What if I had died or gone brain-dead in my sleep?"

"You didn't have a concussion or any kind of brain trauma. The hospital would have kept you overnight."

"And you didn't text because . . . ?" He bites his lip.

Before I lose my nerve, I get up and plop down next to him in what little space is left on the couch. Our thighs touch, fabric to fabric, but he doesn't move away. "Of course I was worried about you," I say begrudgingly, not meeting his eyes. "I'm not that much of a monster."

"So, why didn't you check on me?" He uses this goading tone that relaxes me, just a bit.

"My lawyer told me not to admit guilt and to avoid contact with you."

"Whoa whoa whoa," he laughs, "who said anything about

lawyers?" His breath is minty, like he brushed his teeth recently, or had a piece of gum and removed it before it got old and sucked up all the fresh scent.

"Your brother. When he basically threatened me to stay away from you."

He glances at my lips, then back to my eyes so quickly that I probably imagined it. "You don't take anyone's advice, do you?"

"He's not my boss; Astrid is." I can't help but look at his lips now. It's like he yawned and I have to follow suit. "I would win, anyway. A lawsuit. You didn't look before crossing the street." I grow bold and carefully push his hair away from his forehead so I can see the gory stitching there. His skin is hot and I pull my fingers away like I was burned. "You never look both ways."

"It's a one-way," he says, eyes boring into mine. "And how would you know? Been watching me?"

I shrug, my shoulder rubbing against his arm. "You said it yourself; you're irresistible. I can't keep my eyes off you." We exchange a smile that sends butterflies scattering in my stomach. "In all seriousness, how's it feel?"

Jasper swallows. "A little . . . stiff."

Why does that word instantly make me want to look down? My cheeks blaze to a degree that would have me admitted to the ICU.

"The skin feels tight. It doesn't hurt anymore, though."

"Good." I turn toward him. "About my forgiveness . . . "

"Yeah," he says through a blinding smile, "that's not going to happen."

I scoff. "Why not?"

"Come *on*, Madeline." His grin is contagious, but I fight it with my entire being. "You'll have to work a little harder than that. You got me hit by a car."

Frustration wells up inside me despite his joking tone. While I've already taken the blame, it wasn't really my fault! I was just being nice!

I turn toward him, my knee brushing his thigh. "I wasn't the one driving. That was all you and your stupidity. If you don't want to forgive me, though, that's fine. I don't need forgiveness from an idiot like you anyway."

His mouth goes slack but his eyes follow me, a shine in them like he can't wait to see what brazen thing I'll do next. "Yeah, well, maybe I *am* an idiot." He turns and I have to angle my face up to feel like he's not looming over me. "I must be to like you."

"You'd be smart to like me. I'm great. If you don't like me, it's only because your brain got scrambled the other day when it hit the concrete!"

But that's when it hits me that we're arguing? About? If he? Likes me?

I suck a breath in.

"We already covered the fact that my brain *wasn't* scrambled. I must just be a masochist to be attracted to someone as obviously stubborn and uninterested as you."

"I'm—I'm not uninterested."

I cannot believe I just said that aloud. What's the point in admitting that maybe, possibly, there are feelings inside me that aren't all hatred? I'm not looking for a relationship; there's too much else to focus on and I'm going away to school. But . . . it's already out there.

"In me?" His breath hits the tip of my nose we're so close now.

I try to shrug, as if my nonchalance will somehow stuff my traitorous but truthful words back in my mouth. But my body is too tense with fear to move. I'm really saying this out loud, really acknowledging these feelings. "I guess I'm a masochist, too."

My words are barely out of my mouth before Jasper devours them, his hand wrapping around my neck and pulling me into him. The adrenaline pulses through my body so intensely I think I may collapse. Never—never—has a kiss felt like this before.

When I first imagined kissing Jasper Hamada, I thought it would be a sweet brush of lips, so soft that I could feel the tingle everywhere. But the reality is that there's a pressure to his movements that builds a need deep inside me. Just a few days ago, I thought I'd had more than enough of him, marked him as Did Not Finish, but now I feel like every part of him will remain To Be Read.

I hate how frazzled I feel, how much he's thrown me out of orbit—how much I like it. I force my fingers into the soft patch of hair behind his ears as our mouths move together. His hands are so soft and warm, so big that they span from under my breasts to the bit of skin on my hips that always seems to bulge out even when I'm not wearing tight pants—

I freeze. What do I feel like to his hands? Just mountains of jiggles?

He pulls away, his hair mussed and his lips glossy and red. He watches me through half-closed eyes. "Everything okay?"

His thumbs caress me the same way he had my bare shoulder when I dropped him off at his house: lazily, unconsciously. He doesn't care. He doesn't even realize what's going on in my head. He sees me how I am. He likes me this way.

"I'm fine." He waits for me to make the next move . . . so I do. I push his back against the couch and stare for one moment, two, before gathering the courage to straddle him. My knees sink into the leather of the couch and my lips connect with his for just one blissful moment before his hands land confidently on my ass. And, I don't know, I guess even with the current situation unfolding in wonderful ways, it still surprises me and I jerk up, hitting the underside of the utility shelf sharply, and a book topples onto us with a *whack*.

The book is *Everyone Poops*. Because of course.

We pull away with laughs and heated cheeks, our breaths shallow. I'm only slightly disappointed, but the rest of me is overflowing with relief. I feel ten times lighter, airy, dizzy with happiness. Things with B&M are nowhere near solved, but if Jasper and I have a truce, if we have mutual, *positive* feelings for each other, then maybe it will be okay—maybe it will be easier to focus. This is the turning point in my summer, I can feel it. This is how I had hoped things between us would go at the very beginning. Something light and full of laughter (and kissing).

I slide off him, carefully avoiding the slight bulge in his

pants that he covers immediately with his hands. My face is on fire, but it's probably arctic levels of cold compared to his.

He walks to the table where I put the brownies, his back to me the whole time. "Uh, your mom seems nice," he says, like this is the best change of topic. He adjusts himself, not discreetly enough to prevent the ridiculous pride from building in me like *I've still got it.*

"When did you meet Dahlia?"

He raises an eyebrow over his shoulder. "That day you sent me on a wild-goose chase to find you."

Oh yeah. Benny Betrayal Day. "Yeah, sorry about that."

"Wow, you're just full of apologies now," he says, finally turning toward me with his shirt fully untucked. "It's like someone poked a hole in a dam."

"To be clear," I say, pointing a finger at him, "I'm apologizing for you having to meet Dahlia, not for anything else that happened that day."

"She was really nice, though. Even when she was being pushy and insisting that you said I had to buy a book. She blocked the door when I tried to leave."

"She's tenacious."

"I see where you get it." He grabs a plastic cup and fills it with water from the sink. "And you're also related to Astrid?"

"She's my aunt."

He downs the water and tosses the cup in the trash. "Any other family members working there?"

"Why?" I ask. "Are you going to try to poach them?"

He tries to fix his hair, but it's a wonderfully lost cause.

"Nah, Benny was the only one worth it." He grins. "Just trying to understand your family tree; it doesn't seem as straightforward as mine. No offense."

"It's just Astrid, Dahlia, and me working there. Probably not for long."

There's a beat.

"Because Dahlia's flaky!" I rush to say. Not because of his store kicking my store's ass. This is going to be hard. Whatever *this* is. When's the appropriate time to ask him to define a relationship in a beneficial way for me? Before or after *Everyone Poops* ruins a make-out session? "She comes and goes. Astrid raised Benny and me. And Benny's dad."

His eyes widen. "She raised Benny's dad?"

"No," I say through a laugh. "They both raised Benny and me."

"Oh, okay. What about your dad?"

"Never knew him. Big fan of his child support checks, though."

He stops at the door and stares at his feet. He's quiet for a moment. "That really happened, right?"

"My deadbeat dad sending me money? Yeah, the court made him."

He bites back a smile. "No. You and me. Obviously."

"Yes," I say lightly, sliding closer to him. There's maybe a foot of space between our bodies and I'm ready to experience what his felt like again. And again. "It did."

"Finally."

"What do you mean, *finally*?"

"I've been into you for months, but your little prank war has been throwing off my game." He attempts to smooth out the wrinkled parts of his shirt.

"You think you have game? Were you flirting via sabotage or something?"

"I was trying to. Weren't you?"

"No, I was trying to destroy your store so ours would stay open."

He pulls in his lips but can't hide his smile. "That's a terrible plan. And it's over now, right?"

I raise an eyebrow, my heart rate kicking up a notch. "Maybe."

"We called a truce."

"I think it becomes null and void when you only agree so you can kiss me." It feels freeing to say the words out loud. There isn't much doubt—I mean, there's always *a little* doubt, right?—that he likes me; he said as much, he showed as much. Feelings can change, and I'd never expect them not to, but right now, in this moment, he likes me.

"Who wouldn't?" He holds the door open for me.

"Oh, wow. Manners," I say, passing through.

He places a hand on his chest and matches my pace. "I'm a nice guy. Don't you know that by now?"

"I'm still forming an opinion." I tilt my head to the side, pretending like I'm sizing him up, but I enjoy the view nonetheless. I can't believe what we were just doing. I can't believe any of this. It's almost too good to be true. I fight back the part of me that's screaming to proceed with caution. "You're kind of nice."

"You kiss all the guys you think are *kind of nice*?"

"If you knew my ex—" I stop before calling Eric my boy-friend, because he wasn't, not really. I just keep it at that and continue. "You wouldn't be surprised. He was the king of Kind Of."

The first time Eric and I held hands, he told me mine were dry. But then he offered me lotion, so, it wasn't that bad? The first time we had sex, he called me out for faking my orgasm—it wasn't the best experience, being a virgin with a guy who cares more about his own climax, but then, because he's kind of a nice guy, he still made me orgasm that night.

I blink. *Stop thinking about sex with someone else when Jasper's here smiling at you.*

We reach the front counter. Benny stands there, his eyes slits as he watches us.

"Everything cool?" he asks in a skeptical voice.

"I've accepted her brownies and am willing to share them with you," Jasper says solemnly.

"They have nuts," Benny says with a sigh.

"They have nuts?" Jasper curls his lip at me. "Apology not accepted. I take it *all* back."

"It's too late to take it back." I turn to my brother. "There aren't actually any nuts. I just didn't want you to eat them all before I could give them to Jasper."

He perks up. "I'll be back in fifteen."

He dashes toward the back of the store. There's something uncomfortable about the thought of Benny sitting on the same couch where Jasper got an erection, so I try not to think about it, which is easy when Jasper is right in front of me with a dopey look on his face, his hair trashed from me gripping it between my fingers. I have to resist grabbing it again. Resist mauling him with my mouth and finding out if it's his skin that smells like fresh laundry or his clothes. The only way to tell would be to separate them.

I point toward the door. "I have some planning to do for my Warbeck event. Don't steal that, too," I joke.

His eyes light up. "I'm close to finishing the second book now. They've kept me company the past few days since a certain someone wasn't."

My heart feels like it'll burst with pride. "I'll see you at the event, then? I assume you'll be a huge fan by that point."

"Maybe I hate the books?"

I cock my head to the side, deadpanning. "Goodbye."

"Hate-reading is a thing," he says, watching me retreat.

Yes, I know. Zelda and I do it all the time, just to share the ridiculous parts of books with each other so the other one doesn't have to suffer through it. "*Bye*. I'll text you the date."

"Oh, I already know it. The date's been burned into my mind since I had to take *seventy-eight* flyers for it out of our books."

I salute him—ugh, I fucking *salute* him—backing so close to the doors that they slide open. "I'll text you anyway?" I mean to ask if he'll text me, but something deep inside me says there's still a chance he'll say no, that this was a one-time thing, that he got it out of his system and now we can go our separate ways even though he's not Eric, he's not Dahlia, and if anyone is leaving the other, it'll be me.

"Please," he says, nearly upsetting the book stand by the counter as he tries to back up without looking away. He rights it quickly. "Or I'll text you. I'll definitely text you."

There's one less thing in my way now. One less thing to worry about, to do, to save B&M. It also doesn't hurt that there might be more kissing in my future as a reward.

# EIGHTEEN

It's on a sunny Friday evening that Astrid finally gives Sterling the go-ahead to do the thing he's wanted to do for years: upgrade our inventory system. I don't know whether this is a red flag, like, she doesn't care if it's horrible and hard to use because we're closing, or if it's a white flag, giving up and succumbing to technological advances because we're in this for the long haul thanks to the hard work I've been putting in.

Either way, I'm here with Sterling and ready to kick some book inventory ass.

As soon as the Excel file loads. He accidentally closed it; three minutes have passed, and it's still not open.

Sterling watches the screen before glancing at me. "Is this from 2003?"

"The file?"

"This version of Excel."

"Probably." I think. "Probably both. Computer, too."

He sighs. "This might take a while. Help me unpack the gear."

I push aside our Buns brownies display and he pulls a cardboard box across the counter. Inside, various cords and gadgets are neatly wrapped and stacked, complete with Velcro ties to keep things that way. He pulls out a device that looks similar to what cashiers use to scan big items in carts, but it's connected to a brick-shaped black box.

"What is this stuff?"

His eyes light up and I cut him off before he can go on one of his long tangents about technology using words I try to remember and understand but never do. "Can you give me the short, kindergarten version?"

"I'll connect this"—he holds up something the size of his pointer finger—"to the computer, and then"—he holds up the brick and scanner—"use this to scan in new titles by barcodes."

It takes a second, even despite his second-grade explanation, for me to realize what he's saying. "So, we'll get a book in, scan it, and it'll show up in the computer?"

He grins, his white teeth in stark contrast to his dark skin. "Easy as that."

Take that, Prologue. We're joining the twenty-first century finally. We turn back to the computer screen, him aglow because someone is excited about things he's excited about, and me with a little bubble of hope growing in my chest. There's always room for improvement, and our store needs some if we're going to last past the summer.

"What about the actual inventory, the stuff we already have listed?" I ask.

"I'm going to install a new program, one that won't take forever to launch like this." He taps a key on the keyboard, but nothing happens. "I would install it if this thing wasn't running as slow as you trying to get out of bed in the morning."

The door opens and a little Black boy walks in, hesitant at first, with an older man following after.

"Hi," I say with a smile. "Let me know if you need help finding any—"

The boy squeals, rushing over to our display, and picks up the final book in a sci-fi series. With awe on his face, he shows the cover to the older man.

"This is the one," the boy says, grinning. "I want this one."

They approach the counter where Sterling's mess currently sits and, because the computer's frozen, I jot down the book and price, and give them their change.

"I'm going to restart," Sterling mumbles, bending down to the huge computer tower under the counter. It whirs and hums loudly.

Of course, this is when B&M decides to get busy. On a random Friday at six thirty, when I'm alone because Rhoda newly reinstated Shabbat dinners for Zelda and everyone else has their maximum number of hours scheduled, and the computer is down.

I help a woman find all the romance novels in B&M that feature the same cover model—yes, *cover model*—and she buys them all (four). A teen with glasses three times the size of his eyes buys the last old copy of *The Magnificent Lies of Lasers*. A man joined by three little girls, all wearing tutus—including the man—needs help picking out picture books for the two younger ones and a chapter book for the eldest.

It's around eight o'clock when I'm able to slide over to Sterling to check his progress. He has the equipment hooked up and he's installing the new program, though it's going slowly.

"We close in an hour," I remind him unnecessarily. "Will we be able to test it out on new books tonight?"

Sterling frowns at the computer. "I don't know. It's taking so long to get the software on. It might not work."

Panic jumps in my stomach. "What? No. It has to."

If it doesn't work, Astrid won't allow us to try again. She'll just remind us not to close her Excel file, or restart the computer, or update it. Everything works best for her when it's frozen in time.

"I might have to put together a new setup for you guys—oh my god." Sterling stares at the computer wide-eyed.

"What?" I fling myself so close that he loses balance. Some program is up that I don't recognize. "What's happening?"

"It worked." He grins, but I punch his arm. "I can't believe it. I really thought this dinosaur would just die."

"Don't say that." He knows how I feel about jinxing things. "So . . . we're good?"

I pick up the scanner and the warm black box—the power source, Sterling had said. "Can we try it out?"

"I'm trying to import the Excel file but—"

I can't help it. I'm too excited! I scan the first book in sight and receive a rather malicious-sounding beep.

"—the file is corrupt."

My stomach drops. "What does that mean?"

"Madeline." Something in his voice makes me turn slowly,

wanting to throw the scanner like it's burned me. His face, frustrated and exhausted, sags.

"What?"

"I can't open the list. And the computer's frozen again." He closes his eyes, breathing out a sigh. "You guys have a backup, right?"

My heart thumps wildly in my chest. "Yeah. Yeah, we have one. Astrid does it weekly."

"She should do it daily," he grits out, clearly trying to keep calm.

Dashing around the counter, I point at the large external hard drive plugged into the computer. He stares at it, forced calm lining his eyes, before restarting the computer again. In ten minutes, the computer is up, but it's no relief to either of us.

Because apparently instead of having a backup, we had been working on the file that was on the external hard drive. And it's now corrupted. Or it disappeared. I don't really know what happened, but what I do know is that we're fucked.

Our inventory list is gone.


Sterling stays for two hours, helping to "clean install" the operating system onto the computer and reinstall the new inventory program. The spreadsheet is really gone. No backups ever existed, apparently. Astrid was just saving that one Excel file over and over on the external hard drive while working on it from the external hard drive.

When Sterling packs his things, I tell him I'll lock up in a minute, that I just want to finish scanning a row of books into the inventory. But I stay longer than a minute, and when I finish the row, I keep going until I finish the shelf, my arm aching.

By midnight, with my arms and back on fire, I realize I'm scanning the books to avoid having to face Astrid. Even though she thinks the store will be closing soon, she still needs an inventory to work from and, therefore, this will actually upset her. I should be happier to know I'll finally elicit an appropriate reaction from her, but I'm not. I'm just numb.

I take a break at half-past twelve and raid the break room for food. I only find Zelda's half-eaten turkey sub from four days ago, a rotten apple, and a jar of pickle juice. I grab a bottle of water and throw myself into a seat at the table, unplugging my phone from the outlet where I started charging it hours ago.

My screen is littered with notifications. Zelda sent a dark, blurry picture of what she says is Levi doing a handstand in their pool, but I'd never guess that from looking at it. She also invited me, but that was over an hour ago. Astrid wants to know where I am. She wants to know where I am four times. And I have a missed call from Jasper. From two minutes ago.

I quickly text Astrid. I don't want her to ask what I'm doing at the store. I'm not ready for her to find out.

**Astrid**

Today 12:37 AM

Sorry, I'm at Zelda's

12:37 AM

Swimming

12:37 AM

I send her the photo Zelda sent me.

Be home soon.

12:38 AM

I kind of feel bad for lying to her, but those feelings fly out the window when I switch to my text chain with Jasper.

**Jasper Hamada**

Today 12:39 AM

Need something?

12:39 AM

YOU

12:39 AM

YOUR AWAKE*/

12:39 AM

Would you like to buy a vowel?

12:40 AM

I have no money I spent it all on this beer

12:40 AM

I roll my eyes, but can't stop the smile spreading across my face. I guess he owes me a good tipsy texting after I did the same thing to him a while back. What a difference a few weeks make.

> You're not old enough to buy alcohol
>
> 12:40 AM

YOUR not old enough to by alcohol

12:41 AM

> Would you like to buy multiple vowels?
>
> 12:41 AM

Stop trying to sell me things!!!

12:41 AM

I actually laugh. After the shitty night I've had.

> Did you need something? You called me.
>
> 12:41 AM

Just wanted to talk

12:42 AM

Grant isn't paying me attention

12:42 AM

So

12:42 AM

What are you wearing?

12:43 AM

Heat pools in my stomach. I glance around, even though I know the room is empty. I should go home. I should end this conversation. But what's the harm in continuing it if I respect that he's not quite himself right now? We can laugh about it later when he's sober, and it's not like he might accidentally reveal something I don't know, like that he has a huge crush on me. Just *thinking* that turns my cheeks hot enough to melt an iceberg.

A Minions onesie.

12:47 AM

Have I told you how much I love Minions? Love 'em. So. Much.

12:47 AM

I want to speak to Madeline Moore RIGHT NOW WHAT HAVE YOU DONE WITH HER

12:48 AM

Now that we called a truce, I think it's time you met the real me.

12:48 AM

In all my Minions-loving glory. This is
me, Jasper. Take me or leave me.

12:48 AM

I want a refund

12:48 AM

Well, I want to speak to Jasper Hamada.
We don't always get what we want.

12:48 AM

This is me!

12:50 AM

I don't know. Jasper Hamada never seemed
this needy before. Prove you're really him.

12:50 AM

Tell me what you're wearing.

12:50 AM

I'm wearing a shirt

12:53 AM

Oh shit

12:53 AM

It really is you

12:53 AM

I told you!

12:54 AM

Now that I'm talking to you, Grant wants to hang out

12:54 AM

He tried to stole my phone! I am locked in his
bathroom to make sure he doesn't bother oyu

12:54 AM

Too drunk to kick his ass?

12:55 AM

I'm a lover not a FIGHTER

12:55 AM

I would argue that

12:55 AM

Sre you would you love two argue

12:55 AM

Bless Jasper Hamada's drunken soul, even autocorrect can't
help him now. The sting of sleep creeps into the edges of my
eyes and I know I need to leave while I'm still alert enough
to drive, even if it means pausing or ending our conversation.
Pausing is preferred, but in such new territory with Jasper, it
feels kind of like talking to Dahlia. Like, maybe it will turn

terrible if we give it enough time, so I should end it on a positive note.

> I'll show you what a lover I am
>
> 12:55 AM

> Wanna bang?
>
> 12:56 AM

I stop in my tracks, halfway to the front door, right on a creaky floorboard that scares the shit out of me. He's going to be mortified when he sobers up, regardless of how he feels for me.

> IM JOKINGg
>
> 12:57 AM

> I'm too drunk to get I up
>
> 12:57 AM

> I'm joking again
>
> 12:57 AM

> Shit please say something
>
> 12:57 AM

> Grants trying to take my phone from me
>
> 12:58 AM

I should take control of this conversation. I'm sober, thank-youverymuch. I would want someone to end this conversation if it were me, but I like flirting so much more than fighting.

Shame

12:59 AM

How many chances will I get to see him (okay, read him) like this? After this summer, we'll part ways, so I should enjoy the time I have being not-enemies with him, right? This really *is* harmless this time. I grab my things from behind the counter and shut off the lights, my face a few inches from my phone.

Hahahahaha don't don't start something you can't finish Madeline

12:59 AM

I should let it end here. Let him fall into an inebriated stupor and rub this in his face later when we can both laugh about it, instead of just me.

You'd know all about that, wouldn't you, Limp Dick?

1:00 AM

Your hurting my feels

1:00 AM

I'll just give you the vowel, no need to buy it.

1:00 AM

I tear my gaze from my phone and lock up. Mechanicsburg is an overall safe town, but the bars are letting out, and I don't know where my car is. I let Benny borrow it as an apology for nearly getting him in trouble, even though I'm a little mad at him still—and he's a bit mad at me, too—and he never bothered to tell me where he parked it.

I click the lock button on my key fob, but hear and see nothing. I glance down the street, to the left. There are a few cars, but none that look like mine. Now to the right, there are fewer cars—but one is mine! Benny parked it under a streetlight, so at least he gets points for that. I hit the unlock button, but the car stays silent.

"Stupid thing," I mumble, my throat raw with exhaustion. I hold the fob closer to my eyes, hoping I was hitting the wrong button or something. But no. None of the buttons work and I wonder if the fob battery died.

I approach the car—it's definitely mine because there's a tote full of books I keep forgetting to donate in the back seat—and unlock the door. When I turn the ignition: a clicking sound and nothing else. The eerie silence that follows is surprisingly loud.

"Fuck."

I try again. Just a *click—click—click*.

I lock the doors and pull out my phone. I'm about to tap Astrid's name when I realize she'll wonder why my car died outside B&M as opposed to Zelda's. I can't call Benny because he doesn't have a car. I try Sterling, but he's either sleeping or playing video games with Benny or having some sort of adult version of a social life.

There's Dahlia, but I can't bring myself to ask her for help. Zelda's probably been drinking. Levi, too. And Jasper . . . Why is everyone drunk?

**Jasper Hamada**

Today 1:02 AM

> Did you kill my car in a last-ditch
> effort to gain the upper hand?
>
> 1:02 AM

Why would I do that

1:02 AM

> I guess I'm just used to blaming
> you for all the stress in my life
>
> 1:02 AM

If Jasper's not stressing me out, that leaves room for Dahlia to slide in with more drama, though. And now Benny, who left an overhead light on or a door ajar, draining my battery all night.

> Car won't start. I'm stranded here forever now.
> Remember me for my brownies and not my pranks.
>
> 1:02 AM

Where are you?

1:04 AM

This is Grant

1:04 AM

I'm sober

1:04 AM

I can come give you a jump

1:05 AM

And that's how, weirdly enough, Jasper Hamada ends up knocking on my car window at 1:27 in the morning with a big, cheesy smile on his face. "We've got to stop meeting like this. You stalking me?"

# NINETEEN

I slide out in an overly casual manner, meaning: not casual at all. The truth is my heart is jackhammering in my chest like I've never seen a guy before, let alone an attractive one. I blink away the thoughts of the Prologue break room and give an awkward wave to Grant as he exits his red Honda Civic parked in front of me. This wasn't how I imagined my post-make-out meeting with Jasper to be. I had imagined a little more heat and a little less bags under my eyes.

"Thanks." It's almost like I'm not really talking to Prologue Jasper. This is another person, one who only exists in the middle of the night. Before, I had been pretty dead set on believing Jasper was a robot who powered down in the Prologue storage room every night. But now I just have to wonder if he's a sleep-deprived hallucination. A nightmare that turned into a dream I don't want to wake up from.

Grant pulls jumper cables from his back seat. "Hey, Madeline, can you pop your hood?"

"Sure." I reach into my car and yank on the temperamental latch. "Thank you for the help."

"It's no problem. I couldn't just leave you here." He starts connecting cables and winks. "Literally. Jasper wouldn't stop telling me to help you."

Jasper steps closer and I can practically taste the beer on his tongue when he breathes. "What were you doing here by yourself?"

"I was working." I shift my weight to the opposite foot, my arms crossed. "I don't just hang out here in my spare time if that's what you were thinking. I was doing something important, as opposed to getting drunk and sending joke messages to people I don't like."

He leans against my car, his injured arm extended over the top. He's *very* close. "Come on. You know I like you." He wets his bottom lip. "Did I not make it very clear the other day?"

Behind us, Grant turns his car on. It's not the only thing getting turned on in this vicinity.

"I could probably use some more clarification," I say quietly, under the hum of the engine.

Jasper grins, angling his face toward mine.

I place my hand on his chest. "Maybe when you're not drunk."

"I'm not that drunk. I'm not even drunk. I'm just slightly *inebriated*." He stumbles over the word.

"Go ahead and turn your car on, Madeline," Grant says, his head out his open window.

I open my car door, having to wait for Jasper to move out

of the way. "I have text messages that prove otherwise. Some other time, though."

Inside the car, I turn the ignition and it revs to life.

"You weren't supposed to fix it," Jasper groans to Grant. "Now she has to leave."

Grant gets out of his car, shaking his head. "If you have to detain her, the relationship isn't going to work."

I joke along to counteract all the nervous butterflies flapping in my gut. There will be *no* relationship. "And here you had me convinced my dead battery *wasn't* an act of sabotage. Fool me once."

"It's okay," Jasper says, squatting by my open door, elbows on his knees. "I'll forgive you for being so naive."

"So gracious of you." I stare down my nose at him, taking in his moon-soaked cheeks and lashes. Perfect cheekbones. Perfect eyes. The best hair. I'm in deep.

"*If* you give me more brownies." He stops to consider his words, tilting his head back and forth. "And a kiss." He taps a slender finger against his cheek twice.

I'd be impressed if Grant could hear me whispering over the sound of two cars while he reins in the jumper cables, but I lower my voice regardless. "Brownies take time."

"Kisses don't."

"Kisses? Plural now? You're asking a lot of me here."

"What are you doing, bud?" Grant asks in an amused voice, lowering my hood and looking at us through the windshield. "If you're getting in the car, you might want to try a different door."

It's only now that I've noticed how close Jasper has gotten to me. He's hunching down so he can lean into the car, no longer casually resting by my seat.

"I'm saying goodbye," Jasper says. "It would be awkward if I didn't."

I stifle a laugh, eyes roaming over his hunched position. "Yeah, that's what would be awkward."

He glances at me and I raise an eyebrow, not willing to budge. How did we get to this point? From me having a crush on him, to hating him, to now having him leaning down to me, eyes full of heat. To a point where I know what his lips feel like, what they taste like. To the point where I crave them and could so easily have them.

Grant gently pulls Jasper from the car. "Madeline, could I use the bathroom in the store?"

"Oh, sure." I swipe the store key from my key ring, letting the car stay on.

"Watch the cars, bud?" Grant asks, clasping Jasper on the shoulder. "Madeline's needs to stay running."

Jasper leans against my car as we hop onto the sidewalk.

"Can I put on the radio?" Jasper calls after us. Before I can even answer, music starts playing and Jasper starts nodding to himself.

"I'll have to send you a video of him dancing earlier tonight," Grant says. "He has a measuring tape tied around his head and a fanny pack bouncing at his hip. Not the usual outfit for listening to ska."

We stop outside B&M and I jiggle my key in. "Why was he wearing a fanny pack exactly?"

"Well, as he would say, 'Where else would I keep my to-go

sewing kit?'" He says it like *Duh, Madeline, where do you keep* your *to-go sewing kit?*

"Did he need it?" My eyebrows squish together. "To dance?"

"No, because he was in the middle of altering something." He steps inside the store and then he winces. "I shouldn't be talking about this. Forget I said anything."

I point Grant in the direction of the bathroom and lean against the counter, waiting. I make a mental note to ask Jasper about the book he bought from B&M about sewing. I'll leave out that Grant told me about him dancing, though. After tonight, there's more than enough in my potential blackmail file and I hope I never have to use it for anything more than friendly jabs.

Grant meets me in the front a moment later, wiping wet hands against his jeans. "Thanks."

"It's the least I could do." I smile. "Even if you only helped because Jasper wouldn't stop bothering you."

He laughs. "He only had to ask, like, *twice*."

I snort.

"So . . ."

I face him. "Yeah?"

"This is awkward, I'm sorry, I'm not trying to be, but—" He takes a deep breath in. He whispers, though there's no need. "If you could be gentle with Jasper, that'd be great. He's kind of, I don't know, sensitive. He cares, and he cares hard."

I frown. "Well, we called a truce, so—" So what? I don't exactly know. I'm not going to rush into finding out because that'll just lead to stress and probably heartbreak. If we don't get serious, then no one gets seriously hurt. It's worked in the past, with Eric and . . . others.

He raises an eyebrow. "Okay, not making this easy . . ." We exit the store, me a little slower than Grant, trying to figure out what he's getting at. Is he giving me the Luke Speech?

"I just mean be nice to him. Don't lead him on and let him think there's something here if there's not. He's mentioned you're going away to school soon and he's, like, already obsessed with you and, Jasper, he's a relationship guy. He likes commitment and dedication and the cheesy romance stuff some people like."

"We haven't discussed anything like that yet," I say in a small voice.

Part of me was hoping we could just avoid that discussion until I was away at school and it didn't matter. Sure, it's really nice being on good terms with Jasper now, but I'm not, like, planning our wedding or something. I hadn't thought Jasper was, either. That'd be a huge red flag, anyway. We're both on the same page that this is nothing more than a summer fling . . . I couldn't start something real with him and then leave. I couldn't open myself up to *him* leaving me. No. No, we're not doing anything but having a good, casual time. This is fine. I'm fine. Jasper will be okay with that, "relationship guy" or not, because he'll see reason.

*Shut up, Feelings.*

He smiles sadly. "Yeah. Sure. But, like, there's something there, right?" He delivers a pointed look that I catch when I finish locking up the store.

This is too much pressure to put on me at two in the morning. I lost all my inventory hours ago. Days before, I called a truce with the guy working for the store putting mine out of business and then ended up kissing him. I'd like some time. To enjoy this. To figure it out without someone breathing down my neck. There's already so much going on, too much up in the air for me to make some commitment right now. There are more important things than a summer fling.

# TWENTY

I kept the Jasper kiss thing a secret for a few days, unlike the inventory thing I had to tell Ravi and Zelda about. It was nice to have a few days of that kiss belonging to just Jasper and me, our truce not necessarily a secret, but not something I was broadcasting. But then I told Zelda.

**Zelda from YouTube**

Today 2:03 PM

EVERYONE POOPS

2:03 PM

I'm dying

2:03 PM

I'm dead

2:03 PM

Did he immediately start thinking about poop
and need to leave because it was too awkward?

2:03 PM

It wasn't awkward! It was hilarious.

2:04 PM

I feel like someone needs to meet-
cute the shit out of your life

2:04 PM

No pun intended

2:04 PM

Because I said shit

2:04 PM

Yeah, I got it. You're not subtle.

2:04 PM

I finish lacing up my Vans and leave my room. About a week
ago, Dahlia asked, very nicely, for Benny and me to join her for
a game of mini-golf at some point this summer, and since none
of us work today, we agreed. Last minute. Hoping she'd have
plans with whoever it is she hangs out with when we're not
around for her to bother. Old high school classmates who also
have nothing to do with their days, I assume.

But, alas, no such luck. We are not lucky kids.

My phone starts ringing as I stomp down the stairs. A photo of Zelda with a Sharpie mustache fills my screen.

"Yes?"

"Ugh, sorry," she says, sighing dramatically. "My fingers hurt too much from masturbating so I had to call instead of text."

"Thank you so much for sharing," I say dryly. "Is that all?"

She laughs. "Just kidding. Are you guys going out or just hooking up? Or was it a one-time thing? My fans need to know the fate of Jadeline."

"We didn't really talk about it. We just kissed and now I'm here." I try my best to keep the edge from my voice, but it's a struggle. I don't want to think about it, let alone speak to anyone about it. Why can't people just accept that sometimes people kiss and that's it? Or that they kiss and then they kiss some more and maybe there are other things that happen but *that's it*?

"But you said it's been days. Haven't you talked to him since then?"

I reach the bottom of the stairs and wait for Dahlia near the front door. "Yes, but it hasn't really come up naturally and I don't care for it to."

"You're hopeless." I can practically hear her eye roll. She wasn't a fan of what I did with Eric last year because she felt like I wanted more from him than I did, even when I told her I was fine.

"It's an awkward thing to bring up when I'm leaving in a few weeks anyway. I'll seem so creepy and clingy for asking if he wants to talk about it, and I don't even want a relationship! It's just a summer fling."

"A summer fling means you should be flirting and sending dirty pictures or something. You guys have been filling the town with sexual tension since day one, and you make out, and then nothing?"

"Ready to go?" Dahlia appears at the top of the stairs, sunglasses already over her eyes, her hands slipped into bright blue shorts pockets—shorts that belonged to me a few years ago.

The color blue makes me think of Jasper. I think I can manage to get through today.

"Yep." To my phone, I say, "I have to go. Don't masturbate yourself to death."

I hang up before she can lecture me further about how to have a relationship or a not-relationship.

Dahlia meets me at the door. "Do I want to know who you were talking to just now?"

"I don't know. *Do* you?"

She stares at me for a second before cracking a smile. "Are you driving or me?"

She still doesn't have a car—another sign she's not planning on staying long-term—so I grab my keys from the hook by the door, offer her an obligatory laugh, and gesture for her to walk out.

On the way to the golf course, she says she has a surprise for me. Just the act of her having a surprise for me is a surprise.

"I'm not going to tell you what it is, though, because I don't want you to check out mentally. I take mini-golf very seriously."

So does Benny. I wonder if that's why she chose to do this. Either way, I'm prepared to see her realize her mistake in real time. My brother is the throw-the-putter-while-screaming-profanities-in-front-of-children type of serious mini-golfer and Dahlia doesn't even like when people raise their voice around her—not just to her, but around her.

The surprise, which should inflate a little bubble of excitement in my stomach, sets my gut aflame in dread. Her last surprise wasn't the best, even though Astrid's been kind enough to avoid letting Dahlia and me work too many overlapping shifts. And the surprise before that, Dahlia coming to stay, was The Worst. Surprises suck.

When I pull into the parking lot, there's only two other cars. Probably one for the worker in the little rental booth and the other for the family near the end of the course. Benny's already here, sitting on a bench in the sun. Sterling's nowhere in sight.

I park and turn to Dahlia. "You could have invited Sterling."

She shoots me an open-mouthed look. "I did. He didn't want to come."

It's a likely excuse. She's not the most considerate person unless she's considering herself. And now that I think about it, I haven't seen the two of them interact much this summer. It must be awkward to share a kid. It's possible "he didn't want to" is code for "he ran away screaming at the prospect."

We meet Benny and get our putters, golf balls, and one of those cute little pencils to mark our scorecard. My brother insists on going first.

And that's the place he stays in. He never gets more than

four strokes for each hole, even though some of these twists, hills, and obstacles seem impossible. My best hole is five strokes. Dahlia's is six. She might be serious about mini-golf, but she's not good.

"How's work going, Benny?" she asks him as we move to the sixth hole.

"Fine. No one's gotten me hit by a car."

I glare. This will haunt me forever. At least he doesn't know—or doesn't say, more realistically, because Sterling probably told him—about the inventory flub.

She glances at me, her eyebrow raised above her sunglasses. "What about you? I heard you and Jasper are friends now."

Without looking at her or Benny, I say, "We're fine."

Dahlia exhales through her nose, lining up her golf ball. "Everything's fine, huh?"

Benny and I exchange a look, even though he's halfway down the green, next to one of those windmill obstacles. "Yep," we say in unison.

She messes up her swing, missing the ball. Benny and I laugh, which just causes her face to scrunch up and turn pink. I hate that I'm getting along with him for the sake of not getting along with Dahlia, but it's nice to not put energy into being mad at him anymore.

"When's your soccer camp?" she asks Benny, giving the ball a gentle push. It hits the side wall and rolls back toward her.

"Two weeks." He nods to her ball. "Do you want to redo?"

"No. That's one." She moves to the side and gestures for me to go in front of her. "Your turn."

"You can try agai—"

"I don't want to try again," she snaps, turning away from us. "I just want to keep going."

I hit my ball, not caring where it goes. Benny tilts his head to the side, waiting, but I drop my putter and walk up behind Dahlia. I place my hands on her shoulders and feel her intake of breath.

"What's wrong?" The irony of so much happening in my life and me comforting her isn't lost.

She sniffs quietly, like she's actually trying to hide her tears and not use them to manipulate my feelings. Like she did after missing a video chat with the cast and crew of my eighth-grade musical, *The Little Mermaid*. I played one of Ariel's sisters—"the fat one" was how a few guys referred to me—that disappears after the first few seconds of the play, because, like Dahlia, I am not a great actress, but the musical was mandatory for chorus members.

"Nothing. Did you go?"

I sigh. "Yeah. But I'm not playing anymore until you tell me what's going on. And that'll really piss Benny off."

Her shoulders tense beneath my hands. I move in front of her. "Are you on your period or something?" It's okay for period-havers to ask other period-havers this, I've decided. Especially when the emotional one is your mother and she's supposed to keep her shit together.

"No, it's just—I don't know—I'm trying. I really am. Is he always this—this distant?"

I want to tell her no, to spite her. To make her realize that it's her. But the real answer actually is no. And it's not just her that he's been distant with.

"No," I say, avoiding his heavy stare. He can't hear us, but he has to know we're talking about him. "He's been acting a little weird this summer. I think he's just trying to keep his cool."

"Why?" She swipes a finger under her sunglasses.

"Really?"

"I get that I've been a terrible mom. If you guys think I don't know that, I do." She pushes her glasses up her sweaty nose. "I'm here and I'm trying, though. Can you at least give me that?"

To my surprise, I can and I have. It's Benny who hasn't. He hasn't really given her anything. Just indifference.

"I can't make him forgive you or give you the time of day. But I can tell you that he's here and he didn't have to be."

"You're right." She sucks a deep breath in. "Any advice?"

"Keep trying." I grab my putter and mutter over my shoulder, "Don't disappear on him again."

On either of us.


The rest of the game is slightly less awkward, even after Dahlia randomly mumbles "I'm sorry" in our general direction two holes later. Benny wins and Dahlia offers to buy him ice cream at Reeser's next door. He . . . accepts. Progress.

While I'm eating my way through a large cone of peanut butter soft serve, the weird material covering the benches sticks to my exposed and sweaty thighs.

"The camp is five days. We learn tricks, build up skills we

already have." He takes some Oreo-crusted vanilla onto his spoon and stuffs it into his mouth. "Do volunteer stuff with little kids. Play pranks on the coaches."

"Is it coed or just guys?" She starts in on the brownie part of her brownie sundae, keeping her eyes on him. "Overnights, right?"

Of course Dahlia's mind goes straight to sex. Or is it my mind going straight to sex?

I stuff more ice cream in my mouth, trying to cool my cheeks from the inside, and blink away fantasies of Jasper and me doing a little more than kissing. My phone sits in front of me on the picnic table, but when I check my notifications, there are none from him. Just Zelda, and a text from Astrid wishing me luck with Dahlia.

"Yeah. Coeds and overnights, but they split us into girls and boys like it's the nineties or something."

Dahlia narrows her eyes. "Meaning . . . ?"

"The outdated belief that there are only two genders."

"Oh," she says, nodding. "Got it."

She smiles and then turns to me, the table between us. "I almost forgot your surprise."

The dread returns. Benny mouths: "Run!"

"I found a station that was giving away tickets to your movie premiere."

I choke on the smooth peanut-buttery goodness. "Really? When are they doing it? What do I have to do?"

She grins. "I already won them! Thanks, Google. I'm picking them up from the station tomorrow after work."

"And they're midnight premiere tickets?" I can't believe this. I won't believe this until the paper is in my hands.

"Yeah."

"What was the question?"

"They read a line from the book and asked what chapter it was from. Chapter thirty-four, for your information."

"What was the line, though?" Benny asks.

"Oh. I don't remember." She shrugs and dives back into her sundae, not a care in the world.

"Thank you." I start thinking about what the night will be like, but then reality sets in. "I already had plans to go with Zelda . . ."

"Oh god, Madeline," she laughs. "No worries. I can't stay up that late anyway. It's agony getting old."

"It's not that late."

"I passed out at nine last night." A bit of brownie is stuck between her teeth.

I motion to my own teeth and she gets the memo, laughing behind her hand.

Benny starts telling her a story I've heard a thousand times about one lunch period where none of his friends told him he had Dorito dust around his mouth. I pull up my messages and, even though I have other things on my mind, I laugh when Benny reveals to her I was one of the people who didn't tell him.

**Zelda from YouTube**

Today 4:16 PM

Remember when I said I didn't get tickets to the movie?

4:16 PM

Don't remind me of that cursed day!!!

4:16 PM

DAHLIA GOT US TICKETS

4:16 PM

FUCK

4:16 PM

Not quite the response I was hoping for. Something heavy sinks to the bottom of my stomach.

Like a good fuck?

4:17 PM

Like I didn't think we were going so
Levi mom and I are going to visit dad

4:17 PM

I can't ask her to skip that. Her dad's counselor made it very clear that when they make plans to visit him, and share those plans with him, they need to do everything in their power to keep them. Routine routine routine. Expectation. All the other therapist stuff Zelda says post-visit as she avoids eye contact and plays with her septum ring.

Throughout all my struggles with food and my perception of myself, I never knew fighting food addiction required so many precautions. I can't stand in the way of her seeing him.

I'm sorry. This fucking sucks.

4:18 PM

@ the world: whyyyy

4:18 PM

We can still see it together.

4:18 PM

We better. Didn't you sell Hotmada the books? Will he go, would that be awkward since you guys aren't talking about how you want to bang or whatever

4:18 PM

It seems too soon to utter my thoughts aloud, even if it's just in text form. The thought of going with Jasper gives me butterflies, feels more exciting than seeing it with my best friend and minor YouTube celebrity. I switch to Jasper's message and type out: What's your status with the Discontent series?

I wait impatiently for an answer.

**Jasper Hotmada**

Today 4:23 PM

Loving it. Hating you for recommending
it. It's killing me. I just want them to go
on vacation. Get some sleep.

4:23 PM

That seems like too much to ask.

4:23 PM

I'm a chapter away from finishing book 2
but Luke dumped his yard work on me

4:23 PM

It's so hot out

4:23 PM

I start picturing Jasper outside in the sun, sweat soaking
through his shirt. He should probably just take it off—

"Right, Madeline?"

"What?" My cheeks flush.

"Sometimes you just have to let your sibling have it," Dahlia
says. "Astrid was a monster growing up. She used to make me
so mad that I called the cops on her once."

I can't say I'm surprised that Dramatic Dahlia called the cops
on Astrid.

"It was literally only a second, but they showed up about
ten minutes later to check it out, in case I had been getting
murdered."

"That's nice of them."

"Yeah, but ten minutes?" Benny stuffs his napkin into his empty dish. "You could have been dead by then."

What are you doing?
4:25 PM

Waiting for your thoughts on book 2. It's going to blow your mind.
4:25 PM

I'll finish after I'm done mowing the grass
4:25 PM

Which you're distracting me from
4:25 PM

How hard is it to not answer texts?
4:25 PM

It's very hard when you're the one texting
4:25 PM

That's what he said
4:25 PM

"Ask your sister who she's texting with that stupid smile on her face," Dahlia says, pulling me from my thoughts. "It's obnoxious and cliché when I ask."

"You texting Jasper?" Benny says, his eyebrow raised.

"Shut up."

"Oh, Jasper," she says, clasping her hands together. "You should take him to the movie. Sorry, Zelda."

It's wild how quickly my body fills with relief now that someone else has given life to Zelda's suggestion. Like, it's not a pity suggestion, or one I should feel too bad about. Maybe Dahlia's not so bad.

"I might do that. Zelda can't go anymore and Jasper's reading the series right now."

"He wouldn't stop talking about it on Sunday, even though I told him I hadn't read it." Benny dumped his and Dahlia's trash into the can. "No one wanted to listen to him. His dad was finally like, 'Would you go organize the stock room?' just to get him away."

I can't help but smile. Even if it weren't him, I would. Someone loves the recommendation I gave them. It's a validating experience. The first time I recommended something to Zelda and she didn't like it, I started to preface all my recs with: *It might suck, I don't know!* It took me a while to get out of the habit. I don't normally get to know if my in-store recommendations go over well.

"I told him to read those."

Benny rolls his eyes playfully. "I'm so shocked."

We head home and Benny joins us. I keep my thoughts about this to myself. He's pressing his luck with Dahlia. She doesn't typically get better in larger doses, but he can do what he wants and it's certainly making her happy. Later, Astrid comes home from work and tears up seeing them kicking a soccer ball around the backyard like one of those wholesome two a.m. reruns on Nickelodeon.

"So," Astrid says, sitting at the table with a glass of orange juice, her eyes now dry, "it seems that Sterling got the inventory system working, but—"

*Fuck.* I should have just worked up the courage to tell her. Ice coats my stomach. "I'm sorry. The file was lost."

She frowns. "Yeah . . . Why didn't you tell me? It's been days, according to Ravi."

*That snitch.* Probably just didn't want to be blamed for it, and I can't blame him for that. "I expected more yelling, if I'm being honest."

She gestures for me to join her at the table. "Accidents happen. Especially when you have someone like me who wasn't backing up our information the right way. It's unfortunate but not the end of the world."

"That's it?"

"Do you want me to ground you or something? For a mistake no one's to blame for?"

Not necessarily, but I'd take it if it meant she cared. This set us back, made things more difficult when they're already so difficult.

"If you want to, yes."

She laughs. "I don't want to ground you. You need to tell me these things when they happen, though. I don't know why you wouldn't have called me." She squeezes my hand. "Hiding it from me only makes it worse. We'll get it fixed. I don't like thinking you were dealing with this by yourself. I don't want you to worry."

She sounds like she means it, but it feels like maybe she's telling me not to worry about B&M because there's no point. Or to not worry because things will be fine?

Why can't people say what they mean?

Jasper hasn't texted about the book so I don't know how to invite him to the movie. What if he got to the big last-chapter plot twist and he hated it? Or what if he came to his senses and realizes that he hates *me*?

**Jasper Hotmada**

Today 8:56 PM

. . . alive?

8:56 PM

No.

8:56 PM

Sorry I didn't text

8:56 PM

I finished mowing the lawn, had to shower, then I fell asleep

8:56 PM

Then it was dinner

8:56 PM

Hey did you want to go to the library?
It closes at 10 and I need to get book 3

8:57 PM

I know he doesn't need my supervision to get the third book, and it would be quicker if he went by himself, so I take the hint and embrace my gutterflies (butterflies in my gut). I take a deep breath and tell him to pick me up.

Ten minutes pass in which I go to the bathroom twice—I'm a nervous pee-er—I brush my hair five times, and I reapply my ChapStick three times. As I'm blotting away the latest layer, he texts to let me know he's here and I rush downstairs before Dahlia or Astrid can notice the car in the driveway and tease me.

He pulls into one of the many empty parking spots at the Simpson Library about five minutes later, approximately a song and a half off Halsey's latest album, and turns his car off.

"Well," he says with a laugh, getting out of his car. "That was an uncomfortable car ride."

"Right?" I laugh, relieved that it wasn't just me being ridiculous. "Why?"

"I have no clue."

"We didn't even talk about the book!" We barely spoke at all. I join him on the sidewalk and we make our way into the library, the overhead lights casting weird shadows on our faces. "I assume you liked it if you're coming here for the next one?"

"Yeah, you could say I liked it. Or you could say it *ruined* me."

I grin. "Did you cry?"

"Don't tell anyone." He fake sniffles. "I have to start the last one tonight."

Jasper admits he's only ever been to the New Cumberland Library—understandable, since he can walk there—so I direct us to the Young Adult section. It's like a sixth sense of mine to be able to find books, so I locate *The Inevitable End of Arachnid* quickly and hand it to him like it's made of glass.

"The title is foreboding," he says with a frown.

"Are you sure you're ready to see how it ends?" I watch his eyes zoom over the cover.

"Maybe."

I shift my weight to one foot and tell myself it's not a big deal if he says no. It's okay for people to say no to things and it doesn't mean that I'm awful, ugly, and terrible to be around. "I wanted to ask you. If you end up liking the series, did you want to see the movie?"

He cradles the book to his chest. "Oh, I'm definitely seeing the movie. I'm gonna buy the action figures, the shirts, the lunch boxes. I need this movie to do well so I can see that twist happen on screen."

He's . . . not getting it. Maybe he's being polite. Answering my question—because I didn't specify *with me*, but it was implied—while letting me down easy. Why is a bookstore war and a minor accident and a kiss and a mutual love for books so confusing?

I clear my throat. "I mean with me. Do you want to see it with me? Dahlia got me tickets to the midnight premiere."

His eyes widen. "Yes. Do people dress up for those? Seems like they would, right?"

Relief washes over me, my limbs growing gooey and relaxed. A woman at a nearby table starts packing up her laptop. "Yeah, I assume people will be dressed up."

"Did you want to? We could go as Ammo and Lasers. I guess I'll let you be Lasers, even though she's my favorite and it would be pretty awesome to gender-bend it."

He wants to do cosplay with me. This might be the weirdest thing my heart has ever raced over.

"Um, sure. Yeah. I've never done cosplay before. What if I do it wrong?"

"I won't lead you astray. You'll be entirely unsurprised to hear that this won't be my first time cosplaying. I made a dashing Poe Dameron last year at Comic-Con."

I rest my hand on his bicep, surprised by how intimate the impersonal touch feels. "I'm going to need pictures, a lot of them."

"Only if you promise that I can help make your costume."

"I'll need all the help I can get." This feels like the time to ask, but the thought of him shutting down or not wanting to answer me shrivels the question up. I'll just keep his craft book purchase, Grant's comments, and the sewing machine in his room bottled up until the right moment.

I start moving us toward the checkout desk because the last thing I need is to get swept up in a moment with Jasper in the stacks of a public library or, worse, to end up checking out books of my own, but he stops me.

"I actually need to grab a few more books if that's okay?" His one eyebrow is cocked a little higher in hope. "Do you know where the nonfiction is?"

We head there next, and when I see the particular section we end up in, I don't let my question go unasked. As our shoes pad across the dingy yellow carpet, I ask, "Have you done this a lot? Cosplay?"

"Only twice. Poe and a gender-bent Captain Marvel." He searches the shelf for something out of my reach.

"Definitely need pictures of both. What are we looking for here? A craft book again?"

He plucks one out and shows me the cover. It has a needle and thread, with the thread unspooling to form the title: *Costume Design Basics*. It's a thick book, and wider than I'm used to reading—probably to include pictures.

"I'm working on a portfolio of clothes and costumes." He snags another book, but he doesn't show me it, just adds it to his pile. "I want to go to school for fashion, be a costume designer. Maybe for theater, or film." He says it offhandedly, like maybe he'll do it or maybe he won't, but it doesn't matter to him either way. It feels like something is finally sliding into place, like I've unlocked a new level in Jasper Hamada: The Lost World. I've met his family, his best friend, seen his bedroom, and gotten a hint of what he likes. Now I know what he wants to do with his life. It's more than I thought I'd know when I met him this summer.

"That's really cool." I frown, thinking about how his brother wants him to be a manager. How he said that Jasper didn't have any passions to pursue.

He cringes when he sees my face. "You don't have to lie. You can admit that this is the moment you're totally turned off of the whole prospect of . . . me."

"Oh. No! No." I flail, trying to get us back on track. "Has that happened before?" I move until I'm between him and the shelf, barely any space for breathing. "I think it's cool, *really*. That's what that stuff in your room was for, right? The fabric? The sewing machine?"

He closes his eyes. "I forgot you were in my bedroom."

"There's an offensive first for everything, I guess," I joke. I put my hand on his arm again and squeeze. "I'm being serious. That's awesome. I don't have the skills or determination to do something like that."

Jasper doesn't want to work in his family's bookstore. Luke's words bounce around my head, trying to fight with this new information. Jasper doesn't want to take down B&M. It was never personal to him.

"I've never known someone that wanted to do that before. It sounds hard."

"That's what she said," he mutters to the ceiling.

"Hey." I poke his chest and make him look me in the eye. "My mom was in a few movies. Maybe she knows someone you could talk to, or intern with, or whatever."

242

Who am I kidding? She probably doesn't. It wouldn't be Dahlia if she wasn't disappointingly unhelpful. I open her IMDB page on my phone.

"Oh my god," he says, grabbing my phone. "She's gonna be in that Timothée Chalamet movie?"

"Even my cold heart warmed a little at that." It doesn't go unnoticed by me that we're in precisely the situation I had tried to avoid earlier: Jasper and me alone in a dark corner, surrounded by the things I love the most. It's almost romantic. It's definitely putting ideas in my head about video chats, surprising him on long weekends, holding hands, and celebrating holidays together—the things that create attachments. The things that make up relationships that go on past the summer, that come with labels.

"He's like an attractive Victorian ghost boy."

And the mood lightens as quickly as my laugh flies out. I hurry to stifle myself. Even though there's only a few minutes left until the library closes, it goes against every fiber of my being to be too loud here. "Weirdly accurate description."

"I think I stole it from Twitter, to be honest." He exhales, his shoulders relaxing, and locks eyes with me. "We should probably check these out. They're closing."

"Yeah, of course. One thing first." I glance around to verify we're alone and then balance up on my tiptoes. Before I can plant my lips on his, he sweeps in, dropping the books so he can wrap his arms around my lower back. I'm not even bothered that he might have hurt the books because he holds me so closely and so tightly that I may have a permanent bend to my spine. But in a really nice way. Like puzzle pieces fitting together, me and him.

At least if we're kissing, our mouths are too busy to talk about what this all means. Too busy for him to reject something I didn't even propose, but maybe—just a little bit—might want? One day . . .

If someone had told me about this night at the beginning of the summer, I would have laughed myself to half-death.

# TWENTY-ONE

It's a fucked-up rule of life that as soon as things are going your way, they're about to turn, crash, and burn.

On a Thursday in late July, I say goodbye to Ravi after my shift ends, grabbing one of his experimental mint chocolate chip cake pops he brought in for me—aka his guinea pig—and run to my car as cool rain cuts through the heat. The first crack of thunder sounds as soon as I slide my key into the ignition. I crank up the AC and pull my phone out, nearly dropping the cake pop. It's too risky to hold it and my phone while I text, so I just shove the whole thing in my mouth.

**Zelda from YouTube**

Today 4:59 PM

Are we still meeting at thrifty?

4:59 PM

Yep. Is your boyfriend gonna be there

5:00 PM

He's not my boyfriend and please don't
say anything like that when he's around.

5:00 PM

But yes, he'll be there

5:00 PM

Leaving now. Can't wait to third wheel

5:01 PM

I swear to god, if Zelda even dares to bust out the *So, what
are you guys? Are you dating? Fuck friends? It was a one-time thing?*
I will strangle her with whatever secondhand clothing item is
closest to her.

I've thought about it more and I'm only more confused. I
like Jasper, and I can imagine a bright and shiny future between
us, but only if you take out me leaving for school, his asso-
ciation with the bookstore putting mine out of business, our
rocky start . . . Everything is so uncertain and flawed. I can't
bother if it's not guaranteed. The last thing I need is another
heartbreak this summer, another tragic goodbye, so I'm trying
to stay firmly in the Fun Zone.

Last night, Jasper asked me to meet him so we could find
items for the cosplay he sketched up. He sent a somewhat blurry
photo of it around midnight and, from what I could see, it

looked great, and I'm excited to work on it. But I panicked at the thought of being alone with him again when I've decided, firmly, to not let this flirtation turn into a full-blown relationship, which Grant more than hinted at Jasper wanting, so I invited Zelda, telling him I already had plans with her. The library incident will be one and done unless Jasper keeps things casual with me.

A few times since our truce, I've had to bat away the voice inside my head that says he's just trying to get me to stop messing with Prologue. He apparently doesn't even care about Prologue, not when he's got his eyes on design school, and if I'm being honest, it's not like I was a real threat to their success anyway. It's almost laughable that he doesn't care about books and his store is thriving, while B&M and I are beyond struggling. Ultimately, though, if we keep things relaxed, if we don't put a name or expectations on this, there can be no breakup, can be no hurt feelings. So that's what I plan to do.

Thrifty, the secondhand shop, sits off the Carlisle Pike in a small shopping center housing a movie theater that changes brands every year, a Planet Fitness, a Weis grocery store, and a Five Guys. It fits the area in the same way that none of the other places seem to fit. I find a parking spot and text Zelda and Jasper that I'm here.

As I'm waiting for responses, the rain pours down harder on my car, sounding like hail. It's hard to see the parking lot through my windshield and as soon as I flick my wipers on, it's covered in a sheet of water again. Naturally, I don't have an umbrella.

My phone vibrates in my cup holder.

**Wreck-It Ravi**

Today 5:11 PM

The books came but idk
if these are the right ones

5:11 PM

Wreck-It Ravi sent a photo.

*Holy shit. No.*

I know as soon as I see the thumbnail that the wrong books were delivered. Or ordered. I can't be sure because I trusted Astrid to do it. A hot hint of betrayal stings my gut. How could she possibly mess this up? And did she do it on purpose?

OMG those are the wrong covers!!!

5:12 PM

I opened all the boxes and
that's what was inside tho

5:12 PM

They're all wrong then

5:12 PM

I'm going to call Astrid

5:12 PM

She picks up on the second ring.

"Hey, baby."

"Did you order the wrong books or did they deliver the wrong books?" I put her on speaker so I can send her the photo Ravi sent me.

"What?" There's shuffling on her end.

"Check your texts. Those are the old covers. We were supposed to get a shipment of the new ones. The ones coming out with the movie."

"Hmmm."

"That's all you have to say?" My heart is pounding in my chest. Texts drop down from the top of my phone, from Zelda and Jasper saying they're here and Ravi asking what he should do with the boxes, but I flick them away. Astrid hmms again. "Stop *hmm*-ing."

"I'm just trying to check my records to see what I ordered." She inhales on her end. "No, I ordered the new covers. The one with the girl with red hair in front of the cute boys. In the desert?"

I throw my head back and it hits my seat hard. "So, we have to send them back and order the right ones."

She sighs. "I'll give them a call."

"I'll do it." I want to make sure it gets done right this time.

"I'll handle it."

"*Will you, though?*"

"Madeline, I ordered the right ones. This isn't my fault so you can lose the attitude."

"I'm not saying it's your fault." I just don't believe her when she says it's not. I don't trust her to have cared enough to get this right.

"It took a month to get these. We don't have another month to wait. The ordering site says to give them two weeks to ship anyway, so we might as well just keep these. Didn't you say the old cover is better?"

"When you call them," I grit out, ignoring her, "tell them they made a mistake, to send the new ones rush delivery, and not to charge us." I hate that I have to spell it out for her. She's been running this store my whole life and she's taking a sloth's route to get things done. It makes me want to scream.

We can't be stuck with the old covers. The rest of the world likes New. And we need the rest of the world to like what we have so they'll buy the books. The whole point of Warbeck's tour is to sign copies of the movie tie-in editions.

"I'll handle it," she says firmly, but not exactly sounding like she will. At least, not like she'll handle it the way I want it to be handled.

"Well, you're the fucking boss, I guess," I say, and hang up. She'll be mad at me, but right now I'm mad at her. It's the *you had one job* meme, but in real life, and not funny. I know she claims she ordered the right ones, but . . . I just know she didn't—mistake or not. She doesn't care about keeping the store open. She's proven it time and time again.

I take a few seconds to breathe in and out slowly. According to my texts, Zelda and Jasper have both gone inside, and as Zelda tells me, she's awkwardly waiting there with my boyfriend so I better come inside now before she says something I'll regret.

The rain lightens up a fraction. I grab my bag and make a run for it, the drops cooling my heated skin. I'm mad and nervous and there are butterflies in my stomach trying to avoid the acid Astrid's mistake poured in.

Inside, Jasper and Zelda stand under the bright yellow overhead lighting about four feet away from each other, dripping from the rain. They appear to be talking—and this much I guess just because their mouths are moving and no one else is around—but not facing each other. Jasper's eyes dart to Zelda every two seconds and then look away. Zelda talks while typing on her phone. Mine won't stop vibrating.

"Hi." My wet hair sticks to my forehead. I push it to the side.

"Hey." Jasper's eyes light up, probably because it was so awkward with Zelda and at least it will be less awkward with me. Zelda's "Prologue is ass" comment from all those weeks ago rings in my ears.

"Were you waiting for it to stop raining or something? You texted like five minutes ago," Zelda says, stepping toward me.

"I was on the phone with Astrid. The books for the event aren't right." My insides squeeze. "We got six boxes of the old covers, not the new ones."

Jasper's eyes widen.

Zelda cringes. "Was that Ravi's fault? He's really trying to be better lately."

"No." I almost feel bad at the guilt twisting her expression. "It was Astrid."

"Thank fucking god," she says through an exhale. "He really wants Astrid to give him a good referral if things, you know, don't go the way we want them to." She side-eyes Jasper for a second, but he doesn't catch it.

"She says she ordered the right ones, but I just don't buy it. I think she made a mistake and doesn't want to admit it." I shake my head. "Let's just do some shopping. I don't want to think about it right now." Not when there's nothing I can do about it.

Zelda takes off down an aisle, but I linger behind with Jasper.

"Sorry about the covers," he says with a grimace, fidgeting with his Nope. band T-shirt.

"There's nothing to be done. I don't want to talk about it."

"But—"

"I'm fine," I say, waving away his words. "Zelda's looking for weird vintage shirts, but she usually gives up after a few minutes. She'll help us then."

Jasper swallows and takes the lead, shoving clothing into my arms and tasking Zelda with searching for certain accessories as soon as she finds the perfect item—a Rolling Stones shirt three sizes too large for her thin frame—just as I predicted. She follows Jasper's orders without sarcastic comments, but also spends a lot of time taking photos and videos—of us, mostly, when she thinks I don't notice, and sometimes of the clothes. I can't even imagine the number of times she's caught me glaring and mouthing, "Knock it the fuck off." She always replies with a whispered, "Jadeline."

"This is perfect, but not the right color." Jasper throws the shirt onto the growing pile in my arms anyway. "We could dye it if we have to."

"Don't let Madeline do that. She'll end up dyeing everything but." Zelda pokes me on the nose. "She tries, though."

"That was one time."

"And one huge mess on my living room floor," she says, spinning to face me between two racks of winter coats.

"I thought the dye had set!"

"Rhoda's still mad at me!"

Jasper cuts his body between ours, his hand held up. "I'll dye it."

"Jasper'll dye it," Zelda says, biting back a laugh.

"That was never really in question," I say, following him to the next spot. The clothes are starting to weigh down my arms. I can feel my muscles screaming that I should stop by Planet Fitness after this to sign up for a membership. "He's the professional."

"Whose decision was it to go as the most cosplayed characters in the series?" Zelda asks.

"Your half bitch is showing," I say as I adjust the pile of clothes in my arms.

"They're my favorites," Jasper says, frowning at us. "I just thought it would be fun."

Zelda looks at me behind Jasper's back. "Does he know that they—"

"Not yet, so don't spoil it! He's not done reading." Plus, pointing out that they have a huge slow burn in the last book will be awkward regardless of the state of Jasper's and my relationship/friendship/no-longer-hating-each-other-ship.

He whips toward me. "Oh my god, do they die?"

I freeze. "Can we try these on and eliminate what's not going to work?"

Zelda pats me on the shoulder, making my back muscles

twinge. "That was a solid attempt at distraction. It did not work at all, but A for effort."

Jasper's face tightens. "Yeah, we should try stuff on." He takes the pile.

Zelda's phone rings and she answers with a dramatic groan. "What?"

Jasper nods toward the fitting rooms. "Does she always answer her phone like that?"

"No, sometimes she answers it with 'No, thanks' and then hangs up."

He picks a large dressing room and starts sorting through the pieces, hanging parts of what would be Lasers's outfit on the hooks. Zelda joins us, sliding her phone into her pocket.

"Levi says I'm ten minutes late for dinner at Longhorn, so I need to go," she sighs. "Okay, so bye, Mads. Bye, Hotmada."

And before I can even process what she says, she darts from the store and into the rain . . . leaving me in the imperfect position to be at the receiving end of Jasper wanting to define this relationship, and I'll either have to reject him and end whatever's growing between us now or, I don't know, woman up and take the plunge despite the possibility that *he* might eventually reject *me*?

Jasper shrugs when I glance at him. "I can appreciate someone who shows up, helps, and then disappears when they're not needed anymore. It's something I wish my brother was better at."

I can't say I disagree. Luke was not helpful at all, but he did show up and then disappear, leaving devastation in his aftermath. Half credit.

He frowns. "Didn't you guys have plans to hang out, though? It's only been like twenty minutes."

Oh right. Fuck. "Her mom tends to demand all attention. She probably just decided to go out to dinner on a whim. That's Rhoda for you."

"And did she call me *Hodmada*?" He frowns. "Will you correct her?"

I snort, unconsciously tugging him closer before I can tell myself to maintain some distance. "She called you *Hot*mada. The reasoning behind it is pretty clear."

His expression falls into one of smugness. "Oh, really?"

"Don't let it go to your head."

"Too late." He directs me into the dressing room. "Ditch anything that's too small," he says, laying his own clothes over his arm and backing out. "We can alter larger clothes to be smaller, and, really, that's better for me to work with anyway. Extra fabric. Room for mistakes." He grimaces. "And there will be mistakes. I'm sorry in advance; I'm still learning."

On his way out, he gently closes the dressing room door. I do a little prayer that most of the clothes will be larger, rather than smaller, and pull my dress over my head.

"What else are you working on?" I ask, hanging it on a free hook. Grant made it sound like he had been working on something the night they jumped my car, but it doesn't seem like Jasper's family—or maybe just his brother?—knows much about his career aspirations.

"What?" he asks from the other side of the wall.

A chill runs down my body, leaving goose bumps in its wake. I'm basically naked within a few feet of him. God, I want to kiss him. Among other inappropriate things to do in a dressing room of a secondhand clothes shop.

"You mentioned a portfolio?"

"Oh." His voice comes muffled. "I'm doing a dress for my mom right now. It's a surprise for her birthday."

I slide the first pair of pants off the hanger and try them on. They get up to my hips and won't budge. I avoid the mirror, not in a good enough emotional state to confront how I look. I'm still so annoyed with Astrid that I could probably find a reason to blame her for all the extra pounds of fat my body won't shed. "That's nice of you."

"Yeah, remember? I'm nice."

I kick out of them, try the next pair—a little loose everywhere, thankfully—and slide the first shirt off the hanger.

"Does she know about this? The designing and stuff?"

"Well," he says heavily. "She knows I'm making her a dress, and that I like altering clothes, but she doesn't know I'm going to use the piece to apply to school. I need at least three, and some photos of others I've done. They don't have to be perfect since this is just for admissions, but I want them to be eye-catching at the very least and the bold colors and design of the cosplay will help. My previous cosplay is either *too* flashy or looks like it comes directly out of the pages of *Space Vogue*."

"I can't tell which costume is supposed to fit with which description."

I can hear the smile in his voice. "Good."

I move on to the next shirt when the current one fits. My good pile is as big as my bad pile. "So, you send the outfits to the school?" I was hoping to keep mine, but I guess if things properly end when I leave next month, it's fitting that I won't have any tangible trace of him.

"Photos. Measurements. Fabric details." His voice is muffled again, maybe taking a shirt off. "I write a little report about it and send the whole package in. If I get granted an interview, I take the pieces in so they can check it out in person. Feel it. See how it moves."

"What if I wanted to keep my outfit? Have the closest thing to a Jasper Hamada original, before you get famous?"

His voice comes from a different direction now, on the other side of my door. "May I please borrow it to get into my dream school?"

Dream school. What a concept. Wanting, *needing*, to be admitted to a place where you're stuffed inside a classroom and forced to spend ridiculous amounts of money to be critiqued. I'm only going to school because Astrid told me I had to. I'd rather stay at home and work in my bookstore forever—what Luke apparently wants of Jasper.

I throw my dress back on. My head tingles as my hair rises. Static. Great. "I suppose I'll allow it."

"You're a good friend."

*Is that all I am, though?* I stop the thought. *Isn't that what I want to be?*

"Thanks." I open the door and plaster on a fake smile.

He stands on the other side, fewer clothes draped over his arm. "Do you have any good pieces?"

I pick up my pile and hand them to him. He turns around,

dumping them into a cart he pulled over. It would have been nice to have that while we were shopping. He helps me put the bad clothes onto a giant rack outside the dressing rooms and then stalls, his hands gripping the shopping cart tightly.

"I need, uh, your measurements. To start altering the clothes."

"Oh." My arms itch to cover my stomach. "I don't know them." And I would hate to hear my body's numerical value. Numbers shouldn't make people feel like shit, and yet.

"Most people don't." From his pocket, he pulls out a tape measure. "I was hoping to show Zelda how to do it and have her get them, but she left."

Is this even the same guy who had his hands on my body and his mouth practically inside my own just a few days ago? I mean, I totally get what he's saying and, in this moment, I wish Zelda were here to do what he wanted, but this is a semi-professional sort of thing. He should be able to do it without it being awkward. And I should be able to suck it up. For the love of midnight premiere cosplay, we have to get our shit together.

He likes me how I am. He likes me. He's said as much.

"I don't mind."

He raises an eyebrow. "You're sure?"

I pat down the sides of my dress. "I mean, you do it over my dress, right?"

He barks out a laugh. "Yeah."

We check to see that we aren't being watched before ducking into the room together. We pause inside, both our cheeks turning rosy. He clears his throat and then unrolls the tape.

"Hold out your arms."

I mimic him, my arms feeling the burn from holding all those clothes again, as he measures them and types numbers into his phone. He doesn't make any faces, or say anything, but suddenly I'm wondering if the numbers are too high. Is he rethinking whether he finds me attractive? Does he even find me attractive or was there just a buzz he needed to silence when he kissed me? Was I just someone fun to tease when he was drunk? The only person to reply to him from a long list of people he called or texted that night? Was the library a test I somehow failed?

*Stop caring.*

He puts the tape gently around my neck, types a number, and then hesitates.

"How about you do this?" He gestures to my chest.

"You can do it." Unless he really doesn't want to. But they're boobs. People who are into girls sexually *like* boobs, right? I'm overthinking this.

He stares at me and then glances down at my chest.

For god's sake, aren't we past this? Why are we always bumbling up to the point where one of us kisses the other? I perch myself onto my tiptoes and plant a kiss on his lips. He rests his palm against my cheek, his mouth working against mine at an aching pace. I pull away first—it feels awful and wonderful all at once to have the power, but know I shouldn't be using it. To know how easily I could let it be turned on me.

He laughs at his own dazed expression, then proceeds to gently wrap it around my back and track the number he finds on the front. Without a word of acknowledgment, he moves the tape down to my waist, his hands sending shock waves down my sides. He takes measurements on my lower half and pauses when he needs to get my inseam numbers, kneeling in front of me. I should feel in control with him gazing up at me like he is, but I just feel light-headed.

"Do you want to do it?" His throat sounds constricted.

*Yes. I do want to do it.* And that's the problem right now. That we're not.

"Do I have to kiss you for confirmation that it's okay for you to touch me again?" It's a joke, but I cut off my own laughter because he's asking for consent and not nearly enough people do. "Sorry. You can. Please do."

"I wouldn't mind another kiss," he mumbles lightheartedly as he slides the measuring tape up my thigh, over my dress. There's no skin-to-skin contact, but I still feel charged. His fingers press into my leg, warm over the fabric. He stands, cheeks pink, after typing the numbers into his phone.

He won't meet my eyes. "Uh, should we talk about what happened?"

"What do you mean?"

"Between us?"

"When?"

"Madeline," he says through a breathy chuckle. "You know what I mean. The kiss. The drunken mess. The cosmic shift between us."

"I don't think we need to talk about it. Everything was pretty straightforward." I catch my breath speeding up and try to slow it. He's going to say we should stop, stay friends, and I agree—we can't keep toeing this line. So why do I feel like I'm twelve again and arriving home after book club to find that Dahlia didn't just forget to pick me up, she forgot to tell me she was leaving the state?

"I like you."

I focus on the wall over his shoulder. "You said that."

He rolls the measuring tape up into a little circle around his finger. "I want you to know that it still stands when I'm sober, and when I'm not, like, on drugs."

Heat surges through my body. "Noted."

Something falls over his face, an expression I can't decipher. He's stiffer. "We should talk about what happens next, if there *is* something that happens next." He stuffs the measuring tape into his pocket and rocks on his heels. "You know, whatever."

"Whatever sounds great." I rush to get the words out of my mouth and I stumble over them a bit. What *is* "whatever"? Is it that state of being where you kissed someone and then regret it? The Friend Zone? I want to stay in the Fun Zone, even though it was like standing on a cliff overlooking an endless drop, but if Jasper's not immediately pushing me away or trying to start something just as summer's ending, I think I can accept this. I can work with it. He can't leave me if he's not really with me.

"I'm going to school soon and I have to focus on the store for now, anyway," I say with a shrug. "It works for me."

"So, we're just . . ." He trails off, avoiding my eyes.

"Whatever."

He clears his throat. "Are we *exclusively* whatever?"

My heart kicks a speedy rhythm in my chest. "Sure." I lick my lips and take a deep breath. "What does that mean to you?"

Because, to me, it sounds an awful lot like dating each other and only each other. Like a relationship. Something that will need to end eventually.

"What does it mean to *you*?" He pushes some of his hair away from his eyes.

"That we stay just how we are, until one of us says otherwise?" I count the seconds he pauses after my question. Twelve seconds of silence. So much opportunity to tell me *never mind*.

"I'll agree to that." He angles toward me, pushing me back against the wall with care, no hint of a smile or smirk, but I feel a delightful tingle starting in my limbs. "Can I kiss you now?"

I blush at the breathiness of my voice. "You have to seal this deal somehow."

And he does. And everything's so much easier when we're not talking.

# TWENTY-TWO

I don't know who's more embarrassed: the waitstaff or me.

They finish singing a jazzed-up birthday song and leave me sitting at the table, mortified and hot, as my family members dissolve into laughter and the awkward glances from other customers fade. If anyone thinks I'm sharing this chocolate cake, they have another think coming.

Dahlia leans in, fork in hand. I pull the plate away and shrug when she pouts.

"Maybe we can come here on your birthday." I take one small, sweet bite. "And then this could be all yours."

Sterling, Astrid, Benny, and Dahlia stare at me with sad puppy dog eyes, but no. It's mine. If they made me sit through that, I deserve at least ten of these thinly sliced, free pieces of cake.

Around us, people laugh loudly and the general noise of dinner out increases. Utensils click against plates. Voices fight to be heard over other voices fighting to be heard over music playing.

"Any plans for later?" Sterling cuts into what's left of his steak.

"Night swimming."

It's my tradition with Zelda and Levi. We steal some of Rhoda's wine coolers, which are basically just sugar, and prune in the warm water for hours before setting off fireworks and playing with sparklers in the deserted street. Then Levi, our designated driver, takes us to Taco Bell around one o'clock in the morning and drops me off at home. I wake up feeling severely dehydrated and exhausted. Tradition.

"If you need a ride," Sterling starts, accidentally catching Dahlia's and Astrid's attention, "*because you're too tired from swimming*, call me."

It was *one* time. Levi couldn't stay awake to drive me home last year so I had to call Sterling or else Astrid would have freaked out. I mean, I get it. But how is Sterling going to throw me under the bus like that? On my damn birthday. In front of my quickly disappearing cake.

"Will do."

"Or maybe don't swim so hard," Dahlia says in an attempt to smooth over Sterling's obvious metaphor. She takes a sip of her wine and winks.

"Don't swim until you're twenty-one. Definitely no swimming and driving." Benny leans back in his chair, clasping his hands behind his head, and glances at Astrid. She meets his stare with a hard look and smacks him on the chest. He straightens.

She turns her glare to me, but it softens. I still haven't gotten over the ordering snafu, but I've relaxed with the cold shoulder.

Mistakes happen; it's just so un-fucking-fortunate that it happened.

"What?" I shove my fork into my mouth. "I didn't do anything."

"Just be safe."

"Always." I glance around the table. Everyone stares back at me. "Stop being weird."

Our waitress places the check on the table and tells us there's no rush, but there is. If we stay too long, if I spend more time with Dahlia, something is bound to go wrong. This is her first birthday with me since my second birthday, I think, and it's been surprisingly pleasant. I hadn't known how to react when she gave me her present—a bundle of books she bought from a library sale that she thought I'd like. It was so nice that I didn't even tell her I already owned two of them and one would never get read since it's a cliché adult book about a white man's mid-life crisis.

Astrid slips a coupon into the black check presenter along with cash she gathers from Dahlia and Sterling. Benny asks if there's cake at home, too, and she says, "Of course there is. We're not monsters."

"I'm going to the bathroom really quick." I slide out of my chair and weave toward the restroom tucked into the corner of the dark restaurant.

I push through the door with my elbow and come face-to-face with Preeti, the owner of Buns.

"Hey." I smile, moving out of the door's trajectory. "How are you?"

"Oh, hi—" I can see it on her face, in her wide eyes and open mouth. She totally blanks on my name.

"Madeline."

"Madeline. Yes." She squeezes my hand. "Sorry. It's been a busy week."

"No worries. Not to add to your stress, but did you get our order for next week?" I slip my hands into my pockets. I haven't heard anything about the original agreement we came to. "For Books and Moore?"

The event is in one week exactly. Just thinking about it gives me full-body chills. The movie. Meeting Isla Warbeck. Getting to see B&M succeed and stay open past the month. Astrid was supposed to send in the order for cookies and cupcakes five days ago, but after the book purchasing fiasco, now seems like the best opportunity to casually feel out if she did the right thing this time.

"Um." Her brown eyes flit to the ground. "I did."

"Great. Do you need anything from us? Estimated table space or help carrying the food to the store?" I close my eyes, grimacing. "I'm sorry. We don't need to discuss this now. I'll call you on Monday."

She bites her lip. "Madeline, perhaps you should speak with your manager."

I blink, my heart sinking. "Did she mess something up?"

"She said you guys no longer needed the catering." Her eyebrows rise. "I'm sorry. I think you should speak with her." She darts past me. "Have a nice night."

Cold fear settles heavily in my stomach. I don't even use the bathroom, I just storm back to our table, stomping through happy diners talking over steaming food and half-empty glasses. I stop next to Astrid's chair.

She glances up. "Ready to go?" She takes her cloth napkin from her lap and places it on the table, standing.

"Something wrong?" Dahlia asks hesitantly.

Tears prick my eyes as my family heads toward the door. I do, too, just so I don't cause a scene in the restaurant, in front of all these customers who live in the area, who could be customers to our store one day.

"Feeling okay?" Astrid asks, rubbing my back. "We're almost outside. You can get some fresh air."

We make our way to the car and Astrid opens the driver door. I push it closed from behind her.

She frowns. "What's wrong?"

Dahlia waits near the rear bumper. "Madeline?"

The first tear spills over. "I'll let you explain," I say to Astrid with a wavering voice, "why Preeti says you pulled out of the contract to have Buns cater the event next weekend."

Astrid sighs, leaning against her car. "Look, baby, we couldn't afford it."

"You should have talked to me before you did that. I could have—maybe I could have fixed it. We could have adjusted the order or—or—I don't know! Thought of something together!"

I cross my arms, gripping my elbows to stop from screaming in her face. After all this, after her mistakes and my effort, she's still making decisions without me? For my event? How am I supposed to trust her to keep B&M open when I go away to school if she can't handle one event? We'll need to do an event every month to scrape by. The only reason we didn't need one last month was because of the fundraiser Zelda helped with, but Jasper was right. That can't sustain a business.

"We have all the books and the author coming. That's enough." She pats me on the cheek and I flinch away.

"It wouldn't be enough for Prologue."

"We're not Prologue."

"Yeah, that's pretty clear by our sales and your lack of trying."

She crosses her arms. "My lack of trying? I've been keeping that store open for the last fifteen years, no matter what I had to do. But I'm tired of struggling, Madeline. I'm going along with all your events and ideas and sales, so don't yell at me for accepting the store's fate when they're not enough."

"You're sabotaging the store."

She angles toward me. "The store is sabotaging me! Ever since I got saddled with it after I put my mother into assisted living."

A silence falls between us as it feels like my heart disintegrates in my chest. "How could you say that? You love the store." I pull in a deep breath. "Do you also feel like you got *saddled* with Benny and me?"

She deflates. "No. Of course not. I love you two with all my heart and raising you both has been the best part of my life."

"Well, the store has been a huge part of that. The store

babysat us while you were busy working. It's what kept us so close all these years. It's part of our family."

"It's easy for you to be optimistic and sentimental. You're not the adult; I don't have that luxury, baby. You're not poring over the financial aspects of this store. Even with Benny gone most of the time, we're struggling to pay the bills and get groceries—"

"Groceries? What are you talking about?"

"At home." She grips my shoulders. "With the decrease in sales, it's like trying to keep two homes afloat, baby. I don't have that money. None of us do. Dahlia's working for free. Benny's making a killing at Prologue. I'm ready to move on. It's just you who's not. I'm doing this event for you, so you can feel like you tried. But the store is going to close."

I push her hands off me. "So, you want me to just throw away all these years? All the memories in the store?" *My entire future?* I'm not sure I even exist without B&M. Maybe *I'm* the robot that charges in the store overnight, not Jasper.

She scoffs quietly, shaking her head. "You're being dramatic. The memories are in your head, not the store. All of this because I won't have carbs at the event?"

I groan. "It's not about the food, Mom! It's about putting effort into this event so we can keep the store open—"

"*Mom?*" Dahlia steps forward, her expression nothing short of shattered. "You just called her 'Mom.'"

She looks to Astrid, who drops her shoulders in defeat. "Does she normally call you that?"

I hadn't realized it slipped out. Between the yelling and the

269

tears, and what's happening with the store, how could I care what I call Astrid? For all intents and purposes, she is my mom. Even Dahlia has to know that.

"I didn't mean to." My eyes sting.

Astrid, because she's an unending well of kindness, pats the side of my head. "It's okay. It was an accident."

"It's not okay," Dahlia says, reaching for her sister's arm. "It's not. You promised me you'd never let them call you that."

"It happens," Astrid says in a soft voice. "She's stressed."

More tears leak out of my eyes and I don't know what I'm most upset about anymore. Astrid's lack of faith in the store—in my ability to save it—or the fact that I called Astrid my mother and I'm, I don't know, disappointed in myself? Sad that it matters? Angry that it was me who ruined my birthday and not Dahlia?

"I'm stressed, too, but I don't call people by the wrong names." Dahlia looks in my direction, but I avoid her eyes. "I've been working my ass off this summer to earn that stupid, pointless name and you just accidentally call Astrid it?"

"If it's stupid and pointless, why does it matter?" I wipe my eyes. "Astrid has been working to earn that my whole life. You don't get pity points or props for being here two months in a row. You've never been around two months collectively my entire fucking life. Can we not—" I take a deep breath, sniffing snot from dripping. "Can we not make this about you right now? For once? This is about the store."

Dahlia recoils faster than if I had slapped her. Even Astrid looks disappointed in me.

A man in baggy khakis approaches us cautiously. "Everything okay here, folks?"

"No," I grunt before pulling open the car door and sliding in.

Zelda will have to break out the stronger stuff tonight.

# TWENTY-THREE

I sleep like shit after I drink more than one glass of anything alcoholic, but I still fight all morning to stay unconscious. It doesn't work.

Around noon, when I give up rolling around in the blankets and stuffing my head under my pillow until it's too hot and I feel like I'm suffocating, I sit up. The house around me is quiet, but outside is a buzz of noise: bees flying by my window; birds chatting with each other; lawn mowers chewing on grass; kids splashing in pools, their wild laughter annoying the shit out of me.

I kick out of my blankets, a clammy sweat coating my skin, and unplug my fully charged phone.

**Astrid**

Today 9:35 AM

Out. Be back around dinnertime.

9:35 AM

Ok

12:13 PM

No "ay"—she'll be able to tell I'm not in the forgiving mood that way.

When I was passed out in bed post–Taco Bell, Zelda texted me.

**Zelda from Youtube**

Today 3:09 AM

You seemed so sad tonight so I wanted to say happy birthday again! You're barely a YA protagonist now!

3:09 AM

Was Hotmada naked in your bed when you got home?

3:09 AM

Is that creepy of me? You said he's like 19 right?

3:09 AM

Ravi remembered your birthday but forgot you had off today so there's cake at the store whenever you come in . . . if I don't eat it all

10:47 AM

I hadn't felt like going through the whole thing with Zelda last night, choosing instead to get morosely drunk and heckle

Levi's poor diving form. I leave the messages unanswered for now and take a shower, using the hot water to wash away thoughts of the mess that is my life. After, with my laptop tucked under my arm, I slide a Tupperware container of watermelon from the fridge and head to the porch swing. I don't have to breach the typical wall of humidity today. There's a soft breeze and the sun keeps hiding behind some clouds. I place one of Astrid's outside pillows—this one says *Practice safe sex!*—behind me and crack open my laptop. I start off by withdrawing funds from our GoFundMe so I can pay for rental chairs and color flyers, and to see how much money I have to work with for new catering. If Astrid thought Buns was too expensive, I'll just have to find something less expensive.

But, after thirty minutes of Googling and the beginnings of a mind-numbing spreadsheet made, I'm realizing that carbs are expensive. It's possible that I could perfect my brownies enough to offer them, but that seems so . . . poor. It's as I'm deciding maybe we don't need baked goods at all that Zelda calls.

I answer. "Hey, Z."

"I'm putting a slice of cake in the fridge for you. It's so good." It sounds like her mouth is full of it right now.

"Thanks."

"Hungover?"

"Emotionally and physically. Hey, is Ravi at the store right now?" It's worth a shot. My last shot.

"Yeah. He's up front while I devour my second slice. I'm so sorry. I promise I won't eat yours."

"Can you ask him if he'll make some kind of dessert for the

event next weekend? I can pay him—" I check my list for funds available. "I can pay him fifty dollars for dessert for—I don't know—fifty people? Is that too optimistic?"

"What if it's not enough?"

"Like we could get that lucky. First come, first served."

"Okay. I'll ask him and get back to you."

When I hang up, feeling slightly better, I hear Dahlia walking around inside, talking. I don't know why, but I had assumed quiet house, plus Astrid gone, meant that Dahlia was also gone. I tilt my head toward the open window next to the porch swing.

The tinny sound of speakerphone makes its way to my ears. "It's not a sure thing, but they liked the tape you sent in and want to meet in person."

"Wow," Dahlia says—to her agent? "That's amazing. I'm really happy to hear that."

"Happy enough that you're going to fly in next week to meet with them?"

I can't risk looking inside and catching her attention. Can't risk her realizing I can hear her backing out of her promise that she was here for good. I don't know how she hasn't heard me yet. I'm pretty sure the sound of my heart shattering was loud enough to be heard in the fictional Discontent Desert.

I really don't know what I was expecting. I wouldn't normally be surprised to hear Dahlia is leaving. It's what she does. It's the thing she's best at. I don't even know when I started to care, to want her to be here. Maybe I don't. Maybe I just got used to her being around. Yeah, I called Astrid "Mom" last night, but Dahlia is my mother and she knows that. And, even after two months, she still doesn't care. I should have known if eighteen years hadn't done the trick, two months wouldn't.

I snap my laptop shut without hearing her answer. I don't need to. Dahlia was always searching for the right role because the first one she landed—being a mom—wasn't her dream. And she sure as hell wasn't good at it. Raising Benny and me at eighteen was something that ended up on the cutting room floor so she could one day win a big award and say that stupid line at the Oscars or wherever about how her kids should go to sleep, but the fact of the matter was we wouldn't have been watching.

It's fine.

I'm fine.

I'm used to things throwing me for a loop. I'm lucky I don't get motion sickness.

I charge inside, setting my laptop on the couch, and grab my car keys. I drive to get away from Dahlia, but end up at Jasper's house. Not at Books & Moore, where my problems have usually led me—to organizing and dusting shelves, to putting together displays and signage, to helping someone find the perfect book. It's not a comfort to me anymore.

**Jasper Hotmada**

Today 2:42 PM

Are you home?

2:42 PM

Yeah. Putting finishing touches on
our costumes

2:43 PM

You'll need to try this on so I can
tweak the final fit and stuff but

2:43 PM

Jasper Hotmada sent a photo.

The costume steals my breath away. It looks just like Lasers's outfit in the trailer, except it has things only a reader would remember. The bullet holes in the shape of a smiley face in her pants. Specific swaths of blood. Sand—how did he make the outfit look sandy?

It's perfect

2:43 PM

Can I try it on?

2:43 PM

Thanks ☺

2:44 PM

Yeah let me know when you're available. I
can bring it to you or you can come over..

2:44 PM

Just one period. I didn't mean for that to be
like a . . . situation

2:44 PM

I'm already at your house

2:45 PM

His face appears in the window above the front door, his eyebrows scrunched together. Then he smiles, waving me in. It doesn't look like he has a shirt on and my heart stumbles in my chest. I just need a distraction from Dahlia, from the store, from Zelda's joke about Jasper's birthday present to me. But, of course, even thinking about needing a distraction from the last thought makes me think it all over again. And it doesn't help that when Jasper answers the door, he's wearing plaid pajama bottoms slung low on his hips and a stretched-out tank top, backward and inside out. His arm is no longer bandaged, a few healing cuts visible on his tan skin.

"Hey." He lets me in, pulling his tank top as low as it'll go, over his pants. "My mom has a rule that the air-conditioning can't be on unless there are at least three people in the house, sorry. It's kind of stuffy. . . ."

"It's fine. We barely even have AC at my house." There's a single unit downstairs and a bunch of window and ceiling fans everywhere else. We're an open windows family, but not by choice.

I meet his eyes after I slip my shoes off. "So, you're alone, then?"

I knew this. I did. The cars, or lack thereof.

"Nope. You're here."

"Am I ruining a mental health day or something?" I peek around his house. Blackout curtains have drenched the living room in darkness, making it hard to catch things like discarded bowls of cereal, empty popcorn bags, or anything else he'd probably need to clean up before his parents got home. From what little I can see, the place is still spotless.

His grin lights up the room. "No, I was just working on the pieces. You want to see them?"

"That's why I'm here," I say offhandedly, following him up the stairs. He has two moles on the back of his bicep—whatever that muscle is called—and I want to connect them with a swipe of my finger. Or maybe my tongue.

"Really? Because you were here before I told you I was done." He peers at me over his shoulder. "Everything okay? Did you just miss looking at my ugly mug?"

We hit the landing outside his bedroom and he waits instead of going inside. An invisible tension builds between us, pulling taut like a string.

I point to a photo on the wall of the Hamadas in front of some type of shrine, all of them dressed in kimonos. "This is cute. Where was this?"

He comes to a stop behind me. "Cousin's wedding in Japan."

"Do you have a lot of relatives there?"

"A few. I don't know them very well. My dad keeps in touch, though."

"Did you think about trying to make one of these?" I gesture at their kimonos.

"I thought about it, but I don't think I'm there yet in terms of skill." He blushes. "Right now, I really shine on altering, not so much creating. That's why I want to go to school, to learn."

I nod. "And your family doesn't really know? Or approve?"

He pauses, the words forming slowly on his lips. "Both? They know I'm interested and I dabble a bit with fixing holes and hems, but they don't know about the school yet. I don't want to tell them until I'm in. There's not really a point getting them worried about me abandoning the store for some fruitless career path unless I'm actually *on* that path, you know?"

"I do."

"So, what's going on?" he asks, leaning against his door frame.

"Just not in a great mood."

"And you decided to come here? To me? I haven't been known to help your moods."

I breathe out a laugh. "I couldn't be at home because Dahlia was—she just—she's Dahlia. We're not close and she constantly disappoints me. I don't know why I let her get my hopes up this time. This is where I ended up. I thought maybe you could . . . keep my mind off her. Don't overthink it."

"I'll try not to, but I'm really good at that. It's like my superpower." He pushes open his door, finally. A standing fan oscillates air around the room, stirring a few designs he has pinned to a corkboard above his desk. The manufactured breeze fights with the one coming from the window, his curtains dancing back and forth.

A headless mannequin is wearing my outfit, just like I saw in the photo, but it suddenly feels so real. It's a thing I can touch, so I do.

"It's amazing. You did a really great job." I let the fabric sift through my fingers. "Where's yours?"

He cracks open his closet door and pulls out a few hangers, his outfit ready to be assembled, not a wrinkle in sight. "Fitted and ready to go."

I back away until my calves hit his bed, an appreciative exhale slipping through my lips. I sit with a small bounce and admire the outfit before he tucks it away. "What do you need me to do to help you finish?"

"You'll have to try it on and I'll pin areas that need to be taken in more. It's kind of loose right now because the fabric doesn't really give and I don't want to tear it." He raises an eyebrow. "Did you want to do that now? Or wait until we can get some air-conditioning on?"

It's not that hot. I think it's just us. Our "exclusive whatever" temperature is turned up to one hundred.

The thought of sliding those clothes over my quickly warming body doesn't sound so appealing, but *him* sliding over my quickly warming body does. If I want to kiss him, and he wants to kiss me back, shouldn't we be kissing? Jasper has proved time and time again this summer that he's not interested in rejecting me. And his pants are practically falling off anyway. One good tug would—

"Are you okay?" he asks.

"I'm good. Let's do it." I'm nothing if not subtle.

"So forward of you," he says, smirking. That small, beautiful scar runs away from me and I want to smooth out his face so I can see it again. "Let's do it."

He turns toward the mannequin to pull off the items with

a little laugh. But I don't wait. If I wait, I'll chicken out. Eric liked my body. Most days I don't *hate* my body. Jasper has had his hands on it before. He likes me. He likes kissing me. Just do it. He's sweet, agreeable, and he won't hurt me.

I stand and pull my shirt over my head, exposing my—thank-fucking-god—black bra lined with lace. That's what I get for not doing my own laundry. The only things left are sexy underwear. I drop the shirt and wait for him to turn around.

When he does—as if he really didn't suspect things going in this direction when I showed up out of the blue—he drops the outfit. I want to yell at him because he of all people should know to handle something so perfect with more care.

"I could have left the room." He quickly turns back around, facing the opposite wall and crossing his arms, shoulders high.

What little self-confidence I managed to find just straight-up dies. I swipe my shirt off the floor, covering my chest with it, and fumble for words.

"But you knew that . . ." He glances over his shoulder, slowly, his eyes down. "Right?"

Something happens in my stomach, like a firework of heat, when he locks his gaze on mine.

"Right." I fidget with the shirt, but don't put it on. "I assumed, if you do this at school or as a career, this would happen a lot." No, I hadn't assumed that, but it makes for a good excuse. *Always making excuses.* "And I'm sure you've seen all of this before."

His eyes stick to the floor. "Not you."

I clench my shirt tighter. "What?"

"I've never seen *you* before."

My face is so hot it hurts. "It's not really a big deal. Everyone has a body."

"I don't know, it feels like a big deal. Seeing someone's body is intimate. We wouldn't wear clothes all the time if it wasn't a big deal to see people naked."

I drop my shirt again, letting the words fall out of my mouth with it. "It's just skin under the clothes, Jasper, and you're not really making me feel great about mine right now."

"I'm sorry," he says suddenly, meeting my eyes for half a second and then looking away. "But it's not just skin; it's other things."

"Things you've seen and touched." I'm starting to feel like I'm tainting his innocence right now. "Right?"

He blows out a breath. "Again, not your things."

I cross my arms over my chest. "Is there something wrong with my *things*?"

"God, no," he chokes out. "No. Not at all."

"So, do you want to . . . move beyond kissing?" I step toward him slowly. "It's okay if you don't. It's okay if you haven't before."

His shoulders tense.

"That's it, right? It's not *me*?" *Please don't be me.* "I mean, is it just the act that's freaking you out? That was kind of personal to ask; I'm sorry. We don't have to do anything—"

He gestures loosely over his shoulder. "I think we're at the personal questions moment of our . . . friendship. I just,

I've never—it's never progressed to that point with anyone before."

"Do you want to progress to that point? Sex, or something?" I want to have sex. With him. I won't feel bad about putting it out there into the universe and I *did* say I wanted a distraction. If Jasper's making up a virgin story because he doesn't want to do things with me, he can say no right now. I'll feel like a total Books & Moron, but I'd never fault someone for not wanting to do something so intimate. There are tons of people who don't do this, ever.

He faces me, his high cheekbones splashed with pink. "Yes."

I have to make sure this isn't another movie invite snafu before getting too excited. "With me?"

"Yes."

Relief washes over me, but it's not enough to cool my body down. "Right now?"

"Yes, why are we still talking?"

I laugh and he slides his hand against my waist, directing me back onto his bed. He kisses like he's starving for the taste of me. I pull his tank top over his head, letting my hands fall down his stomach until they brush over the bit of hair leading under his waistband. I tease at the elastic there, but he pulls away, breathing heavily.

"Are you sure?" he asks.

"I am. Are you?"

"Yes." He kisses me deeply, turning my brain to mush. "I've wanted you since the first day I met you." Another kiss, this one with a bit more bite. "It was a Monday. You were wearing this shirt with a quote from the Discontent books on it." He pauses, his face angled into my neck. I feel his words sweep against my skin. "I went home and googled it. I had to wait for a while to get the books or it would have been obvious I was getting them because of you." Kiss.

"I thought you were just stealing ideas from our store."

His body goes a little rigid, his hands stalling mine just as a finger dipped below his waistband. "Yeah, my dad wanted me to just check it out the first time, but I spent most of the time checking you out. And then I kept going, even when he didn't tell me to."

"That's pretty cute," I sigh. "And it's working for me. Do you have a condom?"

"Yeah, one sec—" He stretches toward the nightstand and pulls open the top drawer. He straddles me to free his other hand and tears a condom from a whole strip of them. For a guy who's never had sex, he sure is prepared to have it. I can respect that.

He puts some distance between us reluctantly and moves his hands to my jean shorts, unbuttoning them and sliding down the zipper. "You're good?"

"Yes." I lift my hips so he can push them down my legs. I kick out of them the best I can with him above me, but I nearly knee him in the crotch. When I'm lying there in my underwear and he's ready, I take the condom from him. "I need . . . you. To touch me. Please?"

It's already been established that I'm not the most eloquent, but Jasper knows what I mean instantly. His hand passes my stomach I'm self-conscious about most of the time, and dips underneath my underwear. It's pretty clear in the next few moments that, while a virgin, he does have other experience or maybe he's just gifted. I almost feel guilty when I climax. Almost.

The condom crushes in my hand, unused.

"I meant to stop you, but—" I barely manage to say before Jasper's lips are on mine.

"Was that okay?"

"It was great." I'm breathless, cheeks aflame, but feeling so liquid and loose. "Thank you."

"Thank *you*," he says with a cheesy grin. "That was . . . wow." His gaze trails over my body. "You're . . . wow," he says again, in a whisper.

"I can—" I reach for him—you know, Him—but he takes my hand in his, kissing each knuckle with care.

"I'm sure you can."

If Eric was any indication, I'm at least of average skill level. Although after what Jasper just did for me, I might not be all that impressive.

His phone vibrates on his desk. He ignores it, falling to his side, his elbow bent to prop his head on his hand. His fingers glide against my skin, over my shoulders, cup my cheek. He bends in for another kiss just as I slide my hand down his sweatpants and wrap it around him. His mouth drops open over mine, his eyes closing.

I freeze. "Sorry, this is okay, right?"

He groans into my mouth. "It's more than okay."

Before I can get a rhythm down, his phone vibrates again. And again. Again. Again. Again. His head lolls back and he sighs.

"Might be important," he says, breathless. "I'm sorry. Hold on a second. Please. One second. I'll be right back."

He climbs over me, pulling his pants up as he goes. I watch his lean form stretch and adjust with his motions. He picks up his phone and the moles on his arm dance away from each other.

"*No.*" He drops his phone onto the desk and turns. I sit up, covering my stomach with my arms. "I have to go into work. Raina called off for the five hundredth time."

"Oh."

He laughs dryly. "Trust me. I'm more disappointed than you are."

I smile at him, sliding to the edge of the bed, but before I can collect my clothes from the floor, he's leaning in front of me, his mouth on mine.

"I want to pick this up where we left off. Maybe tomorrow or something?" He searches my eyes. "Or whenever. Or we could do whatever." He wiggles his eyebrows. "You could slip into my room tonight after work if you want."

"I got the feeling your mom wouldn't care if I used the front door."

"Anything to cut down on the cost of tissues."

I nod, though, his nose tickling against mine. I put on my clothes as he gathers fresh ones from his dresser and closet. He backtracks and puts away a pair of skinny jeans. "Way too tight right now."

He excuses himself to the bathroom to change, like I hadn't just had my hand wrapped around part of him a minute ago. Like his fingers hadn't done things to me that made me see stars. I get dressed much faster than he does and entertain myself with snooping around his room, which I'd usually be so against, but I think we've reached That Point.

His desk is a mess of food wrappers, printed-out sewing instructions, and papers marked with PROLOGUE at the top. But one catches my eye amid the clutter. A confirmation for a book order. A hundred copies of *The Magnificent Lies of Lasers*.

I pick up the paper, my eyes scanning it as my fingertips go numb in shock.

The confirmation is not for Prologue.

It's for Books & Moore, and it verifies a change to our original purchase order of the new covers.

Jasper steps out of the bathroom, his hair fixed and his shirt tucked in.

"What's this?" My voice shakes, anger threatening to spill out. I'm having a hard time catching my breath, keeping my hand steady.

His eyes skim the paper I hold out for him and his face sags, eyes wide. "Madeline—"

"No. *No*. What *is* this?" I wave the paper in his face.

"It's a confirmation for an order change."

"For *my* store. Why do you have this?"

He runs his hands down his face. "I—you have to understand."

"You changed the order?" I step forward. "Be very clear."

He tries to reach for my hand, but I pull away. "Madeline."

"Explain."

"I had my dad ask Astrid who she ordered from," he sighs. "Then I called pretending to be from Books and Moore, and told them to change the order."

The paper crumples in my fist, like I wish I could do to him. "So, even after everything, you did this?"

"No, it was before—"

"So then you knew we got the wrong books—you saw how annoyed I was. You knew I blamed Astrid and it wasn't her fault, and you didn't say anything? You didn't try to fix this?" I head for his door. "This has all been fake, hasn't it? You wanted me to drop my guard."

I should have seen it coming. I *did* see it coming, but I convinced myself to just be brave, just do it like a fucking Nike commercial. He stole our store setup. First the signs, then the book displays. Then our customers. My fucking heart.

"No—"

"I'm not going to believe a word you say." I wrench the door open and face him. "You're just like Dahlia. You're a *disappointing piece of shit only looking out for yourself.*"

He stands there gaping, his head shaking slowly. "No . . ."

"You're back on my shit list. Fuck you."

And then I'm gone.

Like our relationship, or our whatevership, is gone.

Like Dahlia will be gone. Like B&M will be gone. Like that blissful feeling in Jasper's bedroom has gone—turned sour.

Nothing's permanent this summer. And those fleeting feelings of happiness, of contentment, can't possibly be worth the emptiness that comes afterward. Can't be worth the anger that sets my body aflame.

# TWENTY-FOUR

The drive home is a blur of red, my mind almost completely on autopilot with an exception for the profanities I attach to Jasper Hamada's name. I park, and then storm up the stairs to my bedroom, tunnel vision blocking everything except the next step in front of me.

Zelda's not answering her phone. I can't even be mad at her for it because 1) my anger is all reserved for Jasper, that lying, manipulative sack of shit, and 2) because she's actually acting professional while on the clock by not answering her phone, something I feel like I haven't done in forever. If I wasn't pulling pointless pranks, I was checking my phone for fundraiser updates, never fully present at B&M anymore because Jasper got me off task in one way or another.

I throw my phone onto my bed. I shouldn't have taken off the whole weekend for my birthday. Zelda has to work. Astrid's out, and she's probably mad at me for being mad at her—and for such stupid (and untrue!) reasons. Dahlia's in and I'm mad at her. Prologue's so busy they need more than one worker, so I'm assuming Benny's at work, too. Would I even want to talk to him if he weren't? I'm feeling a confusing amount of extra hurt now that I know Jasper was behind sabotaging not only B&M, but our biggest event, and Benny works with him. I'm hurt and that hurt is mixing with this brand-new, shiny hurt, and I'm *hurt*, okay?

I pivot toward my desk for my laptop, but it's not here. I left it downstairs. If I want to get it, I'll have to face Dahlia.

No thanks, I'll just die up here.

I'm sure she'll be gone by the end of the night anyway. I can't starve in one night, right? My stomach growls to spite me.

Dahlia knocks on my door then. It's like she has a radar for when she's least wanted. I don't tell her to come in, but she does anyway, my laptop in her hands.

"Hey." She smiles at me, holding it out for me. I take it, lying down on my bed and stretching out so it's very apparent there's no room for her to sit. "You left in such a hurry earlier; I didn't know where you went."

"What does it matter?"

She tilts her head to the side. "As we reestablished yesterday, I'm your mother. So, if you're going somewhere, you should tell me where. When you'll be back. Who you're with—"

"Let me just stop you there. I'm eighteen. And you may have given birth to me, but you're not my mother." I open my laptop. Type my password in even though I don't have anything to work on. I just want to punch things and these keys will do.

I raise an eyebrow, looking at her out of the corner of my eyes when she doesn't budge.

"That was cold, even for you. What's your deal, kid?"

If we're going to get technical, here's my deal with her: She's leaving us. Again. I was a fool to think she'd actually stay this time, an idiot to let my guard down. Why did I never stop to think about what was actually worse: Dahlia staying or Dahlia leaving?

Hot tears build in my eyes.

B&M is dying, my future is a tuition bill for an undecided major that I'll actually have to decide on if B&M is truly not a viable option any longer, I'm stressed, I'm tired, I've barely done anything aside from work this summer and it will have all been pointless, I'm not sure I even like working, my heart has been beaten into a pulp, and I have betrayal whiplash.

"Boy troubles?"

"Yep." It's almost comical how it can be summed up that way.

She steps into the room and leans against the wall, taking my answer as encouragement. "Is Jasper being mean to you?"

"No." "Being" indicates he's currently doing something. He's not doing anything. He's nothing to me. The damage is already done, in the past. I don't elaborate, hoping she'll leave.

Her shoulders sag. "Good. Is it something else? Did you guys fight?"

Who am I kidding? Subtlety has always been lost on her, this woman whose favorite color has been hot pink for the majority of my life. She'll never take a hint. "I'm fine."

She scratches her elbow awkwardly. "Okay, we don't need to talk if you don't want to. Need condoms? Birth control?"

I slam my laptop shut, eyes stinging. "*No.* Your motherly

influence has resulted in me being on birth control since I was thirteen and I know how and when to use condoms. I don't need anything else from you."

She blinks once, twice. "Let me help with whatever it is."

I won't let her get the satisfaction in knowing that maybe I was considering her a permanent fixture. I won't let her know I care if she's not. If she's going to force a conversation out of me, it's not going to be that one.

"Have you ever known someone who hurt you so badly you felt like you'd never bother to like people again?" I mean her. I mean Jasper. I can't trust either of them. I was stupid to. I knew better. *I knew better.*

She actually laughs, not understanding what I'm implying. "Your father."

"So, you're saying you wish you hadn't known him?" Then she wouldn't have me—so yeah, that's exactly what she's saying. This conversation was supposed to be a distraction from the real one we could be having and it's going just as poorly as the other one would have.

"I still would have slept with him," she says, taking a backward seat in my desk chair. "To get you."

"That's so nice of you to say," I say dryly.

"Oh, come on," she laughs. "You know what I mean. You're great, but he sucks. He didn't stick around."

I sit up suddenly, derailed from my Jasper feelings. Or . . . non-feelings. Because he's nothing. "Like *you* did?"

Her face reddens. "I was a baby with a baby. I could barely take care of myself. You expected me to take care of you, too?"

*YES*, I want to scream. *Yes, I did expect you to take care of me because you gave birth to me.* I could have been aborted or put up for adoption, but instead she spent nine months with me in her body and then dumped me into Astrid's arms. She thinks I shouldn't have expected her to take care of me while she expected Astrid to?

"Astrid managed and she's only two years older than you." I stand, too much energy surging through my body. "Sterling managed to be here, too. What's your excuse? What makes you so special that we should all forgive you for the shit you've pulled in the past?"

I want her to say it. I want her to own her actions. To just blurt it out: she didn't want us then and she doesn't want us now. We're just proof of her irresponsibility. Mistakes. I'm the slightly less screwed-up version of her and that's why she can't stand to be around me unless it makes her feel better about herself. If she knew what happened with Jasper, she wouldn't console me—she'd tell me I was overreacting. She'd make jokes about how cute it was that we fought over the stores, that we thought it could work out, like she knows anything about making it work.

"It's hard being a single mom, okay?" She stands, too.

"How would you know! You just ran off to chase some dream that would never become a reality! If you were such a good actress, you could have at least acted like you loved us all these years!"

She doesn't move, doesn't emote. She stares at me until one tear falls. Two, three. "Was there a point to this outburst?" she asks in a shaky voice.

"Of course there was, but now I'm too mad to remember

it." I'm unfortunately not too mad to notice she doesn't say she loves me. Doesn't even try to deny her detachment.

I should have just kept shooting her down until she gave up and left. I grab my phone and leave the room instead of kicking her out. She'll leave on her own accord, like she always does. But that doesn't mean when I stomp through the hallway and spot one of her suitcases, half-unzipped with clothes spilling out, it doesn't stab me directly in the heart.

Benny's not at work, like I had assumed. He answers when I call and I could cry at the warmness in his voice when he tells me to meet him at Sterling's apartment.

Sterling's complex is a clean, welcoming place that I've spent plenty of time at, but never really considered an escape from reality like Benny has. Or, I guess, this is his reality now.

We sit on the faux wooden balcony outside of the apartment, the shade and a breeze fighting away the heat, two sweating water bottles on the little plastic table between us.

"I never asked, how was soccer camp?" I prop my legs up on the black metal railing surrounding the balcony, the heat soaking into my skin. I feel jittery, like I imagine a few cups of coffee make you feel in the mornings.

Benny raises his eyebrow. He wants to ask, *Madeline, why did you call me on the verge of tears only to show up and ask about soccer camp?*

"It was good," he says instead. "They gave out these cheesy awards at the end—you know, everyone gets one—and the one I got was the Most Jaw-Dropping Diagonal Cruyff."

"Congrats." I try to picture the move, but fail. "Which one's that?"

"That fake-out move you like. It's basic, but no one ever saw it coming."

I smile, debating how to bring up Dahlia leaving. Would he even care?

"I also kissed Sanderson."

I whip my head in his direction. "Sexy Sam Sanderson? The guy I graduated with?"

Benny grins, shrugging. "No big deal."

"He's going away to college, though." My heart sinks for my brother. "Are you guys going to be long distance—"

"Whoa," he says, holding up his hand. "It was just a kiss. A good one, but just a kiss."

I can't find regret or sadness on his face or in his voice. It was just a good kiss. Is that all Jasper and I will be? A few good kisses and one great orgasm, followed by the sting of utter betrayal and distrust? I'm so glad I didn't get him off. I'd feel like such a chump right now. As opposed to . . . feeling like an idiot.

"So, you didn't come here to talk about soccer camp."

I bite my lip. "No."

"I heard you got into it with Astrid and Dahlia last night after dinner." He laughs. "I'm almost sad I missed it."

"Yeah, it must be so great having a dad as an excuse to get out of everything mildly uncomfortable."

His face turns blank. "Don't."

I sigh. "I'm sorry, but it's just—"

"No."

I roll my eyes, feeling tears forming at the crests of my lower lids. "Sorry."

"It's not my fault I have a dad that stuck around, just like it's not your fault your dad didn't." He looks out over the little courtyard in front of us. "I don't know why you do that. Why you try to make me feel bad for what I have. I'm your brother, and my dad has always been there for you."

A gnawing feeling tears apart my gut. "You're right."

"And you have Astrid—"

"You have Astrid, too."

"It's not a competition." He swipes at his eye, but I don't see any tears.

I blink. This is not how I thought the conversation was going to go today. "You're right. I'm sorry. I'm just—"

"Jealous."

"Yes." The word sounds more like a breath than a confirmation of all my pent-up feelings. I love Sterling, and he's always been there when I needed him, but he was never mine. Maybe that's why Dahlia leaving again hurts so much. I almost had something mine. *I* was almost hers. Finally.

And maybe that's why losing B&M really hurts. Benny's always had Sterling. A place where he, without a doubt, fits. B&M was always that place for me. The place to run when Dahlia let me down again; when Zelda's dad, pre-rehab, was extra nice to me and it made me sad because I didn't have a dad around to be extra nice to Zelda; the place that I was in control and things were easy. Benny losing B&M, losing Dahlia, would never be a big deal to him because he never had to go searching for things to fill the holes in his heart like I did.

Maybe that's why what Jasper did feels even worse than any other prank we pulled. Because I finally let myself think Jasper was mine, too. But now I don't have him, and he still has a hand in B&M's demise, just like he wanted. Now I could kick myself, thinking of all the times I thought *I* was pumping the brakes on our relationship. He never wanted it to go any further. He knew where it was headed. He knew how it would end. He probably convinced Grant to help him scare me away by saying he had feelings he didn't.

Benny takes a deep breath, unscrewing the cap of his water bottle and taking a large gulp. The sweat falls off the bottle and lands on his cargo shorts.

"I didn't mean to be an asshole," I say quietly.

"No, you never do."

I slide off my chair, coming behind his so I can wrap my arms around him. I rest my head on his shoulder long enough for him to clear his throat and release another shaky breath. To squeeze my arm for a second.

I release him, my mouth feeling hot and swampy, my throat tight. I take a swig of my water.

"Why'd you really come over? It wasn't to be yelled at."

"I deserved it." I sit heavily on the plastic chair, making it scrape against the wood. "Dahlia's leaving again."

He doesn't even look fazed by this. "She does that."

"You don't care?"

"I'm not really hurt by what she does anymore. I'm hurt by you rubbing Sterling in my face, by the thought of Astrid turning my room into a library or something with all the leftover books we'll have from B and M. Not Dahlia, though."

I can't tell if I hate the idea because of B&M closing or love it because that's the perfect use for the room. Not that Astrid would ever change Benny's room. Not even for Dahlia to move out of the basement.

"But Dahlia, she was always meant to pass through. She was never going to stay." He searches my eyes. "Why'd you fall for it this time?"

I slide down the chair, my thighs clinging to the plastic, and drop my head on the backrest. "I don't know."

"You wanted to." He offers a sad smile when I look at him. "You wanted her to stay."

"I don't know. I'm leaving soon anyway. She'd be more of a problem for you if she stayed."

He shrugs. "She's kind of a perfectly fine person if you don't consider she was supposed to be our mom all these years. She's good in small doses as long as you don't bring up the past."

"It would have hurt either way." I pick at the armrest, letting my nail dig in. "Either she leaves or I do."

Earlier in the summer, I thought that if she actually stayed, I would have gotten to be the one to leave her for once when school started up. I thought that maybe the moment would leave me feeling powerful and in control, but when I think about it now, I just feel . . . sad. Despite all the times she abandoned me—despite her leaving me again, as she always does—I can't actually see me getting enjoyment in doing the same to someone else, even her.

We finish our waters outside, the sun setting over the little playground in the courtyard. When Sterling shows up with Chinese food for dinner, we eat on the balcony and end the night with fortune cookies and a tub of Oreo ice cream.

When I go home, Astrid sits at the kitchen table with bills spread out on every available inch of wood, her coffee gone cold next to her. I start making her a turkey sandwich with what's left in the refrigerator and she doesn't even twitch. She finally stops *tap tap tapping* at her calculator when I sit the sandwich down on the bill she's trying to read.

"I'm sorry," I say quietly. The guilt's been slowly eating away at me all day, but when I walked in and saw her sitting alone in the near dark, the last bit of me that didn't feel absolutely terrible for how I yelled at her disappeared.

She meets my eyes for a second and then takes the sandwich, one big bite gone in the blink of an eye. "What for?" she asks between chewing.

She doesn't mean it like, *You have nothing to be sorry for!* but instead like, *There are so many things you should be sorry for.*

"Everything. But mostly for yelling at you yesterday. And for blaming you when the books showed up with the wrong covers. That wasn't your fault." Ultimately, it's kind of my fault. I was the one who started this war with Prologue. But, fuck, if Jasper really ordered the books before our truce, he should have fixed the order. Everything is falling into place and pointing to signs of sabotage.

She sighs. "I don't know. It might have been. My head has been in one big fog. I think Ravi's been less forgetful than I have lately."

"No." I pull her arm out, sliding myself close to hug her. "It was Jasper," I say against her shoulder. "I'm so sorry."

She squeezes me. "What do you mean?"

"He called pretending to work at B and M and he changed the order. I don't want to talk about it. We can't fix it anyway." My eyes sting. What an exhausting day.

"Okay." She rubs my back slowly. "Well, we have the books regardless of the cover. And the author. It'll be fine."

"The whole point of her tour is the new covers. I think Ravi's going to make us some desserts, but Warbeck's going to think we're amateurs."

"No," she says, pulling away to look me in the eyes. "You're planning a great event. I know there have been issues, but I believe in you. This could be it for the store, so let's try to plan the best goodbye party we can. We'll show Prologue what Books and Moore can do."

# TWENTY-FIVE

Jasper texts only four times over the next few days and I answer him precisely none of them. Every time I want to reply, I do something else: pack for school, eat an apple, take a walk, paint my nails, organize what's left in my closet and wonder where the hell Dahlia is hiding my clothes, text someone else, struggle with not devouring the Buns brownies at the register in a childish rage. Et cetera, et cetera. I become even busier than before. Because, in addition to avoiding the Jasper drama, I am also doing the same with Dahlia. She hasn't left yet, or even said anything about leaving, which only sets me on high alert, because she's probably just going to bail without a word. Not that I didn't already say goodbye to her, *essentially*.

"That'll be twenty dollars," I tell the woman with bright orange hair and a lip piercing.

I process her order with a smile and hand over a flyer for the Warbeck event. Despite consistent sales, we're still below the line of keeping the store open. B&M's only hope is to sell all the copies of *The Magnificent Lies of Lasers*, along with all the other copies we have of the rest of the series, along with . . . most of the books we have in stock. For perspective: the majority of these books have been here since the store opened, and for some reason, my grandmother stocked the strangest books that no one wants.

I really don't know why I ever thought I could keep the store open. From this end of the summer, it feels laughably naive.

I sigh, finally heading over to a shelf that caught my eye earlier when I couldn't give it more attention. Zelda's organized books from various sections to spell out: *No cisgender boys allowed*. I work on fixing them, only slightly annoyed when I realize the shelf below has an even raunchier message to "Assper Hatemada." Mostly, I'm happy for the busywork to distract me from the thoughts that flit through my head whenever there's too much empty space.

When I come back home for fall break, this store won't be here. If someone buys or rents the space, they'll tread over the creaky floorboards where I dropped tons of books—accidentally—without a second thought. They might even get the floors replaced, all the creaks and water damage gone. There won't be any more messages left on the bookshelves—there probably won't even be any bookshelves. The new owner could paint over Benny's and my height ticks on the back wall, some off-white color that demolishes any evidence of us. Or worse, this store could just sit here collecting dust, no one to love it, feeling abandoned and useless. Like me.

The door chimes and my heart lurches into my throat when I see Grant walk in.

"Hey," he says cautiously, a brown paper bag swinging in his hand. "Jasper texted me—"

I walk behind the counter, a habit and a protection. "No."

He rolls his eyes, taking a step forward. "Unlike him, I won't be deterred by your stubborn attitude."

"Really? You're going to call me stubborn? Are you here to remind me to *be gentle* with him? After what *he* did to *me*?"

Shuffling from my left steals my attention. Dahlia, who came in to replace Ravi for the night, walks around the shelf closest to her, a customer following. I reel in my anger as best as I can.

"We have an event on Saturday with the author of that book series they just turned into a movie. It's out tomorrow. *The Discontent.*" She smiles at the middle-aged woman and then winks at me, as if she just did the best job selling the books, the event, and the movie.

"The movie is called *The Magnificent Lies of Lasers,*" I say. "It stars Lulu Nex from *The Race to Forever.*"

"Oh," the woman gasps, the lights dancing in her cat-eye glasses. "My daughter loves her. Maybe we'll go see that."

"And come to our event," Dahlia stresses, standing beside me at the counter and handing the woman a flyer.

Dahlia checks the woman out while I stand there, arms crossed, glaring at Grant with a fire growing in my stomach. He stays silent, smiles at the woman, and holds the door open for her. His bag hits the glass heavily.

"What's that?" I ask, curiosity outweighing my annoyance.

He glances down. "The whole reason I'm here. Jasper assumes he's no longer invited to the movie and wanted to give you your costume."

I tilt my head. "Then why isn't he handing me this himself?"

He sighs, his shoulders dropping at least two inches with the action. "You know why." His eyes fall on Dahlia, who is watching us with rapt attention, like we're some reality show that was playing when she turned on the TV and she got sucked in before she could change the channel. "Could we have a minute?"

She looks to my irritated face and then to Grant's desperate one. "I'm working. Why don't *you* go somewhere else to talk?"

He straightens, properly put in his place. "That's fair. Can we talk, Madeline?"

I decide we can, outside, where the breeze helps to cool my cheeks. He hands me the bag and inside are pieces of my costume. Something shatters in my chest. It can't be my heart; that's already broken.

"Look, I said it before and I'll say it again. Jasper likes you. A lot. This whole thing"—he gestures to Prologue and then me—"is a really unfortunate circumstance. Please just let him explain."

I'm not considering anything, but the least I can do, for Grant, is pretend like I am. I would want Jasper to give Zelda the same decency if I were the one who intentionally ruined something Jasper cared about and then barely tried to atone for it.

"Maybe. But not today." There's nothing that could change between today and tomorrow that would make me hear Jasper out. There's nothing new to add to his excuse that would make me forgive him. "Don't you have better things to do besides try to fix his problems?"

"Sometimes," he says with a weak smile, his hair blowing into his face. "But not today."

"He was there the day we got the wrong books. I told him and he didn't say anything. He let things—let things *progress* between us and didn't say a word. That's sneaky and shitty. I hate him and you can tell him so."

I leave him outside before I can second-guess my words and feelings. I don't owe him anything. I don't owe Jasper anything. The betrayal is so fresh, I can still taste it on my tongue. It's like that feeling right before puking, where your mouth starts to water and your vision becomes a tunnel. Except there's no relief like there is post-puke. There's just more nausea. I let him do this to me. The one time I let myself take the tiniest chance, give up the smallest bit of control.

This isn't who I am. I get upset about books, not boys.

I close the door behind me, hoping Grant takes the hint. When I don't hear his voice, don't feel the doorknob turn against my back, I sigh. Dahlia watches me from behind the counter, her chin in hand.

"Want to talk about anything?"

Yeah, because that went so well before. "No, thanks. I'm just going to rip this up and set it on fire and then I'll be back so you can take your break."

I'm sure Ravi has a lighter stashed somewhere in the break room.

She darts out from behind the counter, latching onto my shoulder as I pass.

"Hey." She squeezes my shoulder. "We're going to talk."

She slowly spins me so I face her. I breathe out through my nose, in through my mouth. Two beats. Then I meet her eyes.

"Don't ruin a perfectly good costume. He owes you that, at least."

"I don't want to wear something his traitorous hands touched." Fuck, I don't even want to be in my own skin because of that. I'm so glad we didn't go further, so glad I got something from him that he didn't get from me. Maybe he didn't want to take things further because he knew I'd end up mad at him, or maybe it was because he didn't want to waste his first time with me. If he was even a virgin. He was probably just manipulating me, making me feel like I had the power when he knew I didn't. Or it's all been out of pity, which might be worst.

"Fuck him," she says, invading my thoughts. "He made that for you, so take it. Wear it. Show it off at the premiere."

"I don't even want to go," I croak out, tears threatening to flood my eyes. "I was so excited and he's literally ruined everything."

She rubs her hands up and down my shoulders, her own face breaking into a frown. "Don't let a guy do that. Enjoy things while they last and then let them go."

The words hit me hard. Not only because of Jasper, but because of her. It's kind of what Benny was saying. Dahlia was never meant to stay—she was never going to stay. But instead of being mad at her for disrupting things, maybe we should have just let her swoop in and be the cool mom she tries so hard to be. We've always had Astrid for the important stuff. For the kissing of scraped knees, the life advice, the lunch money and bad haircuts. Maybe all this time, we should have just been enjoying Dahlia while she lasted. While she still tried to make time for us, no matter how short that time was. I don't forgive her, but I kind of get her. She's just not mom material, and I'm tired of being mad at her for it. She's like a firework: burns brightly, loudly, and fades away quickly.

The best thing she could ever have done for Benny and me was give us up.

It takes her a second to realize I'm hugging her when I wrap my arms around her middle. She puts her arms around my shoulders and one hand caresses my hair. My tears leak out, wetting her shirt.

"You're about to go to college and find so many boys— and/or girls or others—and this one won't even matter. He'll be the asshole who made you realize things could be better."

I sniff. "Duncan was your Jasper, huh?"

She rubs my back. "Kind of."

"Sterling's better."

"He is, but I'm not. I wasn't."

I breathe deep and pull away. "You're trying." But, since the knife had been twisted in my gut enough today, I decide to pull it out and twist it in hers, because no matter how nice she's being now, I know there's a plane ticket with her name on it. "I'm happy you're here for good."

⊾ ⩒ ⩘

I don't text Zelda about the movie because it'll only hurt her knowing the ticket is free again and she can't go. I don't take the clothes out of the bag. I don't do much of anything except throw myself onto my bed, light a stick of incense I found in Benny's room, and read my favorite parts of *The Magnificent Lies of Lasers*. The opening scene with Tick. Finding Madison. The fight with the cops. Dahlia was all rah-rah, don't let anybody ruin your good time, which could be the Dahlia motto if we're being serious, and it had inspired me for half a minute, but now I'm feeling miserable and this is the only thing that can properly calm me down.

But then, at around ten o'clock, Dahlia comes home with a brownie-batter-filled doughnut. And the action nearly makes me burst into tears, when I thought all my tears were done trying to escape.

"Shouldn't you be getting dressed and stuff?" she asks.

I sit up. "Will you go with me?" I'm almost as surprised as she is that the words came out of my mouth.

She freezes, her lips parted, then shakes herself loose, clasping her hands together. "If you want me to."

I smile, which makes her smile. "If you can stay awake, I want you to come with me."

"I'll sneak an energy drink into the theater."

"Well, they probably sell them there."

"I'll be giving them enough money for candy as it is. I take movie candy very seriously."

"We could buy a few bags of Reese's Pieces and pour one out in honor of Benny."

"Or we could *eat* them. Who taught you to be so wasteful? I know it wasn't Astrid."

It's as close to an apology she'll get from me, and as close to an apology I'll get from her. We Moores are petty women.

She grabs a shower then—pointless because the costume I'm forcing her into requires heavy makeup on her face—and I finally pull each piece of my costume out, laying them on my bed how they'd appear on my body. She was right. I can't waste something this good just because Jasper's a conniving douche. The fabric is soft under my fingers, the stitching delicate and precise. He even included Lasers's real name's initials on the shirt tag like in the book. The detail nearly steals my breath away, makes me want to cry again, and I'm not sure if it's because that moment in the book made me want to cry—she wears her real identity on her every day and no one knows!—or if it's because Jasper remembered that and included it, even though no one will know it's there besides him and me. I hate having a secret with him, but it's almost like Lasers is in on the secret, too, and that makes me feel better.

From my closet, I snag a tight black shirt I grew out of last year, black pants with rips at the knees, and combat boots I haven't worn since the temperature climbed over seventy-five. I take some flour from the kitchen and smack it into the jeans and shirt, trying to give the clothes a dusty, sandy look.

I take some bright red lipstick from Dahlia, mix it with water, and draw some bloody cuts on her face, using the excess for her arms and exposed knees. She looks a hot mess, but it sends a thrill down my spine. It's obvious she's a random

Discontentee. I don't need Jasper after all.

"Your turn. I want to see this thing," Dahlia says, sitting in my desk chair and nodding toward the outfit laid out on my bed.

"It looks kind of like what you saw in the trailer." I need to change, but then everything starts to feel real. And doubt creeps into my mind—not about Jasper, Dahlia, or the store—but about the movie. It could be terrible. I could get laughed at, whispered about, for this costume no matter how great it is. What if no one else is dressed up?

"I don't think I've actually seen the trailer." She presses a finger at the corner of her mouth where we put the fake blood. "I don't even know what the movie is about."

I pause, my hand clenched around my shirt. "Excuse me?"

She leans away from me, her eyes wide. "Are you gonna hit me?"

"Have you ever been slapped with a four-hundred-and-fifty-three-page paperback?"

I point toward my open laptop, currently playing Hayley Williams. "Bring it up on YouTube. *The Magnificent Lies of Lasers.*"

"Now, are we talking about lasers like the *pew-pew* kind?"

I shake my head, facing the wall and taking my shirt off. "No, it's a nickname."

As her attention is focused on the trailer I've watched at least a hundred times, I finish changing into Lasers's outfit. The clothes are a little loose, but it feels comfortable that way. The image of sitting in the theater and popping a stitch as I try to shove some popcorn in my mouth doesn't even make me laugh. I swallow down the fear. Thinking about coming undone in the theater is going to make me mentally come undone.

The trailer ends as I'm securing a belt around the pants.

She turns to me, her mouth open. "I totally know that guy." She points to the screen, but it's black. She scrubs back a few seconds, right near the end when Grimly, the villain, is revealed.

I feel like I've been punched in the gut. "What? Alex Vander?"

"Yeah, I had no clue he was in this movie."

"You know Alex Vander? Like, personally?" My heart goes from zero to sixty in one second. "Or, like, you know his face, like millions of other people?"

She shrugs, a smile on her face. "I *know* people, Madeline. He's a friend of a friend." She stands, brushing some flour off my chair. "You look really great. That looks exactly like in the trailer."

I want to say thanks, but it's not my compliment to accept. Plus, I'm kind of distracted by the fact that she knows Alex-fucking-Vander.

"If I knew you cared so much about him, I would have mentioned him that day in the airport." She winks.

I smile back, but it's more of a cringe. Spiraling.

"To the concession stand," she cheers, ignoring my meltdown.

"Can you prove you actually know him somehow?" I ask while we wait in line. I believe her, but I want to see a photo or something that makes it more tangible. Right now, it's just words, not even words in a book. Just spoken words that fly away with the breeze.

She stuffs a handful of popcorn into her mouth, from what she calls Bag One (of two), and pushes it into my arms. She reaches into her back pocket and pulls out her phone with some difficulty.

"These pants are so tight," she says over her chewing. "I'm gonna need to be cut out of them."

"Only if you eat all the popcorn yourself."

She raises an eyebrow at me. "That's the plan. You didn't think any of this was for you, right?"

She wipes her fingers on her—my—shirt and swipes the phone screen. She turns the phone and shows me a picture of Alex, her, and someone else I don't know atop Runyon Canyon, the most notable location for the "I work out, but, like, *naturally*" photo op. He has sunglasses perched on the top of his head, his golden waves pushed out of his face, and she's sticking her tongue out at him. The third person, a guy around Dahlia's age, flexes his arm muscles at the camera. She swipes across the phone screen a few times and another shot of them, this time with several others, on the beach with red Solo cups and beer bottles appears. I fight the jealousy—not of knowing a celebrity, but of getting to spend time with Dahlia.

I nod. "Okay."

"That's it?" She pockets her phone and takes back her first bag of popcorn while I hold on to the other. "I expected a bigger reaction to the evidence."

To be honest, I'm having a hard time processing the fact that we're going to see a movie together, let alone a movie that stars someone she knows and is one of my favorite books come to life.

"I will have more thoughts on this post-movie. Did you guys date?"

"Oh, no. We never hung out one on one, but I do have his phone number."

I blow out a breath. "This is information you need to *lead* with."

A preteen girl dressed in an excellent gender-bent Grimly cosplay gestures wildly behind Dahlia and stumbles into her back, sending her bag of popcorn to the floor. A few "oooohs" echo around us as the girl profusely apologizes to Dahlia.

"It's cool," Dahlia says, her tone low and disappointed as she takes in her spilled popcorn.

"I'll buy you some more," the girl says, adjusting the bandana over her mouth, her eyes wide.

"No," Dahlia says, waving her away. "That's not necessary."

She looks around the line. "Can everyone please acknowledge that I've been standing here for a while? I'm gonna go get more popcorn and I don't want a fuss about me cutting the line." She points at the girl and her friends. "Will you guys vouch for me? I'm too old to end up in the front row seats no one wants."

The group laughs, nodding, and Dahlia turns to me. "I'll be right back. Did you want any other snacks?"

I look down at our bag full of candy, the popcorn in my

arms, and the soda in my hand. "No, I think I'm good. For the next several years."

She bounds away, crunching through spilled popcorn as a movie theater employee uses an ancient vacuum to suck it up. "I'm so sorry," she hisses to the worker, who nods solemnly, as if he completely hates his life but has accepted it for how shitty it is.

Without Dahlia, I start folding in on myself. Everyone around me is in groups, talking loudly, excitedly. This should have been me and Jasper—no, me and Zelda. But through a series of unfortunate events, all stemming back to Prologue, I'm here alone. Well, right now. Dahlia is eager and excitable, but she's not a fan. She would have shown up in jeans and a T-shirt had I not forced her into an outfit. All around us are different variations of characters from the books. These are true fans. Motivated fans. People who would—

People who would come to a book signing, *obviously*.

"Oh my god," I say suddenly, grabbing the attention of gender-bent Grimly. I glance at her, then the people in front of me. "Cosplay contest," I whisper.

"Cosplay contest!" I wave my hands in the air, stepping away from the wall so I can face the line. "There'll be a cosplay contest at Books and Moore on Oak Street on Saturday at three o'clock! Isla Warbeck, author of the Discontent series, will be there and she'll judge. The winner gets a video shout-out from Alex Vander, aka Grimly, on Twitter." Here's to hoping Dahlia's not just secretly amazing at Photoshop. "And Zelda, the booktuber from Required Reading, is moderating the event."

I take a deep breath, a smile breaking over my face as people start discussing what I've said. All the pieces were right there all along. "And you'll have the chance to be in one of her videos, too, if you show up!"

A loud cheer erupts from the front of the line as people start pushing forward, their tickets out. Every few seconds I reiterate what I said.

"Book signing and cosplay contest at Books and Moore."

"Isla Warbeck will judge."

"Alex Vander gives a shout-out to the winner."

"Books and Moore on Oak Street."

A lot of people nod at me, typing things on their phone as I speak. I can tell from the excitement in their eyes that they're not ignoring me. They're taking down the information, and they'll be there.

"Great costume."

"Hope to see you Saturday at three."

"Books and Moore on Oak Street."

"There'll be free food, too!" Ravi, in all his culinary art school excitement, had discussed so many different dessert options with me this morning that my stomach felt full after our conversation.

Dahlia slowly walks toward me, a fresh bag of popcorn in her hands. Her fake blood is smudged around her mouth. The last of the people in line sift into the theater, leaving just the two of us.

"I'm sitting in the front, aren't I?"

# TWENTY-SIX

I'm running on no sleep. After the movie—which was amazing, even though I saw it with Dahlia, who was nearly comatose by the time it ended because, apparently, she wasn't meant to see one o'clock in the morning any more than I was meant to see five in the morning—I went straight home to start reworking the flyer for the event to include the cosplay contest and the Required Reading YouTube video, which got Zelda's stamp of approval when she woke up. I also wore Dahlia down so much that she sent a text to Alex asking if he'd please do us this favor, since it was essentially to help promote his movie. Book sales turn into fans turn into movie fans turn into Alex Vander fans. Right? The math made sense in my head at four in the morning.

Regardless of the math, he answers at around ten o'clock this morning and is completely down. This text turns into an hourlong phone call between Dahlia and him in which I'm reminded that she'll be going back to LA soon. I stuff away those feelings and proceed to every public place imaginable to drop the flyers off—including the theater—in between tweeting about the event and recruiting Zelda to boost the message to her followers. I send the tweet link to Dahlia, hoping she's off the phone by now, and ask her to have Alex retweet it.

When I start getting so many notifications that my phone freezes, I know she did.

I'm down to five more flyers—six if I count the one I accidentally sweated on—when I leave the local park near B&M. I posted three flyers to the community corkboard and handed out a flyer to anyone walking the track or sitting in lawn chairs watching the baseball game. I round the corner to my car, but stop at the sight of a food truck parked behind it.

I fold the flyers and stuff them in my back pocket. "Melisa," I call into the open window.

Her head pops into view. "Oh, hey!"

Something clatters to the ground and she swoops out of sight to pick it up.

"How are you?" She folds her arms against the counter in her truck. "I'll be done prepping in about five minutes if you wanted something."

My stomach growls, betraying my schedule. I did not allot time for food or sleep.

"Sure, I'll have the nachos again."

She nods, lifting a pan into view for a moment before placing it down on something hard. "Coming up."

Something sizzles in the truck.

"Hey, Melisa?" I pull out a flyer. "Do you and your truck

have plans tomorrow around three?"

She furrows her brow. "Not really. I was planning on being here again tomorrow. Snag the baseball players after the game. Why, got a lot of hungry friends coming to town?"

"Kind of." I hand off the paper. "Maybe you'd be interested in coming back to the bookstore?"

Blowing a stray piece of dark brown hair from her face, her eyes dart across the flyer. "Is there some kinda catch?"

"We were catered, but my aunt felt we couldn't afford it and backed out." I shrug. "I thought maybe you could just park outside the store and it would be a win-win for both of us?"

She bites her lip. "I can't promise anything, but if there's a spot around two thirty, I'll be there."

I hold my hands up. "That's all I ask."

She nods and I wait by the truck for my food, the heat from the sun and the vehicle making my back sweat. When she hands me the nachos, I add one last stipulation. "Can we also agree that I'll send customers to you and you'll send customers to me?" I offer a big, hopeful smile, all teeth. "It's worked before."

She laughs. "Done."

I salute her with the dish.


If I have to look at a phone or computer ever again, it will be too soon. While I tossed and turned all night, my Twitter feed scrolled past my eyelids. Hashtag Lasers Lies. Hashtag Indie Store. Hashtag Last Chance Books. Zelda linked everyone to our GoFundMe page again. *If you can't be there to buy a book, donate what you can! Save an indie! #LastChanceBooks*

We've raised two thousand dollars total, including the funds we took out for last month's operational needs and for the War-beck event. Double the additional funds we needed per month, in a few weeks. The internet is a wild and generous place, but, like Dahlia, it's not consistent.

"I can't believe you're actually eating that," Dahlia says, nodding at the grilled chicken sandwich on my plate. "Devouring it, even." She shoves a hand over my forehead. "Feeling okay?"

"Hungry. Tired." I take another bite. I checked that the chicken was fully cooked before anything, and, while it's a bit dry, it's not going to make me sick. "Thanks for the food."

"Slow your roll."

"I can't." I woke up late. Really late. "Event's in, like, an hour. See you there."

I gather my bag and keys before my last bite is even chewed. I slide into my car, instantly sweating in the trapped heat, put all the windows down, and grab my phone.

**Zelda from YouTube**

Today 2:06 PM

All hands on deck

2:06 PM

I'm already here with my video equipment

2:07 PM

Whats your excuse ;P

2:07 PM

Mechanicsburg passes outside my windows, air flowing freely through the car and cooling me down. It's a perfect summer day, one of many that arrive late into the season to reassure people that it won't always feel like breathing in hot tub water every time they go outside. I'm thankful for it for many reasons, but the first being that it's not too hot outside and, therefore, people will be out shopping, and the second being that *I'm* not too hot—this is important because sweating in my few layers of cosplay would not be cute. I decided after my shower that I might as well get some more use out of it. I even used some Poser Paste to temporarily dye my hair bright red like Lasers's. In Dahlia's words: uh, it's a *look*.

I haul ass to B&M once I've parked and put my windows up, except for a crack. Two spaces are free right in front of the store, so I drop our display sign in the middle of them, discouraging anyone from parking there. I couldn't get a permit so late from the parking authority this time, but if Melisa gets here soon—which she said she would if there was parking—we should be golden.

My heart practically grows ten sizes, Grinch-style, when I walk inside to find Zelda and Astrid moving the staff table to the front of the store, while Ravi organizes a display of what are labeled "gluten-free, peanut-free" cupcakes in chocolate and vanilla along the checkout counter. I whip a freshly made sign from my bag and hold it up for him in excitement.

He reads it and frowns. "I don't get it. And what did you do to your hair?"

Zelda finishes adjusting the table and takes a look. She burst into laughter. "That's a good one."

The sign, decorated to look worn and wooden, reads *The Discontent Dessert* in scratchy letters, and it's made to be placed behind the desserts—I was worried Ravi wouldn't come through with them, but I guess, if I really think about it, he's been getting better and better about remembering things, and maybe I've been the one unfocused lately.

"Your hair and costume look great, by the way." She glares at Ravi. "It's a book thing," she says offhandedly to him.

"It's not permanent, is it?" Astrid asks, her face scrunched up.

I cock my head to the side. "Wouldn't me dyeing my hair be the least of your concerns right now?"

"It's just a little patchy. If you want to go a bright red like this, we need to see a professional. Bleach your hair."

"Oh," Zelda chimes in, eyes wide. "You'd look good as a blonde. You have those really dark, bushy eyebrows that would contrast it well."

I glare at her.

"Clean that off, please?" Astrid points to the table, stifling laughter.

"Sure thing." Zelda dashes behind the counter for some spray and paper towels.

"Madeline," Astrid says, "could you get the tablecloth from the closet, please?"

I set my bag behind the counter, prop the sign up behind Ravi's cupcakes, and gather the dark red cloth from the musty closet in the break room. I shake it out in the alley behind the store and then help Astrid lay it over the table, smoothing out the fold marks.

"Dahlia should be in with the chairs soon," Astrid says, adding a few piles of *The Magnificent Lies of Lasers* to the table.

The door chimes behind me. I whirl around, a smile on my face. "Welcome to Books and M—my god."

"Excuse me?" Isla Warbeck asks.

All the words my brain knows tumble out of my mouth silently as I fangirl to a very ugly degree. I'm pretty sure I blinked a hundred times in the last ten seconds, and a rather unattractive grunt attacks my throat when I try to say anything more.

"Hi," Astrid says, stepping forward with her hand outstretched. Warbeck accepts, a smile on her face. "I'm Astrid, Books and Moore's owner, and this is Madeline, the manager—and a huge fan of yours, as you can see. This is Ravi and Zelda, more employees."

Astrid places a hand on my shoulder and I wonder if she can feel the goose bumps through my clothes. I'm so stunned that it takes a minute to process my aunt's words. She called me the manager!

"Hi," I choke out in a weird, breathy whisper. "I'm Madeline."

I offer my hand and she accepts it, her bracelets chiming with the motion. "Hello, Madeline. I believe you're the one who reached out to my publicist. I love your outfit. You make a great Lasers."

*Fuck*, I'm still shaking her hand. I pull away. "Thank you *so* much. I'm a big fan."

*Double fuck*. She already knows.

"I'm Zelda," my friend says, offering her hand, too. "I'm

moderating tonight and I was hoping it would be cool if I also made a video for my YouTube channel?"

Warbeck adjusts the bag on her shoulder. "Yes, of course. I love your videos. I saw the one about saving the store." She turns to me. "You said some really nice things about this place, so I'm excited to be here."

"Thank you." Embarrassment floods my cheeks in a hot wave. She knows how desperate we are. How much this event means. My favorite author saw me deer-in-the-headlights-ing all over YouTube.

"I realize I'm a little early, but I like to get a feel for the store beforehand, if I'm not too much of a distraction. I might pop in and out."

"Not a distraction at all," Astrid says. "Madeline was just about to stop being awkward and help her mother with the chairs."

"I was?"

"We'll get more work done if you're not here drooling all over the place," she whispers loud enough that Warbeck can hear. She pushes me gently toward the door, pointing out of the display window where Dahlia stands outside a van marked with our rental company's logo.

Warbeck laughs, her bright white, crooked teeth on display. "I look forward to speaking with you when you aren't so busy."

I spin to face them all, elbowing the door open. "I'll—I'll be back."

"Of course you will," Zelda says with a big grin on her face.

For some unexplainable reason, I do finger guns, clicking noises included. Zelda, behind everyone else, throws her head back in a giant, silent laugh, clutching at her heart. *Not everyone has experience with famous authors, Zelda, give me a break!*

"Need a hand?" I ask Dahlia as the worker hands her another two fold-up chairs to join the several already hanging off her arm.

"Several. Please. And quick," she grunts.

I take a few off her arm and prop them outside the door before joining her again. I avoid looking at Prologue to such a point that my eyes sting. I can't lose focus, not now, not when the event is finally here.

"We'll be back to pick them up by eight o'clock," the man says, shutting the vehicle doors as soon as twenty-eight chairs are leaning against the wall to Books & Moore.

Dahlia and I thank him and start lugging them inside.

"Melisa from On the Menu called to say she was on her way and to save her a parking spot if possible," Astrid says, watching Dahlia and me unfold the chairs and place them side by side in front of the table. "I assume that's why you've blocked out front?"

I nod, grinning. "I told you I could have found us a solution with the Buns thing. Food and desserts!"

She smiles, her glasses riding up her nose. "You've really impressed me. I don't think I've told you how proud I am."

"I'm sorry I've been a brat."

She shrugs. "It's in your genes."

"Hey!" Dahlia says, setting up the last chair and collapsing into it.

"I meant *my* genes."

"That's not how it works," Dahlia says, eyes narrowed and sounding more like a pesky little sister than she ever has before.

"Oh," Astrid says. "Guess she must get it from you, then."

The door chimes and I turn to welcome the visitor, but instead I'm met with a stream of people—eight people, to be exact—half of whom are wearing some kind of cosplay. Parents usher kids inside, teenagers filter through the bookshelves, and enough people snag copies of the book, regardless of the old covers, that we need to replenish the pile at the table. With five minutes until the event officially starts, I make my way back to the break room to get Warbeck and Zelda.

I nearly knock on the door, I'm so nervous.

"Sorry to interrupt," I say quietly, cutting off their conversation before realizing Zelda is filming their discussion.

"It's totally cool, Mads. Get over here." She angles herself toward her camera, Warbeck next to her all smiles, and says, "Everyone, you remember my best friend, Madeline. Madeline," she says, gesturing to the camera, "everyone. Look at her amazing cosplay. We won't get into how she ended up with something this cool, but let's just say I had a hand in it."

She scoffs when I give her a look. "It's not a lie."

She makes me do this awkward twirl on camera before pulling me down so I'm eye level with the camera, snug between her and Warbeck.

"We were just discussing the movie. I told Isla I hadn't seen it yet, but you were at the midnight premiere. What are your thoughts on it?"

"Yeah, how did you like it? Be honest. I saw a rough cut a

few months ago, but they were still tweaking the music and CGI. I'm seeing it again with my daughter tomorrow night when I get home." She takes a sip of her coffee as I try to form words to describe the amazingness that was *The Magnificent Lies of Lasers*. "No spoilers."

I breathe "Of course not" like we're talking sacrilege before her joke sinks in.

"It was just as funny and campy as the book. I knew what was going to happen, but I was still excited and worried for everyone. The twists still had me surprised somehow, and the costumes. And the sets." I pause for a moment, my mouth open as I struggle to find the words. "Everything felt like a character and a piece of the story. It just felt so full."

"I'm so glad to hear that," Warbeck says, nodding. "And you have some kind of a connection to Alex Vander? I met him during my set visit; he was really kind. The total opposite of Grimly."

"That would be my mom, actually. She's an actress." It feels weird saying it out loud, but I guess in a sense it's true. Maybe by the time this video is cut and put on the internet, she'll have secured her big break anyway. Maybe I'll be jinxing her in the best way.

When I walk Zelda and Warbeck out, the people sitting in front of her table start clapping. For all intents and purposes, this event is already a success. No, all the seats aren't filled, but people are here, in costume, with books ready to be purchased and signed, and we only spent three hundred on everything needed for today, so, yes, it's a success in my book, thankyouverymuch.

As Warbeck and Zelda get seated and Ravi sets up Zelda's camera on a tripod, I settle to the back of the audience, sandwiched between Astrid and Dahlia.

My phone buzzes and I dig it out of my pocket.

**Benny**

Today 3:01 PM

HEADS UP

3:01 PM

I have no clue how to interpret the text until Zelda's welcome speech is interrupted by the door chiming. Everyone's attention flicks to the doorway to see *Jasper* waltzing in, dressed in perfect Ammo cosplay, followed by at least fifteen other people.

"Sorry we're late," he says, finding my eyes immediately. "Hope there's room."

# TWENTY-SEVEN

While the newcomers settle in, taking the available seats and crowding in the back with Astrid and Dahlia, I pull Jasper outside by his elbow. I don't even care when I pinch him a little.

"What the hell do you think you're doing?" I yell as quietly as I can manage, hoping not to draw the attention of the people in line at Melisa's truck. I wave at her when she catches my eye and then turn back to Jasper, my glare triggered like an alarm.

He frowns. "I thought—I don't know. Grand gesture?"

"*What?*" He makes it sound like he's not here to somehow mess everything up.

"I sent an email out to our mailing list about your event. Told everyone it was at our store and then brought them over here." He looks at me like *What the hell did you think I was doing?* like it's so obvious.

"I don't think it needs to be said, but you're not welcome here." It would be so easy to reject him, turn him away and make him feel like as much of a loser as he made me feel. As silly, rejected, and used.

"Should I take my customers with me when I leave or . . . ?" He smirks.

My heart flutters weakly in my chest at the sight of him. He looks so good in this outfit, it might as well be a second skin. But, no.

I cross my arms over my chest, trying to look surer than I feel. "You can't just show up here and think I forgive you. I trusted you. Maybe I shouldn't have, but I shouldn't be punished for having finally been a nice person to you."

He sighs. "I agree. I'm sorry." He shifts his weight to one foot. "What if I can get your old covers replaced with new ones?"

"Meaning?"

"Meaning," he says through a deep breath, "I told my family that I don't want to help run the store anymore. That I want to go to design school."

"Did I just black out and miss part of the conversation where you made sense?"

"I told them this so maybe they'd understand why I pulled such a horrible prank to take down your store, so Prologue would have better chances of staying open. I felt . . . guilty, I guess. For wanting to leave Prologue. It was—I'm sorry. It was all so stupid. But I told them, and everyone got mad at me, so they're on your side now, rightfully, and want to help make it right."

The words still aren't adding up, especially connected to his actions.

"The new covers?"

"Oh, yeah." He raises his hand to someone I can't see behind the food truck. Then suddenly Jasper's mom, dad, and brother step onto the sidewalk from between parked cars, huge brown boxes in their arms.

"Madeline," Kira says with furrowed brows as she sets the box down in front of me, "I'm so sorry for what Jasper did. That is *not* how we raised him."

Jasper stays silent.

The need to defend him bubbles up before I can stop myself. "I wasn't acting so great myself." I avoid his eyes, the words growing quieter until I'm sure I'm the only one who can hear them over the sound of Melisa's truck.

"We never wanted to be any sort of enemy to you or your store," his dad says, also putting his box down. "We're just— we're book people. We like being around other book people. It's great to have good relationships with local businesses, but our relationship with Books and Moore was always the most important to us; we never meant to step on any toes and we're sorry that it didn't seem that way."

"Jasper told us everything and we hope you forgive him, too." Luke drops the final box in front of me and cracks it open. It's full to the brim with movie tie-in editions. "I'm also sorry for what I said to you," he adds, his cheeks pinking. "I didn't know he didn't want to work at the store, and even if he did, his behavior matters more than yours—you aren't a Prologue employee or my family. Who was I to tell you how to behave?"

"Thanks." I turn to his parents. "Really. Could we maybe set up a payment plan—"

"No," Jasper says quickly.

I have no problem admitting this is *really* nice, but even though Jasper technically owes me this, I still have a problem accepting it.

"What if we literally exchange the books?" I ask. "You guys can take our copies with the old cover and we'll take the new covers?"

"Keep them all."

"Jasper." I whirl in his direction. "We don't even need this many books. I get what you're trying to do, but I don't do charity."

"Forgive me and we can work out some exchange."

"Jasper Sôta Hamada," his mother says with a tight expression, "act like a gentleman and accept defeat. You did something cruel and she doesn't owe you forgiveness for one act of kindness, especially when she had a right to it!"

I'm aware of more than just Jasper's family watching us now. Melisa's customers who have to filter between our group to get in the store stare as they pass. "Fine, fine. I'll take the books." I face his father. "And I'd love to exchange a book for each one of yours that we sell."

"That sounds more than agreeable."

"Thank you."

His family very quietly and discreetly drops the boxes off inside the store and leaves Jasper and me on the sidewalk. I wish they had taken him with them. I'm still angry, but right now I'm angrier that this kind of makes up for him ruining the order in the first place. But it doesn't make up for him lying about it, hiding it, *whatever*. I peek inside the store and see everyone's attention on Warbeck, who's telling a story. I'm missing so much being out here with him, yet I can't seem to leave just yet.

"I told Grant I wasn't ready to hear you out." I keep my breathing even, will my heart to chill the fuck out. This is getting resolved here and now, no matter how it ends or how it makes me feel.

"He said that you said, very specifically, *not today*." He gives me a pointed look. "It's now two days later."

He grins and a little piece of ice chips away from my heart when the scar by his mouth folds into his smile lines. I resist the urge to press my finger into it.

"Why does it matter if I forgive you? I'm leaving for school next week and anything that was happening between us is over." I swallow back an aching, swollen feeling in my throat. "We can just pretend we didn't meet. Prologue can pretend there was never another store across the street once we close."

"I don't want that." With a pinched expression, he exhales loudly. "I don't want to be just forgiven either. I want to be with you. I want to be your boyfriend. I wanted to be your boyfriend from the beginning."

I shake my head, heart racing. "I haven't forgiven you. You're, like, two thousand miles ahead of yourself right now."

"Well, if I don't say it when I'm already terrified of your reaction, I'll never have the guts to say it." He wipes his hands on his thighs, ruining the dusty effect of his costume. "Might as well get it out of the way now."

I glance inside again, just so he doesn't see the recognition in my eyes: we are cut from the same cloth. Just two bookstore employees afraid of rejection.

"I'm sorry to keep you away from your event," he says. "You can go back inside and I'll just—I'll wait. Let me know when you want to talk—*if* you want to talk."

He starts to walk away, but I grab him by his vest, taking in the patch that says "Ammo" over a pocket. He waits, watching me as I formulate a response.

He said he was sorry. He made up for it. Lasers forgives Ammo so many times throughout the series. I'd be doing the character an injustice to hold a petty grudge against Jasper, especially when the thing he did was spurred from my actions.

I got him *hit by a car* and he *forgave* me.

"You changed our order before we—before you and I got together." I don't know the label to put on it, so I don't put one on it at all, but just the reference to that small moment in time that we were happy makes my heart hammer.

"Yes. I could show you the paperwork. It was before. I promise. It was—it was the day you found out about Benny. After you messed with my car and put the flyers in all the books. I was just so annoyed." He slowly angles toward me, my hand still on his vest. "That's the only reason I even knew you were doing the event. I forgot I had even changed the order until the day the books arrived, and I *did* try to tell you, but you didn't want to talk about it, which was understandable because you were upset and that was my fault. But you said there was nothing to be done because of timing, so I . . . I just let it go. I was scared to bring it up and ruin what was happening between us with something that couldn't be fixed."

I run my hand down his vest, smoothing it out. I guess if I can open myself up to Dahlia, who has been rejecting me my entire life, I could maybe do the same for Jasper. It's not a reason not to try, not to put myself out there. Not to forgive him.

"We should go inside," I say quietly. "We're missing the Q and A."

He frowns. "Madeline, what—?"

"*Why should I waste my time telling you I forgive you when I already forgave you?*" It's one of my favorite Lasers lines. This isn't a test, but if he recognizes it . . .

"*Well, you need to give people a heads-up when they're forgiven because you act pissed off all the time anyway.*"

. . . He'll answer with Ammo's response.

"Thanks." He leans down, his hand cupping my cheek. "About the boyfriend thing, though?"

"We'd break up eventually. Shippensburg is almost an hour away."

"You say that like it's far."

"I just think—" This is not fear stalling me; we are finally on equal footing, after all. This is rational. "I just think we should talk it over. Any kind of distance is a lot of pressure to put on a relationship, especially a new one. I mean, just take Dahlia's and my dysfunctional shitshow, for example—"

"Madeline," he says, cutting me off with a small smile. "We can figure it out."

His kiss is soft, but filled with promises, apologies, and intentions. I offer up my own apologies with the kiss, too, being kind and gentle with Jasper Hamada. Though staying out here making out seems like weirdly good promo for people to get their asses inside to the event, it would probably just deter anyone from entering. Plus, Isla-Freaking-Warbeck is inside right now; I mean, *what are we doing out here?*

Over the course of the afternoon, the weather stays perfect, Melisa makes a killing and sends people in to watch the cosplay contest, and we sell a ton of books—with new covers!—enough that we would have needed a second register if this were a normal occurrence.

Ravi's cupcakes disappear within minutes, Warbeck double-fisting a chocolate and a vanilla, earning the last bit of respect from me that she didn't already have. And when she judges the cosplay contest like it's her full-time job, she awards a girl around my age who *actually* dyed her hair to match Lasers's with a fake medal Zelda bought at the Dollar Tree that says *#1 Dad*.

"Is this another employee?" Warbeck asks of Jasper as the event is coming to an end. "Is that why you didn't enter the contest? That is an *amazing* Ammo costume."

He blushes, stuttering over words. "Thanks. I made it myself."

"He made mine, too. He actually works at the bookstore across the street," I add. "I wouldn't let him enter the contest for the principle of the thing." I wink at Jasper, but he just swallows roughly and smiles at Warbeck.

"Friends working at rival bookstores?" Warbeck gives us an appraising look. "That would make a good story."

"That's what I think!" Zelda says, popping up out of nowhere, her camera in our faces. "Hashtag Jadeline forever!"

"Jadeline," Dahlia says excitedly, also appearing from nowhere, a cupcake in her hand. She gives it to me. "I like that."

I glance between her and Zelda, knowing my cheeks match my hair. "You two need to stay away from each other."

By the end of the night, my heart feels fuller than it has all summer. Maybe fuller than it's ever felt. I go to bed with the scent of new books and Sharpies on my mind, the feel of Jasper's hand in mine, images of Warbeck and Astrid and Dahlia floating across the backs of my eyelids, and five words echoing through my subconscious in a way that turns foreboding fast: enjoy it while it lasts.

# TWENTY-EIGHT

We gather in Books & Moore on the cloudy, misty Sunday morning after the event at nine o'clock on the dot. My heart is thumping out of control, rocking my body with its violent motions, and my breathing comes out shallow. I know how this ends. I do. But I need to hear it said aloud to process it.

I just needed to fight and win the battle before conceding the war.

Zelda's hand clamps around mine. Behind the checkout counter, Astrid types something into the computer, Dahlia watching over her shoulder. Benny joined us in solidarity, his elbows propped on the counter and his Prologue polo straining to escape from where it's tucked into his khakis. Sterling waits beside him, arms crossed and face blank. Ravi leans against the first bookshelf, twiddling an unlit cigarette between his fingers.

We all know what's going to happen. But we need to know with absolute certainty.

The store is silent except for the clicks and clacks of the

keyboard. Finally, Astrid straightens. Dahlia takes a step away. Their eyes stay glued to the screen.

Astrid blinks and a small smile crosses her face, but doesn't reach her eyes.

I hold my breath, choking out, "Well?"

Her eyes flit to mine and I see the tears building up. Fuck.

She shakes her head. "We were close." She wipes at her eyes beneath her glasses and smiles at the others. "We were very close."

Zelda squeezes my hand and I want to pull away, flee into the break room and scream my lungs out. So, I squeeze back instead. There's a hurricane brewing inside me, but it was predicted and I took the necessary precautions to weather the storm.

"Did you factor in the leftover GoFundMe money?" I swipe away a rebellious tear sliding down my cheek.

Astrid nods.

"Say it."

She sighs. "We don't have enough to stay open. The store is definitely closing."

Dahlia pulls Astrid into a hug and Sterling clasps Benny on the shoulder, even though he's not losing as much as the rest of us. He left, like the smart kid he is, and never got his hopes up.

Ravi sighs beside me, getting my attention. "Close."

I frown, a stinging in my eyes. "Close."

Very close to having a slight cushion to work with. So, basically, not close at all. Not in the grand scheme of things.

I tune out the rest. I don't want to hear *If we had just sold X amount of books more, we'd still be open.* I don't want to turn my emotional turmoil into a math problem, don't want to sterilize my feelings.

Pulling myself out of Zelda's sympathetic grasp, I excuse myself. "I need some air. I'll be back."

And when the door chimes a second time, after I've cleared the storefront, it's not Zelda or even Benny or Astrid following me, it's Dahlia.

"I could use some air, too."

Now is not the time for her to lament the loss of a store she's only worked in for a few months. Now is not the time for her to tell me she's leaving. I can't take a double serving of loss right now.

"I want—I think I need some alone air." I watch her expression tighten. "No offense."

"No, none taken." She squeezes my shoulder. "I get it. I just wanted to make sure you're okay."

"I'll be fine." I will. I've had all summer to say goodbye to B&M. This isn't coming as a surprise. Even though I fought to keep the store open, I knew it was a possibility that it could close. I saw the sales numbers, knew we were sinking slowly. And I tried. I really did. I even let others help me, eventually. It was a joint effort, one final push. It just wasn't enough, and that's okay.

"Of course you will. And you'll be at school anyway."

"But Astrid." The thought of her sitting at home, surrounded by books she doesn't want, in an empty house, makes me want to cry. Not even the thought of her making both Benny's and my rooms into libraries can change that.

She bats the air between us. "She'll be fine, too. There are other jobs and I know she's kind of excited to figure out what she likes besides books."

The fear claws its way up my throat. "She'll be alone, though."

Her mouth tips into a frown. "Don't be so dramatic. You'll be home on breaks. Benny's only, like, ten minutes away, and, duh, she's stuck with me."

Another tear slides down my face. I catch it at my jawline. "You're leaving," I whisper as the first drop of rain hits my nose. "I know. I heard you talking to your agent about that audition."

The tension doesn't leave her face. "What?"

"I heard your phone call. You were really excited and—"

"Madeline," she says, crushing me against her chest. "I'm not going anywhere. I told you guys I'm back for good."

A sob explodes out of me, my gut fizzling. "What about the suitcase full of clothes? I saw you packing."

Confusion weighs her brow. "You mean—" She laughs. "Oh, kid, have you not noticed the washer is broken? I was taking my clothes to Sterling's to use his."

I freeze, my breath caught.

She rubs my back. "You're gonna be one of those pathetic college kids who brings their laundry home on the weekends, huh?" She tilts her head to the side, considering. "I guess that's better than being the one who just wears dirty clothes when they don't have to."

No wonder my closet was practically empty—Dahlia wasn't

taking my clothes, they just weren't being washed. I bark out a laugh. "So, you're staying?"

She nods, her chin bumping into my shoulder when she pulls me in for another hug. "I'm staying."

I clench her. "Good." I squeeze harder. "Good for, like, Benny."

She laughs into my hair. "Sure, just for Benny."

"And Astrid."

"Yeah."

"Yeah, she'll need your help with this stuff right now."

"Yep. And absolutely no one else will be happy I'm here or need me or anything."

My fingers dig into her mauve cardigan. "Right."

We stand there in the drizzle, hugging and crying and mourning the loss of B&M, all while a new, bright future forms between us. One where maybe she stays and I don't have to keep my guard up. One where she keeps her promises and I make an effort because she's trying, and if this summer with B&M has taught me anything, it's that trying is the most important part of the process.

# TWENTY-NINE

It's Tuesday, but there are no new books to put out—not any-more.

It's just after eight a.m. and the sun shines through B&M's front window, warming the floor where I sit with my laptop on my thighs. Using the internet tethered from my phone, I open Shippensburg's bookstore site. I didn't declare my major yet—I decided too late, so I'll do that next semester—but I'm going into their hospitality program so I can focus on event planning. I have the next four years to figure out for sure if that's the major for me, but I kind of loved the weird stress of planning the Warbeck event. Putting the pieces together and seeing the outcome; it was fulfilling, even if it didn't save the store. Like finishing a good book series that makes you equally mad, stressed, and happy.

I enter in my course numbers, adding the extremely expen-sive books to my cart, and check out with the credit card Astrid gave me for school purchases only. She says I need to save my personal money for clothes, gas, books for enjoyment. Says I've earned it.

My leg starts going numb so I rock to the side, the floor creaking beneath me, and stretch it. The store is completely silent aside from that and the clicking of my keyboard. Like the place is already closed. It hasn't, and it won't, not for another two weeks. Astrid has to find homes for the books. They're all Last Chance Books now. I left the contact information for the head librarians around here on her nightstand before I slipped out this morning. Jasper's dad even told me they'd be interested in buying some of our stock. So, there's that.

Speaking of Jasper—a gentle knock on the window scares the shit out of me.

I glance over my shoulder and up, right into the smiling, bleary-eyed face of Jasper Hamada. Over the last two days, I've gotten to see his put-together appearance fade into the disheveled mess walking through the door. All over his undoubtedly perfect admissions package.

"Did you turn in your application?" I ask when he walks in, the chime ringing out through the store.

He sits next to me, the sleeve of his crinkled shirt brushing my bare arm. "I stayed up all night proofreading it. Sent it before I left the house."

"Congrats." I knock my shoulder into his arm and smile. "When do you find out if you're getting an interview?"

"The site said no longer than a week."

"Wow. That's harsh judging." My heart flutters a little at the thought of a quick and painful no.

"Don't remind me." He looks around the store with slightly swollen eyes. "Just you here?"

"And you."

He leans toward me, his lips grazing mine. I set my laptop aside without breaking away and slide my hand into his hair. At least I don't have to feel bad about messing it up.

"I'm going to miss you," he says against my lips.

"You'll be busy once you're in school, and you'll find someone else." I say it with as light a tone as I can muster, but the thought—even just the words—crush something deep inside me. I'm still worried about getting a boyfriend right before I leave for school, but Jasper's been great about not pressuring me. Not making me feel guilty for taking the time to think it through. It seems cruel to both of us to start something and then separate.

"Madeline." His finger brushes a strand of my hair off my cheek. "I'll miss you."

"I'll miss you, too."

For a moment, we're silent. Then he says, "You wouldn't have to miss me so much if—"

"*Jasper*," I say through a laugh. Okay, so maybe he's pressuring me *slightly* to decide. For now, we're still exclusively whatever and it's not the worst thing to be.

He leans over me, pulling my computer onto his lap. "Are you going to apply?"

"What?" I look at the screen. It's just showing a confirmation of my order. It tells me to pick them up no later than next Monday. My gut tingles—excited, nervous, scared.

"The job." He zooms in to the bottom of the screen, where there's a Help Wanted ad. He clicks it, opening a new page that shows information about working at the bookstore.

I laugh. "Probably not . . ."

"Why?"

"I don't know. I—I'd feel like a traitor."

He meets my eyes, his filled with sympathy. "The store will be closed."

"Yeah, but I'd still feel that way."

"It might help you," he says gently.

It would be so weird to work anywhere else, let alone another bookstore. Does a school bookstore, filled mostly with textbooks, even count as a bookstore?

"Might help with the homesickness," I say quietly. I start imagining myself studying while fanatic parents buy up all the school merch and stressed freshmen zoom about, searching for textbooks they should have bought months ago. "I'd be good at it."

"You would. And if you stick with event planning, you might not end up in bookstores after school. If a part of you wants to do this, then you should."

Enjoy it while it lasts because nothing lasts forever.

I click open the application.


The night before I leave for school, we have a goodbye dinner that ends up feeling more like a hello.

I bite into my Cowboy Crunch and savor the mix of barbecue sauce and ranch dressing. Neato Burrito is the only proper send-off since I won't be having it for a while anyway. The melted cheese hits the spot.

In two days, I have an interview at my next potential job, the Shipwreck Bookstore, and I'm not feeling guilty about it anymore. I'm pretty much fully excited, with only a little bit of nerves. I never had to interview for my job at B&M. One day I was just there helping and the next day, I was paid for it.

"Jasper," Dahlia says, chewing, "Madeline says you might be leaving Prologue."

He looks up from his plate, where he was cutting a chunk of burrito away. He swallows. "Yeah, that's the plan. I applied to a design school using our cosplay."

I'm ready to explode. He texted before coming over for dinner that he had heard back, but I didn't have a minute alone with him and he hasn't given up whether it's good or bad news—the latter wouldn't be great to share in front of my family.

"I have an interview later this week to see if I'll get admitted, but they seemed optimistic." He grins to himself, proud.

I can't contain myself, and don't know how to properly show how excited I am, so I punch him on the arm. Like, a bro punch. *I give up.* He looks down at the spot where my fist connected with his bicep and fights a bewildered expression.

"Sorry. I'm excited," I squeak out.

"Congrats," Benny says as the others offer their own words. "When does the semester start? My friend is going to an art school and their schedule is accelerated and weird."

Jasper wipes his mouth with his napkin. "I have to get in first, but yeah. I'd be starting late September. My breaks would be a bit different from a state school's—no fall and spring breaks, just holidays—but they'd be longer." He raises an eyebrow at me like *top that*. "And then my year is over in June."

I set my burrito down, anxiety filling my stomach instead. June? That's an awful long time to be away from him just when I finally got him. Or the chance to get him. It's like my decision about our relationship is happening right before my eyes, without me having a say in it.

"Are you done then?" Benny asks. For a second, I thought he was referring to our whatevership.

"No, I have two more years after it, but the last year will be mostly interning. Probably in New York, unless there are any semi-local designers." His eyes meet mine. "I'll only be half an hour away from Madeline at Shippensburg."

My heart stutters in an attempt to race. I had no clue his school was so close to mine. "You never mentioned that!"

He smirks. "You never asked. You're kind of self-centered."

My family bursts into laughter and I'd defend myself, but, shit, I have been so self-centered this summer. "I'm sorry." A smile breaks across my face, fighting away the butterflies and dread and confusion. "Why didn't you mention it unprompted?" Even though it *was* prompted. I told him multiple times I was going away to school and I'd be like an hour away! *Thirty minutes is* half *that time, Jasper!*

He shyly glances around the room, then to me. "You want to talk about this now?"

My eyes flit around the room now, too. I don't know if it'll be better or worse with an audience, but the time has come. "Sure."

"I know I made jokes, but I really didn't want to scare you

off by mentioning it. I thought maybe you were trying to let me down easy, and bringing up that we'd be so close would put pressure on you. And I don't even know if I'm going to get in—"

"You'll get in. And I made my decision, regardless." Something like relief fills me having said the words aloud. Having just been brave enough to say it. I don't want to be done. I want to start. If he's going to be gone in three years, I want to enjoy the time we have now. Even if he doesn't get into the school, an hour isn't far. Dahlia said it, *he* said it. And he'd be the one traveling the distance, so if it doesn't bother him . . .

He avoids the hungry stares of my family, watching us like some reality show. "So," he says in a quiet voice, "will you be my girlfriend, even though we might be far apart?"

"I want you to be my boyfriend no matter what part of the state you're in. No matter what part of the state *I'm* in. Will you? Be my boyfriend?" I know his answer but I still wait, my breath in my throat.

"You should say country to be safe," Benny says, giving me a pointed look.

"Country," I say. "No matter what part of the country."

Astrid tilts her head, eyes narrowed. "Maybe world. Say world."

"Just say universe." Sterling flips his hands like *You're welcome.*

"How about we let him answer?" Dahlia asks loudly. Can she hear my heart pounding?

"Uh." Jasper ducks his head, meeting my eyes. "Yes?"

"Don't sound so sure of yourself, kid," Dahlia says.

"Just give her the honest answer," Sterling says, gesturing with what's left of his burrito.

"But don't say no," Benny adds.

"But don't appease her, either," Astrid says.

I stab my burrito with a fork because I can't stab any of them. "Just let him answer! This was technically his idea!" He better not back out now.

Jasper laughs. "I'll be your boyfriend, if you'll be my girl-friend."

My heart takes off faster than Olympians going for gold. I smother an embarrassing smile. "I could agree to that."

"Under what terms?" He pretends like he's really thinking about it, eyes narrowed.

"Well," I say, tilting my head to the side in thought, "I have a pair of pants that the back pocket has ripped off of and—"

"Deal."

"I guess that bulk package of condoms I got you for school will come in handy, huh?" Dahlia says, her beer halfway to her mouth.

"*Mom*," I choke out loudly enough to be heard over every-one's stunned and uncomfortable laughter. Jasper's cheeks burn so red that I can feel the heat sitting next to him. "Astrid, con-trol your sister."

Astrid shrugs. "It's not appropriate dinner conversation, but I do appreciate that she wants you to be safe."

"Thank you," Dahlia says smugly. But then she turns to me and her face softens. She repeats the words again, with a different meaning behind them: "Thank you."

I change the subject and wait for the embarrassment to fade. When the others clear the table and I walk Jasper to his car, we spend an entire minute staring at each other, silent and totally comfortable. This isn't a goodbye. He'll get into that school, and even if he doesn't, I'll only be an hour away. No, it's not across the street, but we'll make it work. It's not an excuse not to try, not to be happy. I'm done with making excuses.

He leans against his car. "So. Girlfriend." He bites his lip. "Should we seal it with a kiss?"

"It's the only way to make things official, I hear."

He bends, and I tip up on my toes, to meet in the middle. My last kiss of the summer with my first kiss of the summer. My first kiss with my first college boyfriend. With Jasper Hotmada, the boy no longer on my shit list. I did not see this coming. It's weird.

But a good kind of weird.

# ACKNOWLEDGMENTS

I think a lot of people uninvolved in publishing would assume that it takes only one person to write a book. They would be wrong. This book, this one right here in your hands, is the product of so many people putting forth so much effort, creativity, and time, including my fantastic editor, Elizabeth Lynch, who has never for a second made me think she didn't 100 percent get me and my story. Thank you to the fantastic HarperTeen team for making my debut an exciting and smooth experience: Nicole Moreno, Vanessa Nuttry, Aubrey Churchward, and Valerie Wong. Thank you to Jessie Gang and Sarah Long for combining your magical powers to create a cover better than I could have dreamed.

To Bridget Smith, my agent. Each step of the way, you've been a calming presence, and I'm so grateful for your expertise and for the care you put into growing my career.

To Sonia Hartl, this book simply would not exist if it weren't for you. Back in 2016, you scooped me up and have never let me go. You've taught me so much about myself, my writing, and publishing. I can't thank you enough for your guidance and love.

To Rachel Lynn Solomon, you saved this book. When it was just a strange idea that you comped to a movie I had never seen, you encouraged me to make it more complex, have more heart, and evolve. You listened unwaveringly to my rants and whining and made sure I came out the other side stronger.

Thank you to Carlyn Greenwald, Annette Christie, Andrea Contos, Auriane Desombre, Marisa Kanter, Jennifer Dugan, and Susan Lee: Not a day goes by where I'm not asking your opinions, complaining about my own lack of motivation, brainstorming, using your problems as distraction from my own, or just talking about life with one or all of you. There's love in this book and it's because of you.

To my friends and early readers: Jenny Howe, Samantha Goodlin, Sierra Elmore, Haley Neil, Monica Gomez-Hira, Kara McDowell, Roselle Lim, Tara Tsai, Jen DeLuca, Jessica Bibi Cooper, Tori Bovalino, Mike Lasagna, and Emily Suvada.

To Rosiee Thor, Rachel Griffin, and the rest of my Pitch Wars 2016 friends who table-flipped, sprinted, and shared snippets along the way.

To my Team B agent siblings and other Harper authors who have been so kind and welcoming and helpful.

To Claire Ahn, for oftentimes making me feel like I hung the moon when I felt that way about you, your work ethic, your drive, and kindness.

Thank you to Stacy McClain for the Edward Cullen joke.

Special shout-out to my coworkers, Deb and Ilene, for always shouting about every little thing that has happened since I was offered this book deal.

To my mom, Wendy, and my sister, Nicole, for being my first readers and cheerleaders.

And lastly, thank you to my partner, Dylan L. Shaffer, for always respecting writing time, always making me laugh so hard I cry, and for always loving me unconditionally. I'll keep trying to write a love story as amazing as ours.